HOV

This is a work of fiction. Similarities to real people, places, or events are entirely coincidental.

HOW THE STEEL WAS TEMPERED

June 14, 2018.

By Nikolai Ostrovsky
Edited by J.T. Marsh

CREDITS AND ACKNOWLEDGEMENTS

This edition is derived from an edition originally published by the Foreign Languages Publishing House, Moscow, USSR, in 1952. In turn, it was published originally in serial format in the magazine *Young Guard* from 1932 to 1934, then as a two-part novel in 1936. As with many works published in the USSR, translations were made into many foreign languages, including English, although this novel was never distributed widely in the West. Owing to the death of the original author, Nikolai Ostrovsky, in 1936, it has long ago lapsed into the public domain. The English language translation on which this edition is based was obtained from the website of the Communist Party of Australia.

FOREWORD

How the Steel Was Tempered is widely regarded as one of the definitive novels written according to the tenets of the socialist realism aesthetic, the preferred artistic aesthetic that enjoyed official sanction throughout the history of the Soviet Union. Briefly, the socialist realism aesthetic consists of two components: the socialist and the realist. The socialist component seeks to glorify the attributes, ideals, and values of the working class, while denouncing the attributes, ideals, and values of the capitalist class. The realist component seeks to portray its subjects realistically, without the kind of abstractions that characterize avant-garde movements to this day.

How the Steel Was Tempered was inspired by and heavily based on the author's experiences serving in the Red Army and as a member of the Komsomol, the Communist Party's youth wing, and later the Party itself. First published in serial format in the Soviet literary magazine Young Guard, an edited version of How the Steel Was Tempered was later published as a two-part novel, having been edited so as to more closely conform to the tenets of socialist realism. This edition is derived from the novel and not the serial. In the novel, the main protagonist, Pavel Korchagin, grows from an impetuous youth through to a mature, self-disciplined soldier in service of the cause of working class liberation and the construction of a new, socialist society in which the working man should be master of his own destiny. In this, Pavel Korchagin can be seen as emblematic of the Soviet ideal of the 'new man:' dedicated, selfless, his person subordinated to the welfare and the relentless advance of the working class. Although I am a writer who variously seeks to articulate working class values and ideals through my work, I do not subscribe personally to the aesthetic of socialist realism. In fact, I regard socialist realism as an aesthetic as more-or-less obsolete, an artefact in the history of the development of the world's working class and its consciousness as a class for itself rather than merely of itself. Nevertheless, socialist realism continues to have value as an aesthetic as a component of the larger working class movement in art, with all its ebbs and flows the movement in a constant state of evolution, its evolution in turn guided by the changing nature of the working class struggle and the character of the working class itself.

I have chosen to republish this novel as a means of disseminating the ideals of the socialist realism aesthetic, and to increase the availability of a classic work of historical fiction. Most of the edits I have made to this book are perfunctory, serving to present the novel in a manner more amenable to the modern reader, or to reduce printing costs and thus lower the sale price for print editions. Therefore, I present this edition of *How the Steel Was Tempered* as a means of disseminating an example of socialist realism and thus an important component in the broad history of working class literature. This novel is presented as an artefact meant to pay homage to and stimulate discussion and awareness of socialist realism among the readers of today. As scientists credit their predecessors for work that forms the basis for all current and future knowledge, so must authors and other artists credit their predecessors for work that forms the basis for all current and future aesthetic. We all seek to stand on the shoulders of giants, whether we realize it or not.

- J.T. Marsh

his emotions. I feel that you will be a most suitable guide for him, Rita. I wish you success. Don't forget to write me in Moscow.'

Today a new secretary for the Solomensky District Committee was sent down from the Central Committee. His name is Zharky. I knew him in the army.

Tomorrow Dmitri Dubava will bring Korchagin. Let me try to describe Dubava. Medium height, strong, muscular. Joined the Komsomol in nineteen-eighteen, and has been a Party member since nineteen-twenty. He was one of the three who were expelled from the Komsomol Gubernia Committee for having belonged to the 'Workers' Opposition.' Instructing him has not been easy. Every day he upset the program by asking innumerable questions and making us digress from the subject. He and Olga Yureneva, my other pupil, did not get along at all. At their very first meeting he looked her up and down and remarked: 'your getup is all wrong, my girl. You ought to have pants with leather seats, spurs, a Budyonny hat and a sabre. This way you're neither fish nor fowl.'

Olga wouldn't stand for that, of course, and I had to interfere. I believe Dubava is a friend of Korchagin's. Well, enough for tonight. It's time for bed.

The earth wilted under the scorching sun. The iron railing of the footbridge over the railway platforms was burning to the touch. People, limp and exhausted from the heat, climbed the bridge wearily; most of them were not travellers, but residents of the railway district who used the bridge to get to the town proper. As he came down the steps Pavel caught sight of Rita. She had reached the station before him and was watching the people coming off the bridge. Pavel paused some three yards away from her. She did not notice him, and he studied her with new found interest. She was wearing a striped blouse and a short blue skirt of some cheap material. A soft leather jacket was slung over her shoulder. Her suntanned face was framed in a shock of unruly hair and as she stood there with her head thrown slightly back and her eyes narrowed against the sun's glare, it struck Korchagin for

CHAPTER ONE

Midnight. The last tramcar has long since dragged its battered carcass back to the depot. The moon lays its cold light on the windowsill and spreads a luminous coverlet on the bed, leaving the rest of the room in semidarkness. At the table in the corner under a circle of light shed by the desk lamp sits Rita bent over a thick notebook, her diary. The sharp point of her pencil traces the words:

May Twenty-Fourth

I am making another attempt to jot down my impressions. Again there is a big gap. Six weeks have passed since I made the last entry. But it cannot be helped.

How can I find time for my diary? It is past midnight now, and here I am still writing. Sleep eludes me.

Comrade Segal is leaving us: he is going to work in the Central Committee. We were all very much upset by the news. He is a wonderful person, our Lazar Alexandrovich. I did not realise until now how much his friendship has meant to us all. The dialectical materialism class is bound to go to pieces when he leaves. Yesterday we stayed at his place until the wee hours verifying the progress made by our 'pupils.' Akim, the Secretary of the Komsomol Gubernia Committee, came and that horrid Tufta as well. I can't stand that Mr. Know-it-all! Segal was delighted when his pupil Korchagin brilliantly defeated Tufta in an argument on Party history. Yes, these two months have not been wasted. You don't begrudge your efforts when you see such splendid results. It is rumoured that Zhukhrai is being transferred to the Special Department of the Military Area. I wonder why.

Lazar Alexandrovich turned his pupil over to me. 'You will have to complete what I have begun,' he said. 'Don't stop halfway. You and he, Rita, can learn a great deal from each other. The lad is still rather disorganised. His is a turbulent nature and he is apt to be carried away by

the first time that Rita, his friend and teacher, was not only a member of the bureau of the Komsomol Gubernia Committee, but....

Annoyed with himself for entertaining such "sinful" thoughts, he called to her. "I've been staring at you for a whole hour, but you didn't notice me," he laughed. "Come along, our train is already in." They went over to the service door leading to the platform.

The previous day the Gubernia Committee had appointed Rita as its representative at a district conference of the Komsomol, and Korchagin was to go as her assistant. Their immediate problem was to board the train, which was by no means a simple task. The railway station on those rare occasions when the trains ran was taken over by an all-powerful Committee of Five without a permit from whom no one was allowed on the platform. All exits and approaches to the platform were guarded by the Committee's men. The overcrowded train could take on only a fraction of the crowd anxious to leave, but no-one wanted to be left behind to spend days waiting for a chance train to come through. And so thousands stormed the platform doors in an effort to break through to the unattainable cars. In those days the station was literally besieged and sometimes pitched battles were fought.

After vainly attempting to push through the crowd collected at the platform entrance, Pavel, who knew all the ins and outs at the station, led Rita through the luggage department. With difficulty they made their way to car No. Four. At the car door a Cheka man, sweating profusely in the heat, was trying to hold back the crowd, and repeating over and over again: "the car's full, and it's against the rules to ride on the buffers or the roof."

Irate citizens bore down on him, thrusting tickets issued by the Committee under his nose. There were angry curses, shouts and violent pushing at every car. Pavel saw that it would be impossible to board the train in the conventional manner. Yet board it they must, otherwise the conference would have to be called off. Taking Rita aside, he outlined his plan of action: he would push his way into the car, open a window and help her to climb through. There was no other way.

"Let me have that jacket of yours. It's better than any credential." He slipped on the jacket and stuck his gun into the pocket so that the grip and cord showed. Leaving the luggage with Rita, he went over to the car, elbowed through the knot of excited passengers at the entrance and gripped the hand rail. "Hey, comrade, where you going?" Pavel glanced nonchalantly over his shoulder at the stocky Cheka man. "I'm from the Area Special Department. I want to see whether all the passengers in this car have tickets issued by the Committee," he said in a tone that left no doubts as to his authority.

The Cheka man glanced at Pavel's pocket, wiped his perspiring brow with his sleeve and said wearily: "Go ahead if you can shove yourself in." Working with his hands, shoulders, and here and there with his fists, holding on to the ledges of the upper berths to climb over the passengers who had planted themselves on their belongings in the middle of the aisles, Pavel made his way through to the centre of the car, ignoring the torrent of abuse that rained down on him from all sides.

"Can't you look where you're going, curse you!" screamed a stout woman when Pavel accidentally brushed her knee with his foot, as he lowered himself into the aisle. She had contrived to wedge her one-hundred-twenty-kilo bulk onto the edge of a seat and had a large vegetable oil can between her knees. All the shelves were stuffed with similar cans, hampers, sacks and baskets. The air in the car was suffocating.

Paying no heed to the abuse, Pavel demanded: "Your ticket, citizen!" "My what?" the woman snapped back at the unwelcome inspector. A head appeared from the uppermost berth and an ugly voice boomed out: "Vaska, what's this 'ere mug doin' here. Give 'im a ticket to kingdom come, will ya?" The huge frame and hairy chest of what was obviously Vaska swung into view right above Pavel's head and a pair of bloodshot eyes fixed him with a bovine stare.

"Leave the lady alone, can't ya? What d'you want tickets for?" Four pairs of legs hung down from an upper side berth; their owners sat with their arms around one another's shoulders noisily cracking sunflower seeds. One glance at their faces told Pavel who they were: a gang of food sharks, hardened crooks who travelled up and down the country buying up food and selling it at speculative prices. Pavel had no time to waste with them. He had to get Rita inside somehow.

"Whose box is this?" he inquired of an elderly man in railway uniform, pointing to a wooden chest standing under the window. "Hers," replied the other, pointing to a pair of thick legs in brown stockings. The window had to be opened and the box was in the way. Since there was nowhere to move it Pavel picked it up and handed it to its owner who was seated on an upper berth.

"Hold it for a minute, please, I'm going to open the window." "Keep your hands off other people's belongings!" screamed the fat-nosed wench when he placed the box on her knees. "Motka, what's this fella think he's doin'?" she said to the man seated beside her. The latter gave Pavel a kick in the back with his sandaled foot. "Listen 'ere, you! Clear out of here before I land you one!" Pavel endured the kick in silence. He was too busy unfastening the window.

"Move up a bit, please," he said to the railwayman. Shifting another can out of the way Pavel cleared a space in front of the window. Rita was on the platform below. Quickly she handed him the bag. Throwing it onto the knees of the stout woman with the vegetable oil can, Pavel bent down, seized Rita's hands and drew her in. Before the guard had time to notice this infringement of the rules, Rita was inside the car, leaving the guard swearing belatedly outside. The gang of speculators within met Rita's appearance with such an uproar that she was taken aback. Since there was not even standing room on the floor, she found a place for her feet on the very edge of the lower berth and stood there holding on to the upper berth for support. Foul curses sounded on all sides. From above the ugly bass voice croaked: "look at the swine, gets in himself and drags his tart in after 'im!"

A voice from above squeaked: "Motka, poke him one between the eyes!" The woman was doing her best to stand her wooden box on Pavel's head. The two newcomers were surrounded by a ring of evil, brutish faces. Pavel was sorry that Rita had to be exposed to this but there was nothing to be done but to make the best of it. "Citizen, move your sacks away from the aisle and make room for the comrade," he said to the one they called Motka, but the answer was a curse so foul that he boiled with rage. The pulse over his right eyebrow began to throb painfully. "Just wait, you scoundrel, you'll answer for this," he said to the ruffian, but received a kick on the head from above. "Good for you, Vaska, fetch 'im another!" came approving cries from all sides.

Pavel's self-control gave way at last, and as always in such moments his actions became swift and sure. "You speculating bastards, you think you can get away with it?" he shouted, and hoisting himself agilely on to the upper berth, he sent his fist smashing against Motka's leering face. He struck with such force that the speculator rolled down into the aisle onto the heads of the other passengers. "Get out of there, you swine, or I'll shoot down the whole lot of you!" Pavel yelled wildly, waving his gun under the noses of the four.

The tables were turned. Rita watched closely, ready to shoot if anyone attacked Korchagin. The upper shelf quickly cleared. The gang hastily withdrew to the neighbouring compartment.

As he helped Rita up to the empty berth, Pavel whispered: "You stay here, I'm going to see about those fellows." Rita tried to detain him. "You're not going to fight them, are you?" "No," he reassured her. "I'll be back soon." He opened the window again and climbed out onto the platform. A few minutes later he was talking to Burmeister of the Transport Cheka, his former chief. The Lett heard him out and then gave orders to have the entire car cleared and the passengers' papers checked.

"It's just as I said," growled Burmeister. "The trains are full of speculators before they get here." A detail of ten Cheka men cleared the car. Pavel, assuming his old duties, helped to examine the documents of the passengers. He had not broken all ties with his former Cheka comrades and in his capacity as secretary of the Komsomol he had sent some of the best Komsomol members to work there. When the screening was over, Pavel returned to Rita. The car was now occupied by a vastly different type of passenger: Red Army men and factory and office workers travelling on business. Rita and Pavel had the top berth in one corner of the carriage, but so much of it was taken up with bundles of newspapers that there was only room for Rita to lie down.

"Never mind," she said, "we'll manage somehow." The train began to move at last. As it slid slowly out of the station they caught a brief glimpse of the fat woman seated on a bundle of sacks on the platform and heard her yelling: "Hey Manka, where's my oil can gone?"

Sitting in their cramped quarters with the bundles of newspapers screening them from their neighbours, Pavel and Rita munched bread and apples and laughingly recalled the far from laughable episode with which their journey had begun.

The train crawled along. The old, battered and overloaded carriages creaked and groaned and trembled violently at every joint in the track. The deep blue twilight looked in at the windows. Then night came, folding the car in darkness. Rita was tired and she dozed with her head resting on the bag. Pavel sat on the edge of the berth and smoked. He too was tired but there was no room to lie down. The fresh night breeze blew through the open window. Rita, awakened by a sudden jolt, saw the glow of Pavel's cigarette in the darkness. It was just like him to sit up all night rather than cause her discomfort. "Comrade Korchagin! Drop those bourgeois conventions and lie down," she said lightly. Pavel obediently lay down beside her and stretched his stiff legs luxuriously. "We have heaps of work tomorrow. So try and get some sleep, you rowdy." She put her arm trustingly around his neck and he felt her hair touching his cheek.

To Pavel, Rita was sacred. She was his friend and comrade, his political guide. Yet she was a woman as well. He had first become aware of this over there at the footbridge, and that was why her embrace stirred him so much now. He felt her deep even breathing; somewhere quite close to him were her lips. Proximity awoke in him a powerful desire to find those lips, and it was only with a great effort of will that he suppressed the impulse.

Rita, as if divining his feelings, smiled in the darkness. She had already known the joy of passion and the pain of loss. She had given her love to two Bolsheviks. White guard bullets had robbed her of both. One had been a splendid giant of a man, a Brigade Commander; the other, a lad with clear blue eyes. Soon the regular rhythm of the wheels rocked Pavel to sleep and he did not wake until the engine whistled shrilly the next morning.

Work kept Rita occupied every day until late at night and she had little time for her diary. After an interval a few more brief entries appeared:

August Eleventh

The Gubernia conference is over. Akim, Mikhailo and several others have gone to Kharkov for the all Ukrainian conference, leaving all the paper work to me. Dubava and Pavel have been sent to work at the Gubernia Committee. Ever since Dmitri was made secretary of the Pechorsk District Committee he has stopped coming to lessons. He is up to his neck in work. Pavel tries to do some studying, but we don't get much done because either I am too busy or else he is sent off on some assignment. With the present tense situation on the railways the Komsomols are constantly being mobilised for work. Zharky came to see me yester-

day. He complained about the boys being taken away from him, says he needs them badly himself.

August Twenty-Third

I was going down the corridor today when I saw Korchagin standing outside the manager's office with Pankratov and another man. As I came closer I heard Pavel say: "Those fellows sitting there ought to be shot".

"You've no right to countermand our orders," the man says. "The Railway Firewood Committee is the boss here and you Komsomols had better keep out of it." You ought to have seen his mug... And the place is infested with parasites like him!

Pavel followed this up with some shocking language. Pankratov caught sight of me and nudged him. Pavel swung round and when he saw me he turned pale and walked off without meeting my eyes. He won't be coming around for a long while now. He knows I will not tolerate bad language.

August Twenty-Seventh

We had a closed meeting of the bureau. The situation is becoming serious. I cannot write about it in detail just yet. Akim came back from the regional conference looking very worried. Yesterday another supply train was derailed. I don't think I shall try to keep this diary any more. It is much too haphazard anyway. I am expecting Korchagin. I saw him the other day and he told me he and Zharky are organising a commune of five.

One day while at work in the railway shops Pavel was called to the telephone. It was Rita. She happened to be free that evening and suggested that they finish the chapter they had been studying – the reasons for the fall of the Paris Commune.

As he approached Rita's house on University Street that evening, Pavel glanced up and saw a light in her window. He ran upstairs, gave his usual brief knock on the door and went in.

There on the bed, where none of the young comrades were allowed even to sit for a moment, lay a man in uniform. A revolver, kit-bag and cap with the red star lay on the table. Rita was sitting beside the stranger with her arms clasped tightly around him. The two were engaged in earnest conversation and as Pavel entered Rita looked up with a radiant face. The man freed himself from her embrace and rose. "Pavel," said Rita shaking hands with him, "this is..." "David Ustinovich," the man said, clasping Korchagin's hand warmly. "He turned up quite unexpectedly," Rita explained with a happy laugh. Pavel shook hands coldly with the newcomer and a gleam of resentment flashed in his eyes. He noticed the four squares of a company commander on the sleeve of the man's uniform. Rita was about to say something but Pavel interrupted her: "I just dropped in to tell you that I shall be busy loading wood down at the wharves this evening," he said. "And anyhow you have a visitor. Well, I'll be off, the boys are waiting for me downstairs."

And he disappeared through the door as suddenly as he had come. They heard him hurrying downstairs. Then the outside door slammed and all was quiet. "There's something the matter with him," Rita faltered in answer to David's questioning look.

Down below under the bridge a locomotive heaved a deep sigh, exhaling a shower of golden sparks from its mighty lungs. They soared upward executing a fantastic dance and were lost in the smoke. Pavel leaned against the railing and stared at the coloured signal lights winking on the switches. He screwed up his eyes. "What I don't understand. Comrade Korchagin, is why it should hurt so much to discover that Rita has a husband? Has she ever told you she hadn't? And even if she has, what of it? Why should you take it like that? You thought, comrade, it was all platonic friendship and nothing else... How could you have let this happen?" he asked himself with bitter irony. "But what if he isn't her husband? David Ustinovich might be her brother or her uncle... In which case you've done the chap an injustice, you fool. You're no better than any other swine. It's easy enough to find out whether he's her brother or not. Suppose he turns out to be a brother or an uncle, how are you going to face her after the way you've behaved? No, you've got to stop seeing her!"

The scream of an engine whistle interrupted his reflections. "It's getting late. Time to be going home. Enough of this nonsense."

· · · ·

AT SOLOMENKA, AS THE district where the railway workers lived was called, five young men set up a miniature commune. They were Zharky, Pavel, Klavicek, a jolly fair-haired Czech, Nikolai Okunev, secretary of the railway yards Komsomol, and Stepan Artyukhin, a boiler repair man who was now working for the railway Cheka.

They found a room and for three days spent all their free time cleaning, painting and whitewashing. They dashed back and forth with pails so many times that the neighbours began to think the house was on fire. They made themselves bunks, and mattresses filled with maple leaves gathered in the park, and on the fourth day the room, with a portrait of Petrovsky and a huge map on the wall, literally shone with cleanliness.

Between the windows was a shelf piled high with books. Two crates covered with cardboard served for chairs, another larger crate did duty as a cupboard. In the middle of the room stood a huge billiard table, minus the cloth, which the room's inmates had carried on their shoulders from the warehouse. By day it was used as a table and at night Klavicek slept on it. The five lads fetched all their belongings, and the practical-minded Klavicek made an inventory of the commune's possessions. He wanted to hang it up on the wall but the others objected. Everything in the room was declared common property. Earnings, rations and occasional parcels from home were all divided equally; the sole items of personal property were their weapons.

It was unanimously decided that any member of the commune who violated the law of communal ownership or who betrayed his comrades' trust would be expelled from the commune. Okunev and Klavicek insisted that expulsion should be followed by eviction from the room, and the motion was carried.

All the active members of the District Komsomol came to the commune's housewarming party. A gigantic samovar was borrowed from the next-door neighbour. The tea party consumed the commune's entire stock of saccharine. After tea, they sang in chorus and their lusty young voices rocked the rafters:

The whole wide world is drenched with tears
In bitter toil our days are passed
But, wait, the radiant dawn, appears...

Talya Lagutina, the girl from the tobacco factory, led the singing. Her crimson kerchief had slipped to one side of her head and her eyes, whose depths none as yet had fathomed, danced with mischief. Talya had a most infectious laugh and she looked at the world from the radiant height of her eighteen years. Now her arm swept up and the singing poured forth like a fanfare of trumpets:

Spread, our song, o'er the 'world like a flood;
Proudly our flag waves unfurled
It burns and glows throughout the world
On fire from our heart's blood.

The party broke up late and the silent streets awoke to the echo of their hearty young voices.

· · · ·

THE TELEPHONE RANG and Zharky reached for the receiver. "Keep quiet, I can't hear anything!" he shouted to the noisy Komsomols who had crowded in the Secretary's office. The hubbub subsided somewhat. "Hello! Ah, it's you. Yes, right away. What's on the agenda? Oh, the same old thing, hauling firewood from the wharves.

What's that? No, he's not been sent anywhere. He's here. Want to speak to him? Just a minute." Zharky beckoned to Pavel. "Comrade Ustinovich wants to speak to you," he said and handed him the receiver."

"I thought you were out of town," Pavel heard Rita's voice say. "I happen to be free this evening. Why don't you come over? My brother has gone. He was just passing through town and decided to look me up. We haven't seen each other for two years."

Her brother!

Pavel did not hear any more. He was recalling that unfortunate evening and the resolve he had taken that night down on the bridge. Yes, he must go to her this evening and put an end to this. Love brought too much pain and anxiety with it. Was this the time for such things? The voice in his ear said: "Can't you hear me?" "Yes, yes. I hear you. Very well. I'll come over after the Bureau meeting." And he hung up.

He looked her straight in the eyes and, gripping the edge of the oak table, he said: "I don't think I'll be able to come and see you anymore."

He saw her thick eyelashes sweep upward at his words. Her pencil paused in its flight over the page and then lay motionless on the open pad. "Why not?"

"It's very hard for me to find the time. You know yourself we're not having it so easy just now. I'm sorry, but I'm afraid we'll have to call it off..." He was conscious that the last few words sounded none too firm. "What are you beating about the bush for?" he raged inwardly. "You haven't the courage to strike out with both fists." Aloud he went on: "Besides, I've been wanting to tell you for some time – I have difficulty in grasping your explanations. When we studied with Segal what I learned stayed in my head somehow, but with you it doesn't. I've always had to go to Tokarev after our lessons and get him to explain things properly. It's my fault – my noodle just can't take it. You'll have to find some pupil with a bit more brains."

He turned away from her searching gaze, and, deliberately burning all his bridges, added doggedly: "So you see it would just be a waste of time for us to continue." Then he got up, moved the chair aside carefully with his foot and looked at the bowed head and the face that seemed so pale in the light of the lamp. He put on his cap. "Well, goodbye, Comrade Rita. Sorry I've wasted so much of your time. I ought to have told you long before this. That's where I'm to blame."

Rita mechanically gave him her hand, but she was too stunned by his sudden coldness to say more than a few words. "I don't blame you, Pavel. If I haven't succeeded in finding some way of making things clear to you I deserve this."

Pavel walked heavily to the door. He closed it after him softly. Downstairs he paused for a moment – it was not too late to go back and explain.... But what was the use? For what? To hear her scornful response and find himself outside again? No.

. . . .

GRAVEYARDS OF DILAPIDATED railway cars and abandoned locomotives grew on the sidings. The wind whirled and scattered the dry sawdust in the deserted woodyards.

And all around the town in the forest thickets and deep ravines lurked Orlik's band. By day they lay low in surrounding hamlets or in wooded tracts, but at night they crept out onto the railroad tracks, tore them up ruthlessly and, their evil work done, crawled back again into their lair.

And many an iron steed went crashing down the railway embankment. Boxcars were smashed to smithereens. Sleepy humans were flattened like pancakes beneath the wreckage, and precious grain mingled with blood and earth.

The band would swoop down suddenly on some small town scattering the frightened, clucking hens in all directions. A few shots would be fired at random. Outside the building of the Volost Soviet there would be a brief crackle of rifle fire, like the sound of bracken underfoot, and the bandits would dash about the village on their well-fed horses cutting down everyone who crossed their path. They hacked at their victims as calmly as if they were splitting logs. Rarely did they shoot, for bullets were scarce.

The band would be gone as swiftly as it had come. It had its eyes and ears everywhere. Those eyes saw through the walls of the small white building that housed the Volost Soviet, for invisible threads led from the priest's house and the kulaks' cottages to the forest thickets. Thither went cases of ammunition, chunks of fresh pork, bottles of bluish raw spirit and also news that was whispered into the ears of the lesser atamans and then passed on by devious routes to Orlik himself.

Though it consisted of no more than two or three hundred cutthroats, the band had so far eluded capture. It would split up into several small units and operate in two or three districts simultaneously. It was impossible to catch all of them. Last night's bandit would next day appear as a peaceful peasant pottering in his garden, feeding his horse or standing at his gate puffing smugly at his pipe and watching the cavalry patrols ride by with a blank look in his eyes.

Alexander Puzyrevsky with his regiment chased the bandits up and down the three districts with dogged persistence. Occasionally he did succeed in treading on their tail; a month later Orlik was obliged to withdraw his ruffians from two of the districts, and now he was hemmed in on a narrow strip of territory.

· · · ·

LIFE IN THE TOWN JOGGED along at its customary pace. Noisy crowds swarmed its five markets. Two impulses dominated the milling throngs – to grab as much as possible, and to give as little as possible. This environment offered unlimited scope for the energy and abilities of all manner of sharks and swindlers. Hundreds of slippery individuals with eyes that expressed everything but honesty snooped about among the crowds. All the scum of the town gathered here like flies on a dunghill, moved by a single purpose: to hoodwink the gullible. The few trains that came this way spewed out gobs of sack-laden people who made at once for the markets. At night the market places were deserted, and the dark rows of booths and stalls looked sinister and menacing.

It was the bold man who would venture after dark into this desolate quarter where danger lurked behind every stall. And often by night a shot would ring out like the clang of a hammer on iron, and some throat would choke on its own blood. And by the time the handful of militiamen from the nearest beats would reach the spot (they did not venture out alone) they would find nothing but the contorted corpse. The killers had taken to their heels and the commotion had swept away the few nocturnal habitués of the market square like a gust of wind.

Opposite the market place was the "Orion" cinema. The street and pavement were flooded with electric light and people crowded around the entrance. Inside the hall the movie projector clicked away, flashing melodramatic love scenes onto the screen; now and then the film snapped and the operator stopped the projector amid roars of disapproval from the audience.

In the centre of the town and on the outskirts life appeared to be taking its usual course. Even in the Gubernia Committee of the Party, the nerve centre of revolutionary authority, everything was quiet. But this was merely an outward calm.

A storm was brewing in the town. Many of those who came there from various directions, with their army rifles plainly visible under their long peasant overcoats, were aware of its coming. So did those who under the guise of food speculators arrived on the roofs of trains, but instead of carrying their sacks to the market took them to carefully memorised addresses.

But the workers' districts, and even Bolsheviks, had no inkling of the approaching storm. Only five Bolsheviks in town knew what was being plotted. Closely co-operating with foreign missions in Warsaw, the remnants of Petlyura's bands which the Red Army had driven into White Poland were preparing to take part in the uprising. A raiding force was being formed of what remained of Petlyura's regiments. The central committee of the insurgents had an organisation in Shepetovka; it consisted of forty-seven members, most of them former active counter-revolutionaries whom the local Cheka had trustingly left at liberty. Father Vasili, Ensign Vinnik, and Kuzmenko, a Petlyura officer, were the leaders of the organisation. The priest's daughters, Vinnik's father and brother, and a man named Samotinya who had wormed his way into the office of the Executive Committee did the spying.

The plan was to attack the frontier Special Department by night with hand grenades, release the prisoners and, if possible, seize the railway station. Meanwhile officers were being secretly concentrated in the city which was to be the hub of the uprising, and bandit gangs were being moved into the neighbouring forests. From here, contact with Rumania and with Petlyura himself was maintained through trusted agents

• • • •

FYODOR ZHUKHRAI, IN his office at the Special Department, had not slept for six nights. He was one of the five Bolsheviks who were aware of what was brewing. The ex-sailor was now experiencing the sensation of the big game hunter who has tracked down his prey and is now waiting for the beast to spring.

He dare not shout or raise the alarm. The bloodthirsty monster must be slain. Then and then only would it be possible to work in peace, without having to glance fearfully behind every bush. But the beast must not be scared away. In life and death conflicts such as these it is endurance and firmness that win the day.

The crucial moment was at hand. Somewhere in the town amidst the labyrinth of conspiratorial hideouts the time had been set: tomorrow night. But the five Bolsheviks who knew decided to strike first. No, they decreed, the time was tonight.

The same evening an armoured train slid quietly out of the railway yards and the massive gates closed as quietly behind it. Coded telegrams flew over the wires and in response to their urgent summons the alert and watchful men to whom the republic's security had been entrusted took immediate steps to stamp out the hornets nests.

Akim telephoned to Zharky. "Nucleus meetings in order? Good. Come over here at once for a conference and bring the Party District Committee Secretary with you. The fuel problem is worse than we thought. We'll discuss the details when you get here." Akim spoke in a firm, hurried voice. "This firewood business is driving us all potty," Zharky growled back into the receiver.

Litke drove the two secretaries over to headquarters at breakneck speed. As they ascended the stairs to the second floor they saw at once that they had not been summoned here to talk about firewood.

On the office manager's desk stood a machinegun and gunners from the Special Task Force were busy beside it. The corridors were full of silent guards from the town's Party and Komsomol organisations. Behind the wide doors of the Secretary's office an emergency session of the Bureau of the Gubernia Committee of the Party was drawing to a close.

Through a fanlight giving onto the street wires led to two field telephones. There was a subdued hum of conversation in the room. Akim, Rita and Mikhailo were there, Rita in a Red Army helmet, khaki skirt, leather jacket with a heavy Mauser hanging from the belt

– the uniform she used to wear at the front when she had been company political instructor.

"What's all this about?" Zharky asked her in surprise. "Alert drill, Vanya. We're going to your district right away. There is a practice rally in the fifth infantry school. The Komsomols are going there straight from their nucleus meetings. The main thing is to get there without attracting attention."

The grounds of the old military school with its giant old oaks, its stagnant pond overgrown with burdock and nettles and its broad unswept paths were wrapped in silence. In the centre of the grounds behind a high white wall stood the school building, now the premises of the fifth infantry school for Red Army commanders. It was late at night. The upper floor of the building was dark. Outwardly all was serene, and the chance passer-by would have thought that the school's inmates were asleep. Why, then, were the iron gates open, and what were those two dark shapes like monster toads standing by the entrance? The people who gathered here from all parts of the railway district knew that the school's inmates could not be asleep, once a night alert had been given. They had left their Komsomol and Party nucleus meetings immediately after the brief announcement had been made; they came quietly, individually, in pairs, never more than three together, and each of them carried the Communist Party or Komsomol membership card, without which no one could pass through the iron gates.

The assembly hall, where a large crowd had already gathered, was flooded with light. The windows were heavily curtained with thick canvas tenting. The Bolsheviks who had been summoned here stood about calmly smoking their home-made cigarettes and cracking jokes about the precautions taken for a drill. No one felt this was a real alert; it was being done to maintain discipline in the speciality detachments. The seasoned soldier, however, recognised the signs of a genuine alert as soon as he entered the schoolyard. Far too much caution was being displayed. Platoons of students were lining up outside to whispered commands. Machine guns were being carried quietly into the yard and not a chink of light showed in any of the windows of the building.

"Something serious in the wind, Mityai?" Pavel Korchagin inquired of Dubava, who was sitting on a window sill next to a girl Pavel remembered seeing a couple of days before at Zharky's place. Dubava clapped Pavel good-humouredly on the shoulder. "Getting cold feet, eh? Never mind, we'll teach you fellows how to fight. You don't know each other, do you?" he nodded toward the girl. "First name's Anna, don't know her second name, but I know her title, she's in charge of the agitation and propaganda centre."

The girl thus jocularly introduced by Dubava regarded Korchagin with interest and pushed back a wisp of hair that had escaped from under her mauve kerchief. Korchagin's eyes met hers and for a moment or two a silent contest ensued. Her sparkling jet-black eyes under their sweeping lashes challenged his. Pavel shifted his gaze to Dubava. Conscious that he was blushing, he scowled. "Which of you does the agitating?" he inquired, forcing a smile. At that moment there was a stir in the hall. A company commander climbed onto a chair and shouted: "Members of the First Company, line up. Hurry, comrades, hurry!"

Zhukhrai entered with the Chairman of the Gubernia Executive Committee and Akim. They had just arrived. The hall was now filled from end to end with people lined up in formation. The Chairman of the Gubernia Executive Committee stepped on to the mounting of a training machine gun and raised his hand. "Comrades," he said, "you have been summoned here on an extremely serious and urgent matter. What I am going to tell you now could not have been told even yesterday for security reasons. Tomorrow night a counter-revolutionary uprising is scheduled to break out in this and other towns of the Ukraine. The town is full of White guard officers. Bandit units have been concentrated all around the town. Part of the conspirators have penetrated into the armoured car detachment and are working there as drivers. But the Cheka has uncovered the plot in good time and we are putting the entire Party and Komsomol organisations under arms. The first and second Communist battalions will operate together with the military school units and Cheka detachments. The military school units have already gone into action. It is now your turn, comrades. You have fifteen minutes to get your weapons and line up. Comrade Zhukhrai will be in command of the operation. The unit commanders will take their orders from him. I need hardly stress the gravity of the situation. Tomorrow's insurrection must be averted today."

A quarter of an hour later the armed battalion was lined up in the schoolyard. Zhukhrai ran his eye over the motionless ranks. Three paces in front of them stood two men girded with leather belts: Battalion Commander Menyailo, a foundry worker, a giant of a man from the Urals, and beside him Commissar Akim. To the left were the platoons of the first company, with the company commander and political instructor two paces in front. Behind them stood the silent ranks of the Communist battalion, three hundred strong.

Fyodor gave the signal. "Time to begin."

· · · ·

THE THREE HUNDRED MEN marched through the deserted streets. The city slept. On Lvovskaya Street, opposite Dikaya, the battalion broke ranks. It was to go into action here. Noiselessly they surrounded the buildings. Headquarters was set up on the steps of a shop. An automobile came speeding down Lvovskaya Street from the direction of the centre, its headlights cutting a bright path before it. It pulled up sharply in front of the battalion command post. Hugo Litke had brought his father this time. The commandant sprang out of the car, throwing a few clipped Lettish sentences over his shoulder to his son.

The car leapt forward and disappeared in a flash around the bend of the road. Litke, his hands gripping the steering wheel as though part of it, his eyes glued to the road, drove like a demon. Yes, there was need of Litke's wild driving tonight. He was hardly likely to get two nights in the guardhouse for speeding now! And Hugo flew down the streets like a meteor.

Zhukhrai, whom young Litke drove from one end of town to the other in the twinkling of an eye, was moved to voice his approval. "If you don't knock anyone down tonight you'll get a gold watch tomorrow." Hugo was jubilant. "I thought I'd get ten days in jail for that corner...."

* * * *

THE FIRST BLOWS WERE struck at the conspirators' headquarters. Before long groups of prisoners and batches of documents were being delivered to the Special Department.

In House No. Eleven on Dikaya Street lived one Zurbert who, according to information in possession of the Cheka, had played no small part in the Whiteguard plot. The lists of the officers' units that were to operate in the Podol area were in his keeping.

Litke senior himself came to Dikaya Street to make the arrest. The windows of Zurbert's apartment looked out onto a garden which was separated from a former nunnery by a high wall. Zurbert was not at home. The neighbours said that he had not been seen at all that day. A search was made and the lists of names and addresses were found, together with a case of hand grenades. Litke, having ordered an ambush to be set, lingered for a moment in the room to examine the papers.

The young military school student on sentry duty in the garden below could see the lighted window from the corner of the garden where he was stationed. He did not like being there alone in the dark. It was a little frightening. He had been told to keep an eye on the wall. The comforting light seemed very far from his post. And to make matters worse, the blasted moon kept darting behind the clouds. In the night the bushes seemed to be invested with a sinister life of their own

The young soldier stabbed at the darkness around him with his bayonet. Nothingness. "Why did they put me here? No one could climb that wall anyhow, it's far too high. I think I'll go over to the window and peep in." Glancing up again at the wall, he emerged from his dank, fungus-smelling corner. As he came up to the window, Litke picked up the papers from the table. At that moment a shadow appeared on top of the wall whence both the sentry by the window and the man inside the room were clearly visible. With catlike agility the shadow swung itself onto a tree and dropped down to the ground. Stealthily it crept up to its victim. A single blow and the sentry was sprawled on the ground with a naval dirk driven up to the hilt into his neck.

A shot rang out in the garden galvanising the men surrounding the block. Six of them ran toward the house, their steps ringing loudly in the night. Litke sat slumped forward over the table, the blood pouring from the wound in his head. He was dead. The windowpane was shattered. But the assassin had not had time to seize the documents.

Several more shots were heard in the direction of the nunnery wall. The murderer had climbed over the wall to the street and was now trying to escape by way of the Lukyanov field, shooting as he ran. But a bullet cut short his flight.

All night long the searches continued. Hundreds of people not registered in the books of the house committees and found in possession of suspicious documents and weapons were dispatched to the Cheka, where a commission was at work screening the suspects.

Here and there the conspirators fought back. During the search in a house on Zhilyanskaya Street Anton Lebedev was killed by a shot fired point-blank.

The Solomenka battalion lost five men that night, and the Cheka lost Jan Litke, that staunch Bolshevik and faithful guardian of the republic.

But the Whiteguard uprising was nipped in the bud.

. . . .

THAT SAME NIGHT FATHER Vasili with his daughters and the rest of the gang were arrested in Shepetovka.

The tension relaxed. But soon a new enemy threatened the town: paralysis on the railways, which meant starvation and cold in the coming winter.

Everything now depended on grain and firewood.

CHAPTER TWO

Fyodor took his short-stemmed pipe out of his mouth and poked reactively at the ash in the bowl with a cautious finger; the pipe was out

A dense cloud of grey smoke from a dozen cigarettes hovered below the ceiling and over the chair where sat the Chairman of the Gubernia Executive Committee. From the corners of the room the faces of the people seated around the table were only dimly visible through the haze.

Tokarev, sitting next to the Chairman, leaned forward and plucked irritably at his sparse beard, glancing now and again out of the corner of his eye at a short, bald-headed man whose high-pitched voice went on endlessly stringing out phrases that were as empty and meaningless as a sucked egg.

Akim caught the look in the old worker's eye and was reminded of a fighting cock back in his childhood days in the village who had had the same wicked look in his eye just before pouncing on his adversary. The Gubernia Committee of the Party had been in conference for more than an hour. The bald man was the chairman of the railway firewood committee.

Leafing with nimble fingers through the heap of papers before him, the bald man rattled on: "...under these circumstances it is clearly impossible to carry out the decision of the Gubernia Committee and the railway management. I repeat, even a month from now we shall not be able to give more than four hundred cubic metres of firewood. As for the one hundred and eighty thousand cubic metres required, well that's sheer ..." the speaker fumbled for the right word, "...sheer Utopia!" he wound up and his small mouth pursed itself up into an expression of injury.

There was a long silence.

Fyodor tapped his pipe with his fingernail and knocked out the ashes. It was Tokarev who finally broke the silence. "There's no use wasting our breath," he began in his rumbling bass. "The railway firewood committee hasn't any firewood, never had any, and don't expect any in the future... Right?" The bald man shrugged a shoulder. "Excuse me, Comrade, we did stock up firewood, but the shortage of road transport..." He swallowed. Wiped his polished pate with a checked handkerchief; he made several fruitless attempts to stuff the handkerchief back into his pocket, and finally shoved it nervously under his portfolio.

"What have you done about delivering the wood? After all, a good many days have passed since the leading specialists mixed up in the conspiracy were arrested," Denekko observed from his corner. The bald man turned to him. "I wrote the railway administration three times stating that unless we had the proper transport facilities it would be impossible..."

Tokarev stopped him. "We've heard that already." he said coldly, eyeing the bald man with hostility. "Do you take us for a pack of fools?" The bald man felt a chill run down his spine at these words. "I cannot answer for the actions of counter-revolutionaries," he replied in a low voice.

"But you knew, didn't you, that the timber was being felled a long distance from the railway line?'"

"I heard about it, but I could not bring the attention of my superiors to irregularities on a sector outside my province."

"How many men have you on the job?" the chairman of the trade union council demanded. "About two hundred," the bald man replied. "That makes a cubic metre a year for every parasite!" hissed Tokarev.

"The railway timber committee has been allotted special rations, food the workers ought to be getting, and look what you're doing?

What happened to those two cars of flour you received for the workers?" the trade union chairman persisted.

Similar pointed questions rained down on the bald man from all sides and he answered them in the harassed manner of a man trying to ward off annoying creditors. He twisted and turned like an eel to avoid direct answers, but his eyes darted nervously about him. He sensed danger and his cowardly soul craved but one thing: to get away from here as quickly as possible and slink off to his cosy nest, to his supper and his still youthful wife who was probably cosily whiling away the time with a Paul de Kock novel. Lending an attentive ear to the bald man's replies, Fyodor scribbled in his notebook: "I believe this man ought to be checked up on properly. This is more than mere incompetence. I know one or two things about him... Stop the discussion and let him go so we can get down to business."

The Chairman read the note and nodded to Fyodor.

Zhukhrai rose and went out into the corridor to make a telephone call. When he returned the Chairman was reading the resolution: "...to remove the management of the Railway Firewood Committee for sabotage, the matter of the timber workings to be turned over to the investigation authorities."

The bald man had expected worse. True, to be removed from his post for sabotage would raise the question of his reliability in general, but that was a mere trifle. As for the Boyarka business, he was not worried, that was not his province after all. "A close shave, though," he said to himself, "I thought they had really dug up something..."

Now almost reassured, he remarked as he put his papers back into his portfolio: "of course, I am a non-Party specialist and you are at liberty to distrust me. But my conscience is clear. If I have failed to do what was required of me that was because it was impossible." No one made any comment. The bald man went out, hurried downstairs, and opened the street door with a feeling of intense relief.

"Your name, citizen?" a man in an army coat accosted him. With a sinking heart the baldhead stammered: "Cher...vinsky..."

Upstairs as soon as the outsider was gone, thirteen heads bent closer over the large conference table. "See here," Zhukhrai's finger jabbed the unfolded map. "That's Boyarka station. The timber felling is six kilometres away. There are two hundred and ten thousand cubic metres of wood stacked up at this point: a whole army of men worked hard for eight months to pile up all that wood, and what's the result? Treachery. The railway and the town are without firewood. To haul that timber six kilometres to the station would take five thousand carts no less than one month, and that only if they made two trips a day. The nearest village is fifteen kilometres away. What's more, Orlik and his band are prowling about in those parts. You realise what this means? Look, according to the plan the felling was to have been started right here and continued in the direction of the station, and those scoundrels carried it right into the depths of the forest. The purpose was to make sure we would not be able to haul the firewood to the railway line. And they weren't far wrong – we couldn't even get a hundred carts for the job. It's a foul blow they've struck us. The uprising was no more serious than this."

Zhukhrai's clenched fist dropped heavily onto the tracing paper of the map. Each of the thirteen clearly visualised the grimmer aspects of the situation which Zhukhrai had omitted to mention. Winter was in the offing. They saw hospitals, schools, offices and hundreds of thousands of people caught in the icy grip of the frost; the railway stations swarming with people and only one train a week to handle the traffic.

There was deep silence as each man pondered the situation. At length Fyodor relaxed his fist. "There is one way out, Comrades." he said. "We must build a seven-kilometre narrow-gauge line from the station to the timber tract in three months. The first section leading to the beginning of the tract must be ready in six weeks. I've been working on this for the past week. We'll need," Zhukhrai's voice cracked in his dry throat, "three hundred and fifty workers and two engineers. There is enough track and seven locomotives at Pushcha-Voditsa. The Komsomols dug them up in the warehouses. There was a project to lay a narrow-gauge line from Pushcha-Voditsa to the town before the war. The trouble is there are no accommodations in Boyarka for the workers, the place is in ruins. We'll have to send the men in small groups for a fortnight at a time, they won't be able to hold out any longer than that. Shall we send the Komsomols, Akim?" And without waiting for an answer, he went on: "The Komsomol will rush as many of its members to the spot as possible. There's the Solomenka organisation to begin with, and some from the town. The task is hard, very hard but if the youngsters are told what is at stake I'm certain they'll do it."

The chief of the railway shook his head dubiously. "I'm afraid it's no use. To lay seven kilometres of track in the woods under such conditions, with the autumn rains due and the frosts coming..." he began wearily. But Zhukhrai cut him short.

"You ought to have paid more attention to the firewood problem, Andrei Vasilievich. That line has got to be built and we're going to build it. We're not going to fold our hands and freeze to death, are we?"

• • • •

THE LAST CRATES OF tools were loaded on to the train. The train crew took their places. A fine drizzle was falling. Crystal rain drops rolled down Rita's glistening leather jacket. Rita shook hands warmly with Tokarev. "We wish you luck," she said softly.

The old man regarded her affectionately from beneath his bushy grey eyebrows. "Yes, they've given us a peck of trouble, blast 'em," he growled in answer to his own thoughts. "You here had better look to things, so that if there's any hitch over there you can put a bit of pressure on where it's needed. These good-for-nothings here can't do anything without a lot of red tape. Well, time I was getting aboard, daughter."

The old man buttoned up his jacket. At the last moment Rita inquired casually: "Isn't Korchagin going along? I didn't notice him among the boys."

"No, he and the job superintendent went out there yesterday by handcar to prepare for our coming."

At that moment Zharky, Dubava, and Anna Borhart with her jacket flung carelessly over her shoulder and a cigarette between her slender fingers, came hurrying down the platform toward them. Rita had time to ask Tokarev one more question before the others joined them. "How are your studies with Korchagin getting along?" The old man looked at her in surprise. "What studies? The lad's under your wing, isn't he? He's told me a lot about you. Thinks the world of you."

Rita looked sceptical. "Are you quite sure, Comrade Tokarev? Didn't he always go to you for a proper explanation after his lessons with me?" The old man burst out laughing. "To me? Why, I never saw hide or hair of him."

The engine shrieked. Klavicek shouted from one of the cars: "hey, Comrade Ustinovich, give us our Daddy back! What'd we do without him?"

The Czech was about to say something else, but catching sight of the three latecomers he checked himself. Momentarily he encountered the anxious look in Anna's eyes, caught with a pang her parting smile to Dubava and turned quickly away from the window.

• • • •

THE AUTUMN RAIN LASHED the face. Low clouds, leaden-hued and swollen with moisture, crawled over the earth. Late autumn had stripped the sylvan hosts bare; and the old horn-beams looked gaunt and downcast, their wrinkled trunks hidden under the brown moss. Remorseless autumn had robbed them of their luxuriant garments, and they stood there naked and pitiful.

The little station building huddled forlornly in the midst of the forest. A strip of freshly dug earth ran from the stone freight platform into the woods. Around this strip men swarmed like ants. The clayey mud squelched unpleasantly underfoot. There was a ringing of crowbars and a grating of spades on stone over by the embankment where the men were furiously digging.

The rain came down as if through a fine sieve and the chill drops penetrated the men's clothing. The rain threatened to wash away what their labour had accomplished, for the clay slid down the embankment in a soggy mass. Soaked to the skin, their clothing chill and sodden, the men worked on until long after dark. And with every day the strip of upturned earth penetrated further and further into the forest.

Not far from the station loomed the grim skeleton of what had once been a brick building. Everything that could be removed bodily, torn out or blasted loose had long since been carried off by marauders. There were gaping holes in place of windows and doors; black gashes where stove doors had once been. Through the holes in the tattered roof the rafters showed like the ribs of a skeleton.

Only the concrete floor in the four large rooms remained intact. At night four hundred men slept on this floor in their damp, mud-caked clothing. Muddy water streamed from their clothes when they wrung them out at the doorway. And the men heaped bitter curses on the rain and the boggy soil. They lay in compact rows on the concrete floor with its thin covering of straw, huddling together for warmth. The steam rose from their clothing but it did not dry. And the rain seeped through the sacks that were nailed over the empty window frames and trickled down onto the floor. It drummed loudly on the remnants of sheet metal roofing, and the wind whistled through the great cracks in the door.

In the morning they drank tea in the tumbledown barrack that served for a kitchen, and went off to their work. Dinner, day after day with sickening monotony, consisted of plain boiled lentils, and there was a daily allowance of a pound and a half of bread as black as anthracite. That was all the town could provide. The job superintendent, Valerian Nikodimovich Patoshkin, a tall spare old man with two deep lines at his mouth, and technician Vakulenko, a thickset man with a coarse-featured face and a fleshy nose, had put up at the station master's house.

Tokarev shared the tiny room occupied by the station Cheka agent, a small, volatile man named Kholyava. The men endured the hardships with dogged fortitude, and the railway embankment reached farther into the forest from day to day. True, there had been some desertions: at first nine and a few days later, another five. The first major calamity occurred a week after the work started, when the bread supply failed to arrive with the night train. Dubava woke Tokarev and told him the news. The secretary of the Party group swung his hairy legs over the side of the bed and scratched himself furiously under the armpit.

"The fun's beginning!" he growled and began hastily to dress. Kholyava waddled in on his short legs. "Cut down to the telephone and call the Special Department," Tokarev instructed him, and turning to Dubava added, "and not a word to anybody about the bread, mind." After berating the railway telephone operators for a full half hour, the irrepressible Kholyava succeeded in getting Zhukhrai, the assistant chief of the Special Department, on the line, while Tokarev stood by fidgeting with impatience.

"What! Bread not delivered? I'll soon find out who's responsible for that!" Zhukhrai's voice coming over the wire had an ominous ring. "What are we going to give the men to eat tomorrow?" Tokarev shouted back angrily. There was a long pause; Zhukhrai was evidently considering some plan of action. "You'll get the bread tonight," he said at last. "I'll send young Litke with the car. He knows the way. You'll have the bread by morning."

At dawn a mud-stained car loaded with sacks of bread drove up to the station. Litke, his face white and strained after a sleepless night at the wheel, climbed out wearily. Work on the railway line became a struggle against increasing odds. The railway administration announced that there were no sleepers to be had. The town authorities could find no means of shipping the track and locomotives to the construction site, and the locomotives themselves turned out to be in need of substantial repairs. No workers were forthcoming to replace the first batch who had done their share and were now so completely worn out that there could be no question of detaining them.

The leading Party members met in the tumbledown shed dimly lit by a chimneyless oil lamp and sat up late into the night discussing the situation.

The following morning Tokarev, Dubava and Klavicek went to town, taking six men with them to repair the locomotives and speed up the shipment of the track. Klavicek, who was a baker by trade, was sent as inspector to the supply department, while the rest went on to Pushcha-Voditsa.

Out at the construction site the rain poured down without ceasing.

* * * *

PAVEL KORCHAGIN PULLED his foot out of the sticky slime with an effort. A sharp sensation of cold told him that the worn sole of his boot had finally parted from the uppers. His torn boots had been a source of keen discomfort to Pavel ever since he had come to the job. They were never dry and the mud that filtered .in squelched when he walked. Now one sole was gone altogether and the icy mire cut into his bare foot. Pavel pulled the sole out of the mud and regarded it with despair and broke the vow he had given himself not to swear. He could not go on working with one foot exposed, so he hobbled back to the barrack, sat down beside the field kitchen, took off his muddy foot-cloth and stretched out his numb foot to the fire.

Odarka, the lineman's wife who worked as cook's helper, was busy cutting up beetroots at the kitchen table. A woman of generous proportions, still youthful, with broad almost masculine shoulders, an ample bosom and massive hips, she wielded the kitchen knife with vigour and the mountain of sliced vegetables grew rapidly under her nimble fingers. Odarka threw a careless glance at Pavel and snapped at him: "if it's dinner you're hankering after you're a bit early, my lad. Ought to be ashamed of yourself sneaking away from work like that! Take your feet off that stove. This is a kitchen not a bathhouse!"

The cook came in at that point. "My blasted boot has gone to pieces," Pavel said, explaining his untimely presence in the kitchen. The elderly cook looked at the battered boot and nodding toward Odarka he said: "Her husband might be able to do something with it, he's a bit of a cobbler. Better see to it or you'll be in a bad way. You can't get along without boots." When she heard this, Odarka took another look at Pavel and saw that she had been too hasty in her judgement of him.

"I took you for a loafer," she admitted contritely. Pavel smiled to show that there were no hard feelings. Odarka examined the boot with the eye of an expert. "There's no use trying to patch it," she concluded. "But I'll tell you what I can do. I'll bring you an old galosh we've got lying around at home and you can wear it on top of the boot so your foot won't get hurt. You can't go around like that, you'll kill yourself! The frosts will start any day now!"

And Odarka, now all sympathy, laid down her knife and hurried out, returning shortly with a deep galosh and a strip of stout linen.

As he wrapped his foot, now warm and dry, in the thick linen and put it into the galosh, Pavel rewarded Odarka with a grateful look.

* * * *

TOKAREV CAME BACK FROM town fuming. He called a meeting of the leading Communists in Kholyava's room and told them the unpleasant news. "Nothing but obstacles all along the line. Wherever you go the wheels seem to be turning but they don't get anywhere. Far too many of those White rats about, and it looks as if there'll be enough to last our lifetime anyway. I tell you, boys, things look bad. There are no replacements for us yet and no one knows how many there will be. The frosts are due any day now, and we must get through the marsh before then at all costs, because when the ground freezes it'll be too late. So while they're shaking up those fellows in town who're making a mess of things, we here have to double our speed. That line has got to be built and we're going to build it if we die doing it. Otherwise it isn't Bolsheviks we'll be but jellyfish."

There was a steely note in Tokarev's hoarse bass voice, and his eyes under their bushy brows had a stubborn gleam.

"We'll call a closed meeting today and pass on the news to our Party members and tomorrow we'll all get down to work. In the morning we'll let the non-Party fellows go; the rest of us will stay. Here's the Gubernia Committee decision," he said, handing Pankratov a sheet of paper folded in four.

Pavel Korchagin, peering over Pankratov's shoulder, read:

In view of the emergency all members of the Komsomol are to remain on the job and are not to be relieved until the first consignment of firewood is forthcoming.

Signed R. Ustinovich, on behalf of the Secretary of the Gubernia Committee.

The kitchen barrack was jammed. One hundred and twenty men had squeezed themselves into its narrow confines. They stood against the walls, climbed on the tables and some were even perched on top of the field kitchen.

Pankratov opened the meeting. Then Tokarev made a brief speech winding up with an announcement that had the effect of a bombshell: "the Communists and Komsomols will not leave the job tomorrow." The old man accompanied his statement with a gesture that stressed the finality of the decision. It swept away all cherished hopes of returning to town, going home, getting away from this hole.

A roar of angry voices drowned out everything else for a few moments. The swaying bodies caused the feeble oil light to flicker fitfully. In the semidarkness the commotion increased. They wanted to go "home"; they protested indignantly that they had had as much as they could stand. Some received the news in silence. And only one man spoke of deserting.

"To hell with it all!" he shouted angrily from his corner, loosing an ugly stream of invective. "I'm not going to stay here another day. It's all right to do hard labour if you've committed a crime. But what have we done? We're fools to stand for it. We've had two weeks of it, and that's enough. Let those who made the decision come out and do the work themselves. Maybe some folks like poking around in this muck, but I've only one life to live. I'm leaving tomorrow."

The voice came from behind Okunev and he lit a match to see who it was. For an instant the speaker's rage-distorted face and open mouth were snatched out of the darkness by the match's flame. But that instant was enough for Okunev to recognise the son of a Gubernia food commissariat bookkeeper. "Checking up, eh?" he snarled. "Well, I'm not afraid, I'm no thief." The match flickered out. Pankratov rose and drew himself up to his full height.

"What kind of talk is that? Who dares to compare a Party task to a hard-labour sentence?" he thundered, running his eyes menacingly over the front rows. "No, Comrades, there's no going to town for us, our place is here. If we clear out now folks will freeze to death. The sooner we finish the job the sooner we get back home. Running away like that whiner back there suggests doesn't fit in with our ideas or our discipline."

Pankratov, a docker, was not fond of long speeches but even this brief statement was interrupted by the same irate voice. "The non-Party fellows are leaving, aren't they?" "Yes."

A lad in a short overcoat came elbowing his way to the front. A Komsomol card came flying bat -like across the room, struck against Pankratov's chest, dropped onto the table and stood on edge. "There, take your card. I'm not going to risk my health for a bit of cardboard!"

His last words were drowned out by a roar of angry voices: "What do you think you're throwing around!" "Treacherous bastard!" "Got into the Komsomol because he thought he'd have it easy." "Chuck him out!" "Let me get at the louse!"

The deserter, his head lowered, made his way to the exit. They let him pass, shrinking away from him as from a leper. The door closed with a creak behind him. Pankratov picked up the discarded membership card and held it to the flame of the oil lamp. The cardboard caught alight and curled up as it burned.

A shot echoed in the forest. A horseman turned from the tumbledown barrack and dived into the darkness of the forest. A moment later men came running out of the barrack and school building. Someone discovered a piece of plywood that had been stuck into the door jamb. A match flared up and shielding the unsteady flame from the wind they read the scrawled message: "Clear out of here and go back where you came from. If you don't, we will shoot every man jack of you. I give you till tomorrow night to get out. Ataman Chesnok."

Chesnok belonged to Orlik's band.

· · · ·

AN OPEN DIARY LIES on the table in Rita's room.

December Second

We had our first snow this morning. The frost is severe. I met Vyach-eslav Olshinsky on the stairs and we walked down the street together.

I always enjoy the first snowfall,' he said. 'Particularly when it is frosty like this. Lovely isn't it?'

But I was thinking of Boyarka and I told him that the frost and snow do not gladden me at all. On the contrary they depress me. And I told him why.

'That is a purely subjective reaction,' he said. 'If one argues on that premise all merriment or any manifestation of joy in wartime, for example, would have to be banned. But life is not like that. The tragedy is confined to the strip of frontline where the battle is being fought. There life is overshadowed by the proximity of death. Yet even there people laugh. And away from the front, life goes on as always: people laugh, weep, suffer, rejoice, love, seek amusement, entertainment, excitement.'

It was difficult to detect any shade of irony in Olshinsky's words. Olshinsky is a representative of the People's Commissariat of Foreign Affairs. He has been in the Party since nineteen-seventeen. He dresses well, is always cleanly shaven with a faint aura of perfume about him.

He lives in our house, in Segal's apartment. Sometimes he drops in to see me in the evenings. He is very interesting to talk to, he knows a lot about Europe, lived for many years in Paris. But I doubt whether he and I could ever be good friends. That is because for him I am primarily a woman; the fact that I am his Party comrade is a secondary consideration. True, he does not attempt to disguise his sentiments and opinions on this score, he has the courage of his convictions and there is nothing coarse about his attentions. He has the knack of investing them with a sort of beauty. Yet I do not like him.

The gruff simplicity of Zhukhrai is far more to my taste than all Olshinsky's polished European manners.

News from Boyarka comes in the form of brief reports. Each day another two hundred metres are laid. They are laying the sleepers straight on the frozen earth, hewing out shallow beds for them. There are only two hundred and forty men on the job. Half of the replacements deserted. The conditions there are truly frightful. I can't imagine how they will be able to carry on in the frost. Dubava has been gone a week now. They were only able to repair five of the eight locomotives at Pushcha-Voditsa, there were not enough parts for the others.

Dmitri has had criminal charges laid against him by the tramcar authorities. He and his brigade held up all the flatcars belonging to the tram system running to town from Pushcha-Vodista, cleared off the passengers and loaded the cars with rails for the Boyarka line. They brought nineteen carloads of rails along the tram tracks to the railway station in town. The tram crews were only too glad to help.

The Solomenka Komsomols still in town worked all night loading the rails onto railway cars and Dmitri and his brigade went off with them to Boyarka.

Akim refused to have Dubava's action taken up at the Komsomol Bureau. Dmitri has told us about the outrageous bureaucracy and red tape in the tramcar administration. They flatly refused to give more than two cars for the job.

Tufta, however, privately reprimanded Dubava. 'It's time to drop these partisan tactics,' he said, 'or you'll find yourself in jail before you know it. Surely you could have come to some agreement without resorting to force of arms?'

I had never seen Dubava so furious.

'Why didn't you try talking to them yourself, you rotten pen-pusher?' he stormed. 'All you can do is sit here warming your chair and wagging your tongue. How do you think I could go back to Boyarka without those rails? Instead of hanging around here and getting in everybody's hair you ought to be sent out there to do some useful work. Tokarev would knock some sense into you!' Dmitri roared so loudly he could be heard all over the building.

Tufta wrote a complaint against Dubava, but Akim asked me to leave the room and talked to him alone for about ten minutes, after which Tufta came out red and fuming.

December Third

The Gubernia Committee has received another complaint, this time from the Transport Cheka. It appears that Pankratov, Okunev and several other comrades went to Motovilovka station and removed all the doors and window frames from the empty buildings.

When they were loading all this onto a freight train the station Cheka man tried to arrest them. They disarmed him, emptied his revolver and returned it to him only after the train was in motion. They got away with the doors and window frames.

Tokarev is charged by the supply department of the railway for taking twenty poods of nails from the Boyarka railway stocks. He gave the nails to the peasants in payment for their help in hauling the timber they are using for sleepers.

I spoke to Comrade Zhukhrai about all these complaints. But he only laughed. 'We'll take care of all that,' he said.

The situation out on the railway job is very tense and now every day is precious. We have to bring pressure to bear here for every trifle. Every now and then we have to summon hinderers to the Gubernia Committee. And over at the job the boys are overriding all formalities more and more often.

Olshinsky has brought me a little electric stove. Olga Yureneva and I warm our hands over it, but it doesn't make the room any warmer. I wonder how those men in the woods are faring this bitter cold night. Olga tells me that it is so cold in the hospital that the patients shiver under their blankets. The place is heated only once in two days.

No, Comrade Olshinsky, a tragedy at the front is a tragedy in the rear too!"

December Fourth

It snowed all night. From Boyarka they write that everything is snowbound and they have had to stop working to clear the track. Today the Gubernia Committee passed a decision that the first section of the railway, up to the beginning of the timber workings, is to be ready not later than January first, nineteen-twenty-two. When this decision reached Boyarka, Tokarev is said to have remarked: 'We'll do it, if we don't croak by then.'

I hear nothing at all about Korchagin. I'm rather surprised that he hasn't been mixed up in something like the Pankratov 'case.' I still don't understand why he avoids me.

December Fifth

Yesterday there was a bandit raid on the construction site.

The horses trod warily in the soft, yielding snow. Now and then a twig hidden under the snow would snap under a hoof and the horse would snort and shy, but a sharp cut over its laid-back ears would send it galloping after the others.

Some dozen horsemen crossed the hilly ridge beyond which lay a strip of dark earth not yet blanketed with snow. Here the riders reined in their horses. There was a faint clink as stirrup met stirrup. The leader's stallion, its coat glossy with sweat after the long run, shook itself noisily.

"There's a hell of a lot of them here," said the head rider in Ukrainian. "But we'll soon put the fear of god into 'em. The ataman said the bastards were to be chased out of here by tomorrow. They're getting too damned close to the firewood."

They rode up to the station single file, hugging the sides of the narrow-gauge line. In sight of the clearing near the old school building they slowed down to a walking pace and came to a halt behind the trees, not venturing out into the open.

A volley rent the silence of the night. A layer of snow dropped squirrel-like off the branch of a birch that gleamed like silver in the light of the moon. Gunfire flashed among the trees, bullets bored into crumbling plaster and there was a tinkling of broken glass as Pankratov's windowpanes were smashed to smithereens.

The men on the concrete floor leapt up at the shooting only to drop back again on top of one another when the lethal insects began to fly about the room. "Where you going?" Dubava seized Pavel by the coat tail. "Outside." "Get down, you idiot!" Dmitri hissed, "they'll get you the moment you stick your head out."

They lay side by side next to the door. Dubava was flattened against the floor, with his revolver pointing toward the door. Pavel sat on his haunches nervously fingering the drum of his revolver. There were five rounds in it – one chamber was empty. He turned the cylinder another notch.

The shooting ceased suddenly. The silence that followed was weighted with tension.

"All those who have weapons come this way," Dubava commanded in a hoarse whisper. Pavel opened the door cautiously. The clearing was deserted. Snowflakes were falling softly.

In the forest ten horsemen were whipping their mounts into a gallop.

· · · ·

THE NEXT DAY A RAIL car arrived from town. Zhukhrai and Akim alighted and were met by Tokarev and Kholyava. A Maxim gun, several crates of machinegun belts and two dozen rifles were unloaded onto the platform.

They hurried over to the construction site. The tails of Fyodor's long greatcoat trailed a zigzag pattern in the snow behind him. He still walked with the clumsy rolling gait of the seaman, as if he were pacing the pitching deck of a destroyer. Long-legged Akim walked in step with Fyodor, but Tokarev had to break into a trot now and again to keep up with them.

"The bandit raid is not our worst trouble. There's a nasty rise in the ground right in the path of the line. Just our bad luck. It'll mean a lot of extra digging."

The old man stopped, turned his back to the wind and lit a cigarette, cupping his hand over the match. After blowing out a few puffs of smoke he hurried to catch up with the others. Akim had stopped to wait for him, but Zhukhrai strode on ahead. "Do you think you'll be able to finish the line on time?" Akim asked Tokarev. Tokarev paused a while before replying.

"Well, it's like this, son," he said at last. "Generally speaking it can't be done. But it's got to be done, so there you are." They caught up with Fyodor and continued abreast.

"Here's how it is," Tokarev began earnestly. "Only two of us here, Patoshkin and I, know that it's impossible to build a line under these conditions, with the scanty equipment and labour power we have. But all the others, every last man of them, know that the line has got to be built at all costs. So you see that's why I said if we don't freeze to death, it'll be done. Judge for yourselves; we've been digging here for over a month, the fourth batch of replacements are due for a rest, but the main body of workers have been on the job all the time. It's only their youth that keeps them going. But half of them are badly chilled. Makes your heart bleed to look at them. They're splendid lads, none better. But this cursed hole will be the death of more than one of them."

· · · ·

THE READY NARROW-GAUGE track came to an end a kilometre from the station. Beyond that, for a stretch of about one and a half kilometres, the levelled roadbed was covered by what looked like a log palisade blown down by wind – these were the sleepers, all firmly planted in place. And beyond them, all the way to the rise, there was only a level road.

Pankratov's construction group No. one was working at this section. Forty men were laying ties, while a carroty-bearded peasant wearing a new pair of shoes was unhurriedly emptying a load of logs on the roadbed. In the distance several more sleds were being unloaded in like manner. Two long iron bars lay on the ground – these were used to level up the sleepers properly. Axes, crowbars and shovels were all used to tamp down the ballast. Laying railway sleepers is slow, laborious work. The sleepers must be firmly imbedded in the earth so that the rails press evenly on each of them.

Only one man in the group knew the technique of laying sleepers. That was Talya's father, the line foreman Lagutin, a man of fifty-four with a pitch-black beard parted in the middle and not a grey hair in his head: He had worked at Boyarka since the beginning of the job, sharing all the hardships with the younger men and had earned the respect of the whole detachment. Although he was not a Party member, Lagutin invariably held a place of honour at all Party conferences. He was very proud of this and had given his word not to leave until the job was finished.

"How can I leave you to carry on by yourselves? Something's bound to go wrong without an experienced man to keep an eye on things. When it comes to that, I've hammered in more of these here sleepers up and down the country in my time than I can remember," he would say good-humouredly each time the question of replacements came up. And so he stayed.

Patoshkin saw that Lagutin knew his job and rarely inspected his sector. When Tokarev with Akim and Zhukhrai came over to where they were working, Pankratov, flushed and perspiring with exertion, was hewing out a hollow for a sleeper. Akim hardly recognised the young docker. Pankratov had lost much weight, his broad cheekbones protruded sharply in his grimy face which was sallow and sunken. "Well, well," he said as he gave Akim a hot, moist hand, "the big chiefs have come!" The ringing of spades ceased. Akim surveyed the pale worn faces of the men around him. Their coats and jackets lay in a careless heap on the snow.

After a brief talk with Lagutin, Tokarev took the party to the excavation site, inviting Pankratov to join them. The docker walked alongside Zhukhrai. "Tell me, Pankratov, what happened at Motovilovka? Don't you think you overdid it disarming that Cheka man?" Fyodor asked the taciturn docker sternly.

Pankratov grinned sheepishly. "It was all done by mutual consent," he explained. "He asked us to disarm him. He's a good lad. When we explained what it was all about he says: 'I see your difficulty, boys, but I haven't the right to let you take those windows and doors away. We have orders from Comrade Dzerzhinsky to put a stop to the plunder of railway property. The station master here has his knife in me. He's stealing stuff, the bastard, and I'm in his way. If I let you get away with it he's bound to report me and I'll be tried by the Revolutionary Tribunal. But you can disarm me and clear off. And if the station master doesn't report the matter that will be the end of it.' So that's what we did. After all, we weren't taking those doors and windows for ourselves, were we?"

Noting the twinkle in Zhukhrai's eye, he went on: "You can punish us for it if you want to, but don't be hard on that lad, Comrade Zhukhrai."

"That's all over and done with. But see there's no more of that in the future, it's bad for discipline. We are strong enough now to smash bureaucracy in an organised way. Now let's talk about something more important." And Fyodor proceeded to inquire about the details of the bandit raid.

• • • •

ABOUT FOUR AND A HALF kilometres from Boyarka station a group of men were digging furiously into a rise in the ground that stood in the path of the line. Seven men armed with all the weapons the detachment possessed – Kholyava's rifle and the revolvers belonging to Korchagin, Pankratov, Dubava and Khomutov—stood on guard. Patoshkin was sitting on top of the rise jotting down figures in his notebook. He was the only engineer on the job. Vakulenko, the technician, preferring to stand trial for desertion rather than death at a bandit's hand, had fled that morning. "It will take two weeks to clear this hill out of the way. The ground's frozen hard," Patoshkin remarked in a low voice to the gloomy Khomutov standing beside him.

"We've been given twenty-five days to finish the whole line, and you're figuring fifteen for this," Khomutov growled, chewing the tip of his moustache.

"Can't be done, I'm afraid. Of course, I've never built anything before under such conditions and with workers like these. I may be mistaken. As a matter of fact I have been mistaken twice before."

At that moment Zhukhrai, Akim and Pankratov were seen approaching the slope. "Look, who's that down there?" cried Pyotr Trofimov, a young mechanic from the railway workshops in an old sweater torn at the elbows. He nudged Korchagin and pointed to the newcomers. The next moment Korchagin, spade in hands, was dashing down the hill. His eyes under the peak of his helmet smiled a warm greeting and Fyodor lingered over their handshake.

"Hello there, Pavel! Hardly recognised you in this outfit." Pankratov laughed dryly. "Outfit isn't the word for it. Plenty of ventilation holes anyway. The deserters pinched his overcoat, Okunev gave him that jacket – they've got a commune, you know. But Pavel's all right, he's got warm blood in his veins. He'll warm himself for a week or two more on the concrete floor – the straw doesn't make much difference – and then he'll be ready for a nice pinewood coffin," the docker wound up with grim humour.

Dark-browed, snub-nosed Okunev narrowed his mischievous eyes and objected: "Never mind, we'll take care of Pavlushka. We can vote him a job in the kitchen helping Odarka. If he isn't a fool he can grab a bit of extra grub and snuggle up to the stove or to Odarka herself." A roar of laughter met this remark; it was the first time they had laughed that day.

Fyodor inspected the rise, then drove out with Tokarev and Patoshkin by sled to the timber working. When he returned, the men were still digging with dogged persistence into the hill. Fyodor noted the rapid movement of the spades, and the backs of the workers bent under the strain. Turning to Akim, he said in an undertone: "No need of meetings. No agitation required here. You're right, Tokarev, when you said these lads are worth their weight in gold. This is where the steel is tempered."

Zhukhrai gazed at the diggers with admiration and stern, yet tender pride. Some of them only a short time back had stood before him bristling with the steel of their bayonets. That was on the night before the insurrection. And now, moved by a single impulse, they were toiling in order that the steel arteries of the railway might reach out to the precious source of warmth and life.

· · · ·

POLITELY BUT FIRMLY Patoshkin showed Fyodor that it was impossible to dig through the rise in less than two weeks. Fyodor listened to his arguments with a preoccupied air, his mind clearly busy with some problem of its own. "Stop all work on the cut and carry on farther up the line. We'll tackle that hill in a different way," he said finally.

Down at the station he spent a long time at the telephone. Kholyava, on guard outside the door, heard Fyodor's hoarse bass from within.

"Ring up the chief of staff of the Military Area and tell him in my name to transfer Puzyrevsky's regiment to the construction site at once. The bandits must be cleared out of the area without delay. Send an armoured train over with demolition men. I'll take care of the rest myself. I'll be back late. Tell Litke to be at the station with the car by midnight."

In the barrack, after a short speech by Akim, Zhukhrai took the floor and an hour fled by in comradely discussion. Fyodor told the men there could be no question of extending the January time limit allotted for the completion of the job. "From now on we are putting the work on a military footing," he said. "The Party members will form a special task company with Comrade Dubava in command. All six work teams will receive definite assignments. The remainder of the job will be divided into six equal sectors, one for each team. By January all the work must be completed. The team that finishes first will be allowed to go back to town. Also, the Presidium of the Gubernia Executive Committee is asking the Government to award the Order of the Red Banner to the best worker in the team that comes out first."

The leaders of the various teams were appointed as follows: No. one, Comrade Pankratov, No. two, Comrade Dubava, No. three, Comrade Khomutov, No. four, Comrade Lagutin, No. five, Comrade Korchagin, No. six, Comrade Okunev. "The chief of the construction job, its political and administrative leader will, as before, be Anton Nikiforovich Tokarev," Zhukhrai wound up with an oratorical flourish.

Like a flock of birds suddenly taking wing, the hand-clapping burst forth and stern faces relaxed in smiles. The warm whimsical conclusion to the speech relieved the strained attention of the meeting in a gust of laughter.

Some twenty men trooped down to the station to see Akim and Fyodor off. As he shook hands with Korchagin, Fyodor glanced down at Pavel's snow-filled galosh. "I'll send you a pair of boots," he said in a low voice. "You haven't frozen your feet yet, I hope?"

"They've begun to swell a bit," Pavel replied, then remembering something he had asked for a long time ago, he caught Fyodor by the arm. "Could you let me have a few cartridges for my revolver? I believe I only have three good ones left." Zhukhrai shook his head in regret, but catching Pavel's disappointed look, he quickly unstrapped his own Mauser.

"Here's a present for you." Pavel could not believe at first that he was really getting something he had set his heart on for so long, but Zhukhrai threw the leather strap over his shoulder saying: "take it, take it! I know you've had your eye on it for a long time. But take care you don't shoot any of our own men with it. Here are three full clips to go with it."

Pavel felt the envious eyes of the others upon him. "Hey, Pavka," someone yelled, "I'll swap with you for a pair of boots and a coat thrown in."

Pankratov nudged Pavel provokingly in the back. "Come on, I'll give you a pair of felt boots for it. Anyway you'll be dead before Christmas with that galosh of yours."

With one foot on the step of the rail car for support, Zhukhrai wrote out a permit for the revolver.

• • • •

EARLY THE NEXT MORNING an armoured train clattered over the switches and pulled up at the station. The engine spouted plumes of steam as white as swansdown that vanished in the crystal-clear frosty air. Leather-clad figures emerged from the steel cars. A few hours later three demolition men from the train had planted in the earth of the hill two large black pumpkin-like objects with long fuses attached. They fired a few warning shots and the men scattered in all directions away from the now deadly hill. A match was put to the end of the fuse which flared up with a tiny phosphorescent flame.

For a while the men held their breath. One or two moments of suspense, and then the earth trembled, and a terrific force rent the hill asunder, tossing huge chunks of earth skywards. The second explosion was more powerful than the first. The thunder of it reverberated over the surrounding forest, filling it with a confusion of sound.

When the smoke and dust cleared a deep pit yawned where the hill had just stood, and the sugary snow was sprinkled with earth for dozens of metres all around.

Men with picks and shovels rushed into the artificial cavity formed by the explosion.

* * * *

AFTER ZHUKHRAI'S DEPARTURE, a stubborn contest for the honour of being the first to finish the job commenced among the teams.

Long before dawn Korchagin rose quietly, taking care not to wake the others, and stepping cautiously on numb feet over the chilly floor made his way to the kitchen. There he heated the water for tea and went back to wake up his team. By the time the others were up it was broad daylight.

That morning Pankratov elbowed his way through the crowded barrack to where Dubava and his group were having their breakfast. "Hear that, Mityai?" he said heatedly. "Pavka went and got his lads up before daylight. I bet they've got a good ten sagenes laid out by now. The fellows say he's got those railway carshop boys all worked up to finish their section by the twenty-fifth. Wants to beat the rest of us hollow. But I say nothing doing!"

Dubava gave a sour smile. He could understand why the secretary of the river port Komsomol had been touched on the raw by what the railway carshop men had done. As a matter of fact friend Pave! had stolen a march on him, Dubava, as well. Without saying a word to anyone he had flung a challenge to the whole company. "Friends or no friends, it's the best man who wins." Pankratov said.

Around midday Korchagin's team was hard at work when an unexpected interruption occurred. The sentry standing guard over the rifles caught sight of a group of horsemen approaching through the trees and fired a warning shot. "To arms, lads, Bandits!" cried

Pavel. He flung down his spade and rushed over to the tree where his Mauser hung.

Snatching their rifles the others dropped down straight in the snow by the edge of the line. The leading horsemen waved their caps. "Steady there, comrades, don't shoot!" one of them shouted. Some fifty cavalrymen in Budyonny caps with bright red stars in front came riding up the road.

A unit of Puzyrevsky's regiment had come on a visit to the job. Pavel noticed that the commander's horse, a handsome grey mare with a white patch on her forehead, had the tip of one ear missing. She pranced restlessly under her rider, and when Pavel rushed forward and seized her by the bridle, she shied away nervously.

"Why, Lyska old girl, I never thought we'd meet again! So the bullets didn't get you, my one-eared beauty." He embraced her slender neck tenderly and stroked her quivering nostrils. The commander stared at Pavel for a moment, then cried out in amazement: "Well, if it isn't Korchagin! You recognise the mare but you don't see your old pal Sereda. Greetings, lad!"

· · · ·

IN THE MEANTIME BACK in town pressure was being exerted in all quarters to expedite the building of the line, and this was felt at once at the construction job. Zharky had literally stripped the Komsomol District Committee of all the male personnel and sent them out to Boyarka. Only the girls were left at Solomenka. He got the railway school to send out another batch of students.

"I'm left here with the female proletariat," he joked, reporting the results of his work to Akim. "I think I'll put Talya Lagutina in my place, hang out the sign 'Women's Department' on the door and clear out to Boyarka myself. It's awkward for me here, the only man among all these women. You ought to see the nasty looks they give me. I'm sure they're saying: 'Look, the sly beggar, sent everybody off, but stays on himself.' Or something worse still. You must let me go.''

But Akim merely laughed at him.

New workers continued to arrive at Boyarka, among them sixty students from the railway school. Zhukhrai induced the railway administration to send four passenger cars to Boyarka to house the newcomers.

Dubava's team was released from work and sent to Pushcha-Voditsa to bring back the locomotives and sixty-five narrow-gauge flatcars. This assignment was to be counted as part of the work on their section.

Before leaving, Dubava advised Tokarev to recall Klavicek from town and put him in charge of one of the newly-organised work teams at Boyarka. Tokarev did so. He did not know the real reason for Dubava's request: a note from Anna which the newcomers from Solomenka had brought.

Anna wrote:

Dmitri!

Klavicek and I have prepared a pile of books for you. We send our warmest greetings to you and all the other Boyarka shock workers. You are all wonderful! We wish you strength and energy to carry on. Yesterday the last stocks of wood were distributed. Klavicek asks me to send you his greetings. He is wonderful. He bakes all the bread for Boyarka, sifts the flour and kneads the dough himself. He doesn't trust anyone in the bakery to do it. He managed to get excellent flour and his bread is good, much better than the kind I get. In the evenings our mutual friends gather in my place – Lagutina, Artyukhin, Klavicek , and sometimes Zharky.

We do a bit of reading but mostly we talk about everybody and everything, chiefly about you in Boyarka. The girls are furious with Tokarev for refusing to let them work on the job. They say they can endure hardships as well as anyone. Talya declares she's going to dress up in her father's clothes and go out to Boyarka by herself. 'Let him just try to kick me out,' she says.

I wouldn't be surprised if she kept her word. Please give my regards to your dark-eyed friend.

Anna.

The blizzard came upon them suddenly. Low grey clouds spread themselves over the sky and the snow fell thickly. When night came the wind howled in the chimneys and moaned in the trees, chasing the whirling snowflakes and awakening the forest echoes with its malevolent whine.

All night long the storm raged in a wild fury, and although the stoves were kept warm throughout the night the men shivered; the wrecked station building could not hold the warmth.

In the morning they had to plough through the deep snow to reach their sections. But high above the trees the sun shone in a blue sky without a single cloudlet to mar its clear expanse.

Korchagin and his men went to work to clear the snowdrifts from their section. Only now did Pavel realise how much a man could suffer from the cold. Okunev's threadbare jacket gave him scant protection and his galosh was constantly full of snow. He kept losing it in the snow, and now his other boot was threatening to fall apart. Two enormous boils had broken out on his neck – the result of sleeping on the cold floor. Tokarev had given him his towel to wear in place of a scarf.

Gaunt and red-eyed, Pavel was furiously plying his wooden snow shovel when a passenger train puffed slowly into the station. Its expiring engine had barely managed to haul it this far; there was not a single log of wood in the tender and the last embers were burning low in the firebox.

"Give us fuel and we'll go on, or else shunt us onto a siding while we still have the power to move!" the engine driver yelled to the station master. The train was switched onto a siding. The reason for the halt was explained to the disgruntled passengers and a storm of complaints and curses broke out in the crowded cars.

"Go and talk to that old chap," the stationmaster advised the train guards, pointing to Tokarev who was walking down the platform. "He's the chief of the construction job here. Maybe he can get wood brought down by sled to the engine. They're using the logs for sleepers."

"I'll give you the wood, but you'll have to pay for it," said Tokarev when the conductors applied to him. "After all, it's our building material. We're being held up at the moment by the snow. There must be about six or seven hundred passengers inside your train. The women and children can stay inside but let the men come and lend a hand clearing the snow until evening and I'll give you firewood. If they refuse they can stay where they are till New Year's."

. . . .

"LOOK AT THE CROWD COMING this way! Look, women too!" Korchagin heard a surprised exclamation at his back. He turned round. Tokarev came up. "Here are a hundred helpers for you," he said. "Give them work and see none of them is idle." Korchagin put the newcomers to work. One tall man in a smart railway uniform with a fur collar and a warm caracul cap indignantly twirled the shovel in his hands and turned to his companion, a young woman wearing a sealskin hat with a fluffy pom-pom on top.

"I am not going to shovel snow and nobody has the right to force me to do it. As a railway engineer I could take charge of the work if they ask me to, but neither you nor I need to shovel snow. It's contrary to the regulations. That old man is breaking the law. I can have him prosecuted. Where is your foreman?" he demanded of the worker nearest him.

Korchagin came over. "Why aren't you working, citizen?" The man examined Pavel contemptuously from head to foot. "And who may you be?" "I am a worker." "Then I have nothing to say to you. Send me your foreman, or whatever you call him..." Korchagin scowled. "You needn't work if you don't want to. But you won't get back on that train unless your ticket is countersigned by us. That's the construction chief's orders."

"What about you, citizen?" Pavel turned to the woman and was struck dumb with surprise. Before him stood Tonya Tumanova!

Tonya could hardly believe that this tramp who stood before her in his tattered clothing and incredible footwear, with a filthy towel around his neck and a face that had not been washed for many a day, was the Korchagin she once knew. Only his eyes blazed as fiercely as ever. The eyes of the Pavel she remembered. And to think that only a short while ago she had given her love to this ragged creature. How everything had changed!

She had recently married, and she and her husband were on their way to the city where he held an important position in the railway administration. Who could have thought that she would meet the object of her girlish affections in this way? She even hesitated to give him her hand. What would Vasili think? How awful of Korchagin to have fallen so low. Evidently the young stoker had not been able to rise above navvy work.

She stood hesitating, her cheeks burning. Meanwhile the railway engineer, infuriated by what he considered the insolence of this tramp who stood staring at his wife, flung down his shovel and went over to her side. "Let us go, Tonya, I can't stand the sight of this lazzarone." Korchagin had read Giuseppe Garibaldi and he knew what that word meant.

"I may be a lazzarone, but you're no more than a rotten bourgeois," he said hoarsely, and turning to Tonya, added curtly: "Take a shovel. Comrade Tumanova, and get into line. Don't take an example from this prize bull here... Excuse me if he is any relation of yours." Pavel glanced at Tonya's fur boots and smiled grimly, adding casually: "I wouldn't advise you to stop over here. The other night we were attacked by bandits." With that he turned on his heel and walked off, his galosh flapping as he went.

His last words impressed the railway engineer, and Tonya succeeded in persuading him to stay and work. That evening, when the day's work was over, the crowd streamed back to the station. Tonya's husband hurried ahead to make sure of a seat in the train. Tonya, stopping to let a group of workers pass, saw Pavel trudging wearily behind the others, leaning heavily on his shovel.

"Hello, Pavlusha," she said and fell into step beside him. "I must say I never expected to find you in such straits. Surely the authorities ought to know you deserve something better than navvy's work? I thought you'd be a commissar or something like that by now. What a pity life has been so unkind to you..."

Pavel halted and surveyed Tonya with surprise. "Nor did I expect to find you so ... so stuffy," he said, choosing the most polite word he could think of to express his feelings. The tips of Tonya's ears burned. "You're just as rude as ever!" Korchagin hoisted his shovel onto his shoulder and strode off. After a few steps he stopped. .

"My rudeness, Comrade Tumanova," he said, "is not half as offensive as your so-called politeness. And as for my life, please don't worry about that. There's nothing wrong with it. It's your life that's all wrong, ever so much worse than I expected. Two years ago you were better, you wouldn't have been ashamed to shake hands with a workingman. But now you reek of camphor balls. To tell the truth, you and I have nothing more to say to each other."

· · · ·

PAVEL HAD A LETTER from Artem announcing that he was going to be married and urging Pavel to come to the wedding without fail.

The wind tore the sheet of paper out of Pavel's hand and it flew off into the air. No wedding parties for him. How could he leave at this juncture? Only yesterday that bear Pankratov had outstripped his team and spurted forward at a pace that amazed everyone. The docker was making a desperate bid for first place in the contest. His usual nonchalance had forsaken him and he was whipping up his waterfront workers to a furious tempo.

Patoshkin, noting the silent intensity with which the men worked, scratched his head perplexedly. "Are these men or giants?" he marvelled. "Where do they get their incredible strength? If the weather holds out for only eight more days we'll reach the timber workings! Well, live and learn! These men are breaking all records and estimates."

Klavicek came from town bringing the last batch of bread he had baked. He had a talk with Tokarev and then went off to hunt for Korchagin. The two men shook hands warmly. Klavicek with a broad smile dived into his kitbag and produced a handsome fur-lined leather jacket of Swedish make.

"This is for you!" he said stroking the soft leather. "Guess from whom? What! You don't know? You r dense, man! It's from Comrade Ustinovich. So you shouldn't catch cold. Olshinsky gave it to her. She took it from him and handed it straight to me with orders to take it to you. Akim told her you've been going about in the frost with nothing but a thin jacket. Olshinsky's nose was put out of joint a bit. 'I can send the comrade an army coat,' he says. But Rita only laughed. 'Never mind,' she said, 'he'll work better in this jacket.'"

The astonished Pavel took the luxurious-looking jacket and after some hesitation slipped it over his chilled body. Almost at once he felt the warmth from the soft fur spreading over his shoulders and chest.

Rita wrote in her diary:

December Twentieth

We have been having a bout of blizzards. Snow and wind. Out at Boyarka they had almost reached their goal when the frosts and storms halted them. They are up to their necks in snow and the frozen earth is not easy to dig. They have only three quarters of a kilometre to go, but this is the hardest lap of all.

Tokarev reports an outbreak of typhoid fever.

Three men are down with it.

December Twenty-Second

There was a plenary session of the Komsomol Gubernia Committee but no one from Boyarka attended. Bandits derailed a trainload of grain seventeen kilometres from Boyarka, and the Food Commissariat representative ordered all the construction workers to be sent to the spot.

December Twenty-Third

Another seven typhoid cases have been brought to town from Boyarka. Okunev is one of them. I went down to the station and saw frozen corpses of people who had been riding the buffers taken off a Kharkov train. The hospitals are unheated. This accursed blizzard, when will it end?

December Twenty-Fourth

Just seen Zhukhrai. He confirmed the rumour that Orlik and his whole band attacked Boyarka last night. The fight lasted two hours. Communications were cut and Zhukhrai did not get the exact report until this morning. The band was repulsed but Tokarev has been wounded, a bullet went right through his chest. He will be brought to town today. Franz Klavicek, who was in charge of the guard that night, was killed. He was the one who spotted the band and raised the alarm. He started shooting at the raiders but they were on him before he had time to reach the school building. He was cut down by a sabre blow. Eleven of the builders were wounded. Two cavalry squadrons and an armoured train are there by now.

Pankratov has taken charge of the construction job. Today Puzyrevsky caught up with part of the band in Gluboky village and wiped it out. Some of the non-Party workers started out for town without waiting for a train; they are walking along the track.

December Twenty-Fifth

Tokarev and the other wounded men arrived, and were placed in hospital. The doctors promise to save the old man. He is still unconscious. The lives of the others are not in danger.

A telegram came from Boyarka addressed to us and the Gubernia Party Committee. 'In reply to the bandit assault, we builders of the narrow-gauge line gathered at this meeting together with the crew of the armoured train For Soviet Power and the Red Army men of the cavalry regiment, vow to you that notwithstanding all obstacles the town shall have firewood by January first. Mustering all our strength we are setting to work. Long live the Communist Party, which sent us here! Chairman of the meeting, Korchagin. Secretary, Berzin.

Klavicek was given a military funeral at Solomenka.

The cherished goal was in sight, but the advance toward it was agonizingly slow, for every day typhoid fever tore dozens of badly needed hands from the builders' ranks.

One day Korchagin, returning from work to the station, staggered along like a drunkard, his legs ready to give way beneath him. He had been feverish for quite some time, but today it gripped him more fiercely than usual.

Typhoid fever, which had thinned the ranks of the building detachment, had claimed a new victim. But Pavel's sturdy constitution resisted the disease and for five days in succession he had found the strength to pick himself up from his straw pallet on the concrete floor and join the others at work. But the fever had taken possession of him and now neither the warm jacket nor the felt boots, Fyodor's gift, worn over his already frost-bitten feet, helped.

A sharp pain seared his chest with each step he took, his teeth chattered, and his vision was blurred so that the trees seemed to be whirling around in a strange merry-go-round.

With difficulty he dragged himself to the station. An unusual commotion there caused him to halt, and straining his fever-hazed eyes, he saw a long train of flatcars stretching the entire length of the platform. Men who had come with the train were busy unloading narrow-gauge locomotives, rails and sleepers. Pavel staggered forward and lost his balance. He felt a dull pain as his head hit the ground and the pleasant coolness of the snow against his burning cheek.

Several hours later he was found and carried back to the barrack. He was breathing heavily, quite unconscious of his surroundings. A medic summoned from the armoured train examined him and diagnosed pneumonia and typhoid fever. His temperature was over forty-one Celsius. The medic noted the inflammation of the joints and the ulcers on the neck but said they were trifles compared with the pneumonia and typhoid which alone were enough to kill him. Pankratov and Dubava. who had arrived from town did all they could to save Pavel.

Alyosha Kokhansky, who came from the same town as Pavel, was entrusted with taking him home to his people. With the help of all the members of Korchagin's team, and mainly with Kholyava acting as battering ram, Pankratov and Dubava managed to get Alyosha and the unconscious Korchagin into the packed railway car. The passengers, suspecting typhus, resisted violently and threatened to throw the sick man out of the train en route.

Kholyava waved his gun under their noses and roared: "His illness is not infectious! And he's going on this train even if we have to throw out the whole lot of you! And remember, you swine, if anyone lays a finger on him, I'll send word down the line and you'll all be taken off the train and put behind the bars. Here, Alyosha, take Pavka's Mauser and shoot the first man who tries to put him off," Kholyava wound up for additional emphasis.

The train puffed out of the station. Pankratov went over to Dubava standing on the deserted platform. "Do you think he'll pull through?" The question remained unanswered. "Come along, Mityai, it can't be helped. We've got to answer for everything now. We must get those locomotives unloaded during the night and in the morning we'll try warming them up."

Kholyava telephoned to all his Cheka friends along the line urging them to make sure that the sick Korchagin was not taken off the train anywhere. Not until he had been given a firm assurance that this would be done did he finally go to bed.

· · · ·

AT A RAILWAY JUNCTION further down the line the body of an unknown fair-haired young man was carried out of one of the cars of a passenger train passing through and set down on the platform. Who he was and what he had died of no one knew. The station Cheka men, remembering Kholyava's request, ran over to the car, but when they saw that the youth was dead, gave instructions for the corpse to be removed to the morgue, and immediately telephoned to Kholyava at Boyarka informing him of the death of his friend whose life he had been so anxious to save.

A brief telegram was sent from Boyarka to the Gubernia Committee of the Komsomol announcing Korchagin's death.

In the meantime, however, Alyosha Kokhansky delivered the sick Korchagin to his people and came down himself with the fever.

January Ninth

Why does my heart ache so? Before I sat down to write I wept bitterly. Who would have believed that Rita could weep and with such anguish? But are tears always a sign of weakness? Today mine are tears of searing grief. Why did grief come on this day of victory when the horrors of cold have been overcome, when the railway stations are piled high with precious fuel, when I have just returned from the celebration of the victory, an enlarged plenary meeting of the City Soviet where the heroes of the construction job were accorded all honours. This is victory, but two men gave their lives that it might be – Klavicek and Korchagin.

Pavel's death has opened my eyes to the truth – he was far dearer to me than I had thought.

And now I shall close this diary. I doubt whether I shall ever return to it. Tomorrow I am writing to Kharkov to accept the job offered me in the Central Committee of the Ukrainian Komsomol.

CHAPTER THREE

B ut youth triumphed. Pavel did not succumb to the typhoid fever. For the fourth time he crossed the borderline of death and came back to life. It was a whole month, however, before he was able to rise from his bed. Gaunt and pale, he tottered feebly across the room on his shaky legs, clinging to the wall for support. With his mother's help he reached the window and stood there for a long time looking out onto the road where pools of melted snow glittered in the early spring sunshine. It was the first thaw of the year.

Just in front of the window a grey-breasted sparrow perched on the branch of a cherry tree was preening its feathers, stealing quick uneasy glances at Pavel. "So you and I got through the winter, eh?" Pavel said, softly tapping a finger on the windowpane.

His mother looked up startled. "Who are you talking to out there?" "A sparrow... There now, he's flown away, the little rascal." And Pavel gave a wan smile.

By the time spring was at its height Pavel began to think of returning to town. He was now strong enough to walk, but some mysterious disease was undermining his strength. One day as he was walking in the garden a sudden excruciating pain in his spine knocked him off his feet. With difficulty he dragged himself back to his room. The next day he submitted to a thorough medical examination. The doctor, examining Pavel's back, discovered a deep depression in his spine and grunted in surprise. "How did you come by this?"

"That was in the fighting at Rovno. A three-inch gun tore up the highway behind us and a stone hit me in the back." "But how did you manage to walk? Hasn't it ever bothered you?" "No. I couldn't get up for an hour or two after it happened, but then it passed and I got into the saddle and carried on. This is the first time it has troubled me since then."

The doctor's face was very grave as he carefully examined the depression. "Yes, my friend, a very nasty business. The spine does not like to be shaken up like that. Let us hope that it will pass."

The doctor watched his patient dress with sympathy and a distress he could not disguise.

. . . .

ARTEM LIVED WITH HIS wife's people. His wife Styosha was a plain-featured young peasant woman who came from a poverty-stricken family. Pavel went out one day to see his brother. A grimy slant-eyed urchin playing in the small, filthy yard fixed Pavel with a stare and picking his nose stolidly, demanded: "What d'you want? Maybe you're a thief? You'd better clear off or you'll get it from mother!"

A tiny window was flung open in the shabby old cottage and Artem looked out. "Come on in, Pavel!" he called. An old woman with a face like yellowed parchment was busy at the stove. She flung Pavel an unfriendly look as he passed her and resumed her clattering with the pots. Two girls with stringy pigtails clambered onto the stove and stared down from there at the newcomer with the gaping curiosity of little savages.

Artem, sitting at the table, looked somewhat uncomfortable. He was aware that neither his mother nor his brother approved of his marriage. They could not understand why Artem, whose family had been proletarian for generations, had broken off with Galya, the stonemason's pretty daughter and a seamstress by trade whom he had been courting for three years, to go and live with a dull, ignorant woman like Styosha and be the breadwinner in a family of five. Now after a hard day's work at the railway shops he had to toil at the plough in an effort to revive the run-down farm.

. . . .

ARTEM KNEW THAT PAVEL disapproved of his desertion to what he called the "petty-bourgeois elements," and he now watched his brother take stock of his surroundings. They sat for a while exchanging the usual insignificant remarks that might pass between two people who have casually met. Presently Pavel rose to go, but Artem detained him.

"Wait a bit, and have a bite with us. Styosha will bring the milk in soon. So you're going away again tomorrow? Are you sure you're quite strong enough, Pavka?"

Styosha came in. She greeted Pavel, and asked Artem to go with her to the barn and help her carry something. Pavel was left alone with the dour old woman. Through the window came the sound of church bells. The old woman laid down her pothook and began to mutter sourly.

"Lord above, with all this cursed housework a body can scarce find time to pray!" She took off her shawl and eyeing the newcomer askance went over to the corner where hung the holy images, dreary and tarnished with age. Pressing together three bony fingers she crossed herself. "Our Father which art in Heaven, hallowed be thy name!" she whispered through withered lips.

The urchin playing outside in the yard leapt astride a black lop-eared hog. He dug his small bare heels smartly into its sides, clung to its bristles and shouted to the running, snorting beast: "Gee-up, gee-up! Whoa! Now, whoa!" The hog with the boy on its back dashed madly about the yard in a desperate effort to throw him, but the slant-eyed imp kept his seat firmly. The old woman stopped praying and stuck her head out of the window.

"Get down off that pig at once, you little hell-hound, or I'll tan the hide off you. A plague on you!"

The hog finally succeeded in shaking his tormentor off his back, and the old woman, mollified, returned to her icons, composed her features into a pious expression and continued: "thy kingdom come..."

At that moment the boy appeared in the doorway, his face grimy with tears. Wiping his smarting nose with his sleeve and sobbing with pain, he whined: "Gimme a pancake, grandma!"

The old woman turned on him in a fury. "Can't you see I'm praying, you cross-eyed devil, you? I'll give you pancakes, you limb of Satan! ..." And she snatched a whip from the bench. The boy was gone in a flash. The two little girls on top of the stove snickered.

The old woman returned to her devotions for the third time. Pavel got up and went out without waiting for his brother. As he closed the gate behind him he noticed the old woman peering suspiciously out at him through the end window of the house.

"What evil spirit lured Artem out here? Now he's tied down for the rest of his life. Styosha will have a baby every year. And Artem will be stuck like a beetle on a dunghill. He may even give up his work at the shops." Thus Pavel reflected gloomily as he strode down the deserted streets of the little town. "And I had hoped to be able to interest him in political work."

Pavel rejoiced at the thought that tomorrow he would be leaving this place and going to the big town to join his friends and comrades, all those dear to his heart. The big city with its bustling life and activity, its endless stream of humanity, its clattering trams and hooting automobiles drew him like a magnet. But most of all he yearned for the huge brick factory buildings, the sooty workshops, the machines, the low hum of transmission belts. He yearned for the mad spinning of the giant flywheels, for the smell of machine oil, for all that had become so much a part of him. This quiet provincial town whose streets he now roamed filled him with a vague feeling of depression. He was not surprised that he felt a stranger here now. Even to take a stroll through the town in daytime had become an ordeal. Passing by the gossiping housewives sitting on their stoops, he could not help overhearing their idle chatter: "Now, who could that scarecrow be?"

"Looks like he had the consumption, lung trouble, that is." "A pretty fine jacket he's got on. Stolen, I'll be bound." And plenty more in the same vein. Pavel was disgusted by it all.

He had torn himself up by the roots away from all this long since. He felt a far closer kinship now with the big city to which he was bound by the strong, vitalising bonds of comradeship and labour.

He emerged from his reflections to find himself at the pinewoods, and he paused a moment at the parting of the way. To his right stood the old prison cut off from the woods by a high spiked fence, and beyond it the white buildings of the hospital.

It was here on this broad common that the hangman's noose had choked the warm life out of Valya and her comrades. Pavel stood in silence on the spot where the gallows had been, then walked over to the bluff and descended to the little cemetery where the victims of the White terror lay in their common graves.

Loving hands had laid spruce branches on the graves and built a neat green fence around the graveyard. The pines grew straight and slender on the top of the bluff and the young grass spread a silky green carpet over the slopes.

There was a melancholy hush here on the outskirts of the town. The trees whispered gently and the fresh scent of spring rose from the regenerated earth. ... On this spot Pavel's comrades had gone bravely to their deaths that life might be beautiful for those born in poverty, those for whom birth itself had been but the beginning of slavery.

Slowly Pavel raised his hand and removed his cap, and an over-powering sadness pervaded his whole being.

Man's dearest possession is life, and it is given to him to live but once. He must live so as to feel no torturing regrets for years without purpose, never know the burning shame of a mean and petty past; so live that, dying, he can say: all my life, all my strength were given to the finest cause in all the world – the fight for the Liberation of

Mankind. And one must make use of every moment of life, lest some sudden illness or tragic accident cut it short.

With these reflections, Korchagin turned away from the cemetery.

· · · ·

AT HOME HIS MOTHER was unhappily preparing for her son's departure. Watching her, Pavel saw that she was hiding her tears from him. "Perhaps you'll stay, Pavlusha?" she ventured. "It's hard for me to be left alone in my old age. It doesn't matter how many children you have, they all grow up and leave you. Why must you run off to the city? You can live here just as well. Or perhaps some bob-haired magpie there has caught your fancy? You boys never tell your old mother anything. Artem went and got married without a word to me, and you're worse than him in that respect. I only see you when you get yourself crippled," his mother grumbled softly as she packed his meagre belongings into a clean bag.

Pavel took her by the shoulders and drew her toward him. "No magpies for me, mother! Don't you know that birds choose mates of their own species? And would you say I was a magpie?" His mother smiled in spite of herself. "No, mother, I've given my word to keep away from the girls until we've finished with all the bourgeois in the world. Bit long to wait, you say? No. mother, the bourgeoisie can't hold out very long now. Soon there will be one big republic for all men, and you old folk who've worked all your lives will go to Italy, a beautiful warm country by the sea. There is no winter there, mother. We'll install you in the rich men's palaces, and you'll lie about in the sun warming your old bones while we'll go and finish off the bourgeoisie in America."

"That's a lovely fairy tale, son, but I shan't live to see it come true. You're just like your Granddad, the sailor, always full of ideas he was. A regular brigand, God forgive him! Finished up in the Sevastopol war and came home with one arm and one leg missing. They hung two crosses on his chest and two tsarist silver pieces on ribbons. He lived to a ripe old age and died in terrible poverty. He was awful bad-tempered too, hit some official over the head once with his crutch and was sent to jail for about a year. Even his military crosses didn't help him then. Yes, it's your Granddad you take after and no mistake."

"Now then, ma, we can't have such a depressing farewell, can we? Let me have my accordion. I haven't touched it for a long time."

He bent his head over the mother-of-pearl keys and began to play. His mother, listening, marvelled at the new quality that had crept into his music. He never used to play like this. The dashing, rollicking tunes with the trills and runs, the intoxicating rhythms for which the young accordionist had been famed all over town were gone. His fingers had lost none of their power or skill, but the melody that flowed from under them was richer and deeper.

• • • •

PAVEL WENT TO THE STATION alone. He had persuaded his mother to stay at home for he knew that the final parting would upset her too much. The waiting crowd piled pell-mell into the train. Pavel climbed onto one of the topmost shelves and sat there watching the shouting, excited passengers arguing and gesticulating down below.

There was the usual abundance of packs and bundles which were hastily hidden out of sight under the seats.

When the train got into motion the hubbub subsided somewhat and the passengers settled down to the business of stuffing themselves with food.

Pavel soon fell asleep.

• • • •

ON ARRIVING IN KIEV, Pavel set out at once for Kreshchatik Street in the heart of the city. Slowly he climbed onto the bridge.

Everything was as it had been, nothing had changed. He walked across, sliding his hand over the smooth railings. He paused before descending. There was not a soul on the bridge. Night's boundless vistas presented a majestic spectacle to his enchanted eyes. The horizon was wrapped in the velvety folds of darkness, the stellar hosts sparkled and glittered with a phosphorescent glow. And down below, where the earth merged with the sky at some invisible point, the city scattered the darkness with a million lights...

Voices raised in argument invaded the stillness of the night and roused Pavel from his reverie.

Someone was coming this way. Pavel tore his eyes away from the city lights and descended the stairs. At the Area Special Department the man on duty informed Pavel that Zhukhrai had left town a long time ago.

He questioned Pavel searchingly to ascertain whether the young man really was a personal friend of Zhukhrai and finally told him that Fyodor had been sent to work in Tashkent on the Turkestan front. Pavel was so upset by the news that he turned on his heel and walked out without asking for further details. Overcome by a sudden wave of weariness he had to sink down onto the doorstep to rest.

A tramcar clattered by, filling the street with its din. An endless stream of people flowed past him. Pavel caught snatches of the gay laughter of women, a rumbling bass, the high-pitched treble of a youth, the wheezy falsetto of an old man. The ebb and flow of hurrying crowds never ceased. Brightly-lit trams, glaring automobile headlights, electric lights ablaze over the entrance to a cinema nearby... And everywhere – people, filling the street with their incessant hum of conversation. A big city at night!

The noise and bustle of the avenue dulled the edge of the pain caused by the news of Fyodor's departure. Where was he to go now? It was a long way to Solomenka where his friends lived. He had a vision of the house on University Street not far from here. Of course he would go there. After all, the first comrade he longed to see, after Fyodor, was Rita. And perhaps he could arrange to spend the night at Akim's place.

He saw a light in the end window from afar. Controlling his emotion with an effort he pulled open the heavy oaken outer door. For a few seconds he paused on the landing. Voices issued from Rita's room and someone was strumming on a guitar. "Aha, so she allows guitars nowadays, must have relaxed the regime," he said to himself. Then he tapped lightly on the door, biting his lip to quell his inner excitement.

The door was opened by a young woman with corkscrew curls. She looked questioningly at Korchagin. "Whom do you want?" She held the door ajar and a brief glance within told Pavel that his errand was fruitless. "May I see Ustinovich?" "She's not here. She went to Kharkov last January and I hear she's in Moscow now."

"Does Comrade Akim still live here or has he left as well?" "Comrade Akim isn't here either. He is the Secretary of the Odessa Gubernia Komsomol now." There was nothing for Pavel to do but turn back. The joy and excitement of his return to the city faded. Now the immediate problem was to find somewhere to spend the night.

"You can walk your legs off trying to look up old friends who aren't there," he grumbled to himself, swallowing his disappointment. Nevertheless he decided to try his luck once more and see whether Pankratov was still in town. The docker lived in the vicinity of the wharves and that was nearer than Solomenka.

By the time he reached Pankratov's place he was utterly exhausted. "If he isn't here either," Pavel vowed to himself as he knocked at a door that had once boasted a coat of yellow paint. "I'll give up the search. I'll crawl under a boat and spend the night there." The door was opened by an old woman with a scarf tied under her chin. It was Pankratov's mother. "Is Ignat home, mother?" "He's just come in."

She did not recognise Pavel, and turned round to call: "Ignat, someone to see you!" Pavel followed her into the room and laid his kit-bag on the floor. Pankratov, sitting at the table eating his supper, glanced quickly at the newcomer over his shoulder. "If it's me you want, sit down and fire away, while I get some borscht into my system," he said. "Haven't had a bite since morning." Whereupon he picked up a giant wooden spoon.

Pavel sat on a rickety chair to one side. He took off his cap and, relapsing into an old habit, wiped his forehead with it. "Have I really changed so much that even Ignat doesn't recognise me?" he asked himself. Pankratov dispatched a spoon or two of borscht, but since his visitor said nothing, he turned his head to look at him. "Well, come on! What's on your mind?"

His hand with the piece of bread in it remained suspended in mid-air. He stared at his visitor blinking with astonishment. "Hey...What's this? Well, of all the..!" The sight of the confusion and bewilderment on Pankratov's red face was too much for Pavel and he burst out laughing.

"Pavka!" cried the other. "But we all thought you were a goner! Wait a minute, now? What's your name again?"

Pankratov's elder sister and his mother came running in from the next room at his shouts. All three began showering Pavel with questions until at last they finally satisfied themselves that it really was Pavel Korchagin and none other.

Long after everyone in the house was fast asleep Pankratov was still giving Pavel an account of all that had happened during the past four months.

"Zharky and Mityai went off to Kharkov last winter. And where do you think they went, the beggars? To the Communist University, no more no less! Got into the preparatory course. There were fifteen of us at first. Yours truly also got into the spirit of the thing and applied. About time I got rid of some of the sawdust in my noodle, I thinks. And would you believe it, that examination board went and flunked me!"

Pankratov sniffed angrily at the memory and went on: "at first everything went swimmingly. I fitted in on all counts; I had my Party card, I'd been in the Komsomol long enough, nothing wrong with my background and antecedents, but when it came to political knowledge I got into hot water.

"Me and one of the comrades on the examining board got into an argument. He comes at me with a nasty little question like this: 'Tell me, Comrade Pankratov, what do you know about philosophy?' Well, the fact is I didn't know a damned thing about philosophy. But there was a fellow used to work with us at the wharves, a grammar school student turned tramp, who had taken a job as a docker for the fun of it. Well, I remember him telling us about some brainy fellows in Greece who knew all the answers to everything, philosophers they called them, he said. Well, there was one chap, can't remember his name now, Diogineez or something like that, he lived all his life in a barrel.... The smartest of them all was the one who could prove forty times over that black was white and white was black. A lot of spoofers, you see? So I remember what that student told me and I says to myself: 'Aha, he's trying to trip me up.' I see that examiner looking at me with a twinkle in his eye and I let him have it. 'Philosophy,' I says, 'is plain eyewash and poppycock, and I'm not going to have any truck with it, Comrades. The history of the Party, now, that's another matter. I'll be only too glad to have a crack at that.' Well they went for me good and proper, wanted to know where I'd gotten those queer ideas of mine about philosophy. So I told them about that student fellow and some of the things he'd said and the whole commission nearly split their sides. The laugh was on me all right. But I got sore. 'Take me for a fool, eh?' I says and walks out.

"Later on that examiner fellow got a hold of me in the Gubernia Committee and lectured me for a good three hours. It turns out that the student down at the docks had got things mixed up. It seems philosophy is all right, dashed important, as a matter of fact.

"Dubava and Zharky passed the exams. Mityai was always good at studies, but Zharky isn't much better than me. Must have been his Order that got him by. Anyway I was left back here. After they went I was given a managing job at the wharves – assistant chief of the freight wharves. I always used to be scrapping with the managers about the youth and now I'm a manager myself. Nowadays if I come across some slacker or nitwit I haul him over the coals as the manager and the Komsomol secretary at the same time. He can't throw dust in m my eyes! Well, enough about me. What else is there to tell you? You know about Akim already; Tufta is the only one of the old crowd left in the Gubernia Committee. Still on his old job. Tokarev is Secretary of the District Committee of the Party at Solomenka. Okunev, your fellow commune member, is in the Komsomol District Committee. Talya works in the political education department. Tsvetayev has your job down in the carshops. I don't know him very well. We only meet occasionally in the Gubernia Committee; he seems to be quite a brainy fellow, but a bit stand-offish. Remember Anna Borhart? She's at Solomenka too, head of the Women's Department of the District Committee of the Party. I've told you about all the others. Yes, Pavlusha the Party's sent lots of folk off to study. All the old activists attend the Gubernia Soviet and Party School. They promise to send me too next year."

It was long past midnight when they retired for the night. By the time Pavel awoke the next morning, Pankratov had gone to the wharves. Dusya, his sister, a strapping lass bearing a marked resemblance to her brother, served Pavel tea, keeping up a lively patter of talk all the while. Pankratov the elder, a marine engineer, was away from home.

As Pavel was preparing to go out, Dusya reminded him: "don't forget now, we're expecting you for dinner."

• • • •

THE GUBERNIA COMMITTEE of the Party presented the usual scene of bustling activity. The front door opened and closed incessantly. The corridors and offices were crowded, and the muffled clicking of typewriters issued from behind the door of the administration department.

Pavel lingered in the corridor for a while in search of a familiar face, but finding no one he knew, he went straight in to see the Secretary. The latter, dressed in a blue Russian shirt, was seated behind a large desk. He looked up briefly as Pavel entered and went on writing.

Pavel took a seat opposite him and studied the features of Akim's successor. "What can I do for you?" the Secretary in the high-necked shirt asked as he finished what he had been writing. Pavel told him his story. "What has to be done now, Comrade, is to resurrect me in the membership lists, and then send me to the railway workshops," he wound up. "Please issue the necessary instructions."

The Secretary leaned back in his chair. "We'll put you back on the lists, of course, that goes without saying," he replied with some hesitation. "But it'll be a bit awkward to send you to the workshops. Tsvetayev is there. He's a member of the Gubernia Committee. We'll have to find something else for you to do."

Korchagin narrowed his eyes. "I don't intend to interfere with Tsvetayev's work," he said. "I'm going to work at my trade and not as Party Secretary. And as I am still rather weak in health I would ask you not to assign me to any other job."

The Secretary agreed. He scribbled a few words on a slip of paper. "Give this to Comrade Tufta, he'll make all the arrangements."

In the personnel department Pavel found Tufta giving a dressing down to his assistant. Pavel stood for a minute or two listening to the heated exchange, but seeing that it threatened to last for a long time, he cut short the personnel man's flow of eloquence. "You'll finish the argument another time, Tufta. Here's a note for you about fixing up my papers." Tufta stared uncomprehending now at the paper, now at Korchagin, until it finally dawned on him.

"Whoa, now, wait a bit! So you didn't die after all? Tut, tut, what are we going to do now? You've been struck off the lists. I myself turned in your card to the Central Committee. What's more, you've missed the census, and according to the circular from the Komsomol C.C. those who weren't registered in the census are out. So the only thing you can do is to file an application again in the regular way." Tufta's tone brooked no argument.

Pavel frowned. "Up to your old tricks, eh? You're a young man but you're worse than the mustiest old archive rat. When will you grow up, Volodka?"

Tufta sprang up as if a flea had bitten him. "I would thank you not to lecture me. I am in charge here. Circular instructions are issued to be obeyed and not violated. As for your insults I'll teach you to call me a 'rat.'"

The last words were uttered in a threatening tone, and with a demonstrative gesture indicating that the interview was over, Tufta drew the pile of unopened mail toward him.

Pavel walked slowly to the door, then remembering something he went back to the desk and picked up the Secretary's slip that lay before Tufta. The latter watched him closely; there was something at once unpleasant and ludicrous about this personnel clerk who was as fussy and ill-tempered as an old man and whose large ears seemed perpetually on the alert.

"All right," Pavel said in a calm mocking voice. "You can accuse me of disorganising statistics if you like, but, tell me, how on earth do you manage to wangle reprimands for people who go and die without giving formal notice in advance? After all, anyone can get sick if he wants to, or die if he feels like it, and there's nothing in the instructions about that, I bet."

"Ha! Ha! Ha!" guffawed Tufta's assistant, no longer able to pre-
serve his neutrality. The point of Tufta's pencil broke and he flung it
on the floor, but before he had time to retort to his adversary several people burst into the room talking and laughing . Okunev was
among them. There was much excitement when Pavel was recognised
and endless questions were fired at him. A few minutes later another
group of young people came in, Olga Yureneva with them. Dazed by
the shock and delight of seeing Pavel again, Olga clung to his hand
for a long time.

And Pavel had to tell his story all over again. The sincere joy of
his comrades, their undisguised friendship and sympathy, the warm
handshakes and friendly slaps on the back made Pavel forget about
Tufta for the moment.

But when he ha d finished his account of himself and told his
comrades about his talk with Tufta there was a chorus of indignant
comments. Olga, with an annihilating look at Tufta, marched into
the Secretary's office.

"Come on, let's all go to Nezhdanov," cried Okunev. "He'll take
care of him." And with these words he took Pavel by the shoulders

and the whole group of young friends trooped after Olga into the office of the Secretary.

"That Tufta ought to be taken off the job and sent down to the wharves to work as a loader under Pankratov for a year. He's a hidebound bureaucrat!" stormed Olga. The Gubernia Committee Secretary listened with an indulgent smile when Okunev, Olga and the others demanded that Tufta be dismissed from the personnel department.

"Korchagin will be reinstated without question," he assured Olga. "A new card will be issued him at once. I agree with you that Tufta is a formalist," he went on. "That is his chief failing. But it must be admitted that he has not done so badly on the job. Komsomol personnel statistics wherever I have worked have always been in a state of indescribable chaos, not a single figure could be relied on. In our personnel department the statistics are in good order. You know yourselves that Tufta often sits up nights working.

Here's how I look at it: he can always be removed, but if his place is taken by some free and easy chap who knows nothing about keeping records, we may not have any bureaucracy but neither will we have any order. Let him stay on the job. I'll give him a good talking to. That will help for a while and later on we'll see."

"All right, let him be," Okunev agreed. "Come on, Pavlusha, let's go to Solomenka. There's a meeting of the active at the club tonight. Nobody knows you're back yet. Think what a surprise they'll get when we announce: 'Korchagin has the floor!' You're a great lad, Pavlusha, for not dying. What good would you be to the proletariat dead?" And Okunev threw his arm around his friend and piloted him down the corridor.

"Will you come, Olga?"

"Of course I will!"

* * * *

KORCHAGIN DID NOT RETURN to the Pankratov's for dinner, in fact he did not go back there at all that day. Okunev took him to his own room in the House of Soviets. He gave him the best meal he could muster, then placed a pile of newspapers and two thick files of the minutes of the District Komsomol Bureau meetings before him with the advice:

"Glance through this stuff. Lots of things happened while you were frittering away your time with the typhus. I'll come back toward evening and we'll go to the club together. You can lie down and take a nap if you get tired."

Stuffing his pockets full of all kinds of papers and documents (Okunev scorned the use of a portfolio on principle and it lay neglected under his bed), the District Committee Secretary said good-bye and went out.

When he returned that evening the floor of his room was littered with newspapers and a heap of books had been moved out from under the bed. Some of them were piled on the table. Pavel was sitting on the bed reading the last letters of the Central Committee which he had found under his friend's pillow.

"A fine mess you've made of my quarters, you ruffian!" Okunev cried in mock indignation. "Hey, wait a minute, comrade! Those are secret documents you're reading! That's what I get for letting a nosy chap like you into my den!" Pavel, grinning, laid the letter aside. "This particular one doesn't happen to be secret," he said, "but the one you're using for a lampshade is marked 'confidential.' Look, it's all singed around the edges!"

Okunev took the scorched slip of paper off the lamp, glanced at the title and struck himself on the forehead in dismay. "I've been looking for the damn thing for three days! Couldn't imagine where it had got to. Now I remember! Volyntsev made a lampshade out of it the other day and then he himself searched for it high and low." Okunev folded the document carefully and stuffed it under the mattress. "We'll put everything in order later on," he said reassuringly. "Now for a bite and then off to the club. Pull up to the table, Pavel!"

From one pocket he produced a long dried herring wrapped in newspaper and from the other, two slices of bread. He spread the newspaper out on the table, took the herring by the head and whipped it smartly against the table's edge.

Sitting on the table and working vigorously with his jaws, the jolly Okunev gave Pavel all the news, cracking jokes the while.

• • • •

AT THE CLUB OKUNEV took Korchagin through the back entrance behind the stage. In the corner of the spacious hall, to the right of the stage near the piano sat Talya Lagutina and Anna Borhart with a group of Komsomols from the railway district. Volyntsev, the Komsomol secretary of the railway shops, was sitting opposite Anna. He had a face as ruddy as an August apple, hair and eyebrows the colour of ripe corn. His extremely shabby leather jacket had once been black. Next to him, his elbow resting negligently on the lid of the piano, sat Tsvetayev, a handsome young man with brown hair and finely chiselled lips. His shirt was unbuttoned at the throat.

As he came up to the group Okunev heard Anna say: "some people are doing everything they can to complicate the admission of new members. Tsvetayev is one."

"The Komsomol is not a picnic ground," Tsvetayev snapped with stubborn disdain. "Look at Nikolai!" cried Talya, catching sight of Okunev. "He's beaming like a polished samovar tonight!"

Okunev was dragged into the circle and bombarded with questions. "Where have you been?" "Let's get started." Okunev raised his hand for silence. "Hold on, lads. As soon as Tokarev comes we'll begin." "There he comes now," remarked Anna. Sure enough the Secretary of the District Party Committee approached. Okunev ran forward to meet him.

"Come along, pa, I'm going to take you backstage to meet a friend of mine. Prepare for a shock!" "What're you up to now?" the old man growled, puffing on his cigarette, but Okunev was already pulling him by the sleeve.

Okunev rang the chairman's bell with such violence that even the most garrulous members of the audience were silenced. Behind Tokarev the leonine head of the genius of the Communist Manifesto, in a frame of evergreen, surveyed the assembly. While Okunev opened the meeting Tokarev could not keep his eyes off Korchagin who stood in the wings waiting for his cue. "Comrades! Before we begin to discuss the current organisational questions on the agenda, a comrade here has asked for the floor. Tokarev and I move that he be allowed to speak."

A murmur of approval rose from the hall, whereupon Okunev rapped out: "I call upon Pavka Korchagin to address the meeting!" At least eighty of the one hundred in the hall knew Korchagin, and when the familiar figure appeared before the footlights and the tall pale young man began to speak, a storm of delighted cries and thunderous applause broke from the audience.

"Dear Comrades!" Korchagin's voice was steady but he could not conceal his emotion. "And so, friends, I have returned to you to take my place in the ranks. I am happy to be back. I see here a great number of my friends. I understand that the Solomenka Komsomol has thirty per cent more members than before, and that they've stopped making cigarette lighters in the workshops and yards, and the old carcasses are being hauled out of the railway cemetery for capital repairs. That means our country is getting a new lease on life and is mustering its strength. That is something to live for! How could I die at a time like this!" Korchagin's eyes lit up in a happy smile.

Amid a storm of applause and greetings he descended the platform and went over to where Anna and Talya were sitting. He shook the hands outstretched in greeting, and then the friends moved up and made room for him between them. Talya laid her hand on his and squeezed it tight. Anna's eyes were still wide with surprise, her eyelashes quivered faintly and the look she gave Pavel was one of warm welcome.

· · · ·

THE DAYS SLIPPED SWIFTLY by. Yet there was nothing monotonous about their passage, for each day brought something new, and as he planned his work in the morning Pavel would note with chagrin that the day was all too short and much of what he had planned remained undone. Pavel had moved in with Okunev. He worked down at the railway shops as an assistant electrical fitter.

He had had a long argument with Okunev before the latter agreed to his temporary withdrawal from work in the Komsomol leadership. "We're too short of people for you to cool your heels in the workshops," Okunev had objected. "Don't tell me you're sick. I hobbled about with a stick myself for a whole month after the typhus. You can't fool me, Pavka, I know you, there's more to this than meets the eye. Come on, out with it," Okunev insisted. "You're right, Kolya, there is," Pavel said. "I want to study."

"There you are!" Okunev cried exultantly. "I thought there was something! Do you think I don't want to study too? Downright egoism on your part. Expect us to put our shoulders to the wheel while you go off to study. Nothing doing, my lad, tomorrow you start as organiser."

Nevertheless, after a lengthy discussion Okunev gave in. "Very well, I'll leave you alone for two months. And I hope you appreciate my generosity. But I don't think you'll get along with Tsvetayev, he's a bit too conceited."

Pavel's return to the workshops had put Tsvetayev on the alert. He was certain that Korchagin's coming would mark the beginning of a struggle for leadership. His self-esteem was wounded and he prepared to put up a stiff resistance. He soon saw, however, that he had been mistaken. When Korchagin learned that there was a plan afoot to make him a member of the Komsomol bureau he went straight to the Komsomol secretary's office and persuaded him to strike the question off the agenda, giving his understanding with Okunev as the excuse. In the Komsomol shop nucleus Pavel took a political study class, but did not ask for work in the bureau. Nevertheless, although he had officially no part in the leadership, Pavel's influence was felt in all phases of the collective's work. In his comradely, unobtrusive fashion he helped Tsvetayev out of difficulties on more than one occasion.

Coming into the shop one day Tsvetayev was amazed to see all the members of the Komsomol nucleus and some three dozen non-Party lads busy washing windows, scraping many years' accumulation of filth off the machines and carting heaps of rubbish out into the yard. Pavel, armed with a huge mop, was furiously scrubbing the cement floor which was covered with machine oil and grease.

"Spring-cleaning? What's the occasion?" Tsvetayev asked Pavel. "We're tired of all this muck. The place hasn't been cleaned for a good twenty years, we'll make it look like new in a week," Korchagin replied briefly. Tsvetayev shrugged his shoulders and went away.

Not content with cleaning out their workshop, the electricians tackled the factory yard. For years the huge yard had served as a dumping ground for all manner of disused equipment. There were hundreds of car wheels, and axles, mountains of rusty iron, rails, buffers, axle boxes – several thousand tonnes of metal lay rusting under the open sky. But the factory management put a stop to the young people's activities. "We have more important problems to attend to. The yard can wait," they were told.

And so the electricians paved a small area of the yard outside the entrance to their shop, placing a wire mat outside the door and left it at that. But inside their shop the cleaning continued after working hours. When Strizh, the chief engineer, dropped in a week later he found the workshop flooded with light. The huge iron barred windows, freed from their heavy layer of dust and oil, now admitted the sunlight which was reflected brightly in the polished copper parts of the Diesel engines. The heavy parts of the machines shone with a fresh coat of green paint, and someone had even painted yellow arrows on the spokes of the wheels. "Well, well..." Strizh muttered in amazement.

In the far corner of the shop a few of the men were finishing their work. Strizh went over. On the way he met Korchagin carrying a tin of paint. "Just a moment, my friend," the engineer stopped him. "I fully approve of what you have done here. But where did you get that paint? Haven't I given strict orders that no paint is to be used without my permission? We can't afford to waste paint for such purposes, We need all we have for the locomotive parts."

"This paint was scraped out of the bottoms of discarded cans. We spent two days on it but we scraped out about twenty-five litres. We're not breaking any laws here, Comrade Engineer." The engineer snorted again, but he looked rather sheepish. "Then carry on, of course. Well, well. Now this is really interesting. How do you explain this...what shall we call it...this voluntary striving for cleanliness in a workshop? All this was done after working hours, I take it?"

Korchagin detected a note of genuine perplexity in the engineer's voice. "Of course it was," he said. "What did you suppose?" "Yes, but..." "There is nothing to be surprised at, Comrade Strizh. Who told you that the Bolsheviks are going to leave dirt alone? Wait till we get this thing going properly. You have some more surprises in store for you."

And carefully skirting the engineer so as to avoid splashing him with paint, Korchagin moved on.

Every evening found Pavel in the public library where he lingered until late. He had made friends with all the three librarians, and by bringing all his powers of persuasion to bear he had finally won the right to browse freely among the books. Propping the ladder against the tall bookcases he would sit there for hours leafing through volume after volume in the search of the reading matter he desired. Most of the books were old. Modern literature occupied one small bookcase—a few odd civil war pamphlets, Marx's Capital The Iron Heel by Jack London and several others. Rummaging among the old books he came across Spartacus. He read it in two nights and when he finished it he placed it on the shelf alongside the works of Maxim Gorky. This gradual selection of the more interesting books with a modern revolutionary message lasted for some time.

The librarians did not object: it was all the same to them.

• • • •

THE CALM ROUTINE OF Komsomol life at the railway shops was suddenly disturbed by what appeared at first to be an insignificant incident: repair worker Kostya Fidin, member of the nucleus bureau, a sluggish lad with a snub nose and a pockmarked face, broke an expensive imported drill on a piece of iron. The accident was the result of downright carelessness; worse, it looked like deliberate mischief on Fidin's part.

It happened in the morning. Khodorov, senior repair foreman, had told Kostya to drill several holes in a strip of iron. Kostya refused at first but on the foreman's insistence he picked up the iron and started to drill it. The foreman, an exacting taskmaster, was not popular with the workers. A former Menshevik, he took no part in the social life of the plant and did not approve of the Young Communists. But he was an expert at his job and he performed his duties conscientiously. Khodorov noticed that Kostya was drilling "dry," he had not oiled his drill. He hurried over to the machine and stopped it.

"Are you blind or what? Don't you know better than to use a drill that way!" he shouted at Kostya, knowing that the drill would not last long with such handling. Kostya snapped back at him and restarted the lathe. Khodorov went to the department chief to complain. Kostya in the meantime, leaving the machine running, hurried off to fetch the oiling can so that everything would be in order by the time the chief appeared. When he returned with the oil the drill was broken. The chief submitted a report recommending Fidin's dismissal. The bureau of the Komsomol nucleus, however, took up the cudgels on Fidin's behalf on the grounds that Khodorov had a grudge against all active Komsomol members. The management insisted on Fidin's dismissal, and the case was put before the Komsomol bureau of the workshops. The fight was on.

Three of the five members of the bureau were in favour of giving Kostya an official reprimand and transferring him to other work. Tsvetayev was one of the three. The other two did not think Fidin should be punished at all.

The bureau meeting to discuss the case was called in Tsvetayev's office. Around a large table covered with red cloth stood several benches and stools made by the Young Communists of the carpenter shops. There were portraits of the leaders on the walls, and the railway workshops' banner was spread over one entire wall behind the table.

Tsvetayev was now a "full-time" Komsomol worker. He was a foundry man by trade, but his organisational ability had caused his promotion to a leading post in the Komsomol: he was now a member of the Bureau of the Komsomol District Committee and a member of the Gubernia Committee besides. He had worked in the foundry of a machinery plant and was a newcomer to the railway shops. From the first he had taken the reins of management firmly into his hands. Self-assured and hasty in his decisions, he had suppressed the initiative of the other Komsomol members from the outset. He insisted on doing everything himself and when he found himself unable to cope with all the work, stormed at his assistants for their inactivity.

Even the office had been decorated under his personal supervision. He conducted the meeting sprawled in the only soft armchair in the room which had been brought from the club. It was a closed meeting. Khomutov, the Party organiser, had just asked for the floor, when there was a knock on the door which was closed on the latch. Tsvetayev scowled at the interruption. The knock was repeated. Katya Zeienova got up and opened the door. Korchagin stood on the threshold. Katya let him in.

Pavel was making his way to a vacant seat when Tsvetayev addressed him. "Korchagin, this is a closed meeting of the bureau." The blood rushed to Pavel's face, and he turned slowly to face the table. "I know that. I am interested in hearing your opinion on the Fidin case. I have a point to raise in connection with it. What's the matter, do you object to my presence?"

"I don't object, but you ought to know that closed meetings are attended only by bureau members. The more people there are the harder it is to thrash things out properly. But since you're here you might as well stay." Korchagin had never suffered such a slight. A new crease appeared on his forehead. "What's all the formality about?" Khomutov remarked disapprovingly, but Korchagin stopped him with a gesture, and sat down. "Well, this is what I wanted to say," Khomutov went on. "It's true that Khodorov belongs to the old school, but something ought to be done about discipline. If all the Komsomols go smashing up drills, there'll be nothing to work with. What's more, we're giving a rotten example to the non-Party workers. In my opinion the youngster ought to be given a serious warning."

Tsvetayev did not give him a chance to finish, and began voicing his objections. Ten minutes passed. In the meantime Korchagin saw which way the wind was blowing. When the matter was finally put to the vote he got up and asked for the floor. Tsvetayev reluctantly permitted him to speak. "I should like to give you my opinion of the

Fidin case, Comrades," Pavel began. His voice sounded harsh in spite of himself.

"The Fidin case is a signal, and it is not Kostya's action in itself that's most important. I collected some figures yesterday." Pavel took a notebook out of his pocket. "I got them from the timekeeper. Now listen carefully: twenty-three per cent of our Komsomols come to work from five to fifteen minutes late every day. That has become a rule. Seventeen per cent don't report for work at all one or two days out of every month; the percentage of absenteeism among young non-Party workers is fourteen per cent. These figures sting worse than a whiplash, Comrades. I jotted down a few more: four per cent of our Party members are absent one day a month, and four per cent report late for work. Of the non-Party workers eleven per cent miss one day in the month while thirteen per cent regularly report late for work. Ninety per cent of breakages are accounted for by young workers, seven per cent of whom are newcomers. The conclusion to be drawn from these figures is that we Komsomols are making a far worse showing than the Party members and adult workers. But the situation is not the same everywhere. The foundry record is excellent, the electricians are not so bad, but the rest are more or less on the same level. In my opinion Comrade Khomutov said only a fraction of what ought to be said about discipline. The immediate problem now is to straighten out these issues. I don't intend to begin agitating here, but we've got to put a stop to carelessness and sloppiness. The old workers are frankly admitting that they used to work much better for the master, for the capitalist, but now we're the masters and there's no excuse for working badly. It's not so much Kostya or any other worker who's to blame. We ourselves, all of us, are at fault because instead of fighting the evil properly we sometimes defend workers like Kostya under one or another pretext.

"Samokhin and Butylyak have just said here that Fidin is a good lad, one of the best, an active Komsomol and all that. What if he did bust a drill, it could happen to anybody. He's one of us, while the foreman isn't... But has anyone ever tried to talk to Khodorov? Don't forget that grumbler has thirty years of working experience behind him! We won't talk about his politics. In the given case he is in the right, because he, an outsider, is taking care of state property while we are smashing up valuable tools. What do you call such a state of affairs? I believe that we ought to strike the first blow now and launch an offensive on this sector.

"I move that Fidin be expelled from the Komsomol as a slacker and disorganiser of production. His case should be discussed in the wall newspaper, and these figures published in an editorial article openly without fear of the consequences. We are strong, we have forces we can rely on. The majority of the Komsomol members are good workers. Sixty of them have gone through Boyarka and that was a severe test. With their help and their assistance we can iron out the difficulties. Only we've got to change our attitude to the whole business once and for all."

Korchagin, usually calm and reticent, spoke with a passion that surprised Tsvetayev. He was seeing the real Pavel for the first time. He realised that Pavel was right, but he was too cautious to agree with him openly. He took Korchagin's speech as a harsh criticism of the general state of the organisation, as an attempt to undermine his, Tsvetayev's authority, and he resolved to make short shrift of his opponent. He began his speech by accusing Korchagin of defending the Menshevik Khodorov.

The stormy debate lasted for three hours. Late that night the final point was reached. Defeated by the inexorable logic of fads and having lost the majority to Korchagin, Tsvetayev made a false step. He violated the rules of democracy by ordering Korchagin to leave the room just before the final vote was taken.

"Very well, I shall go, although your behaviour does not do you credit, Tsvetayev. I warn you that if you continue to insist on your viewpoint I shall put the matter before the general meeting tomorrow and I am sure you will not be able to win over the majority there. You are not right, Tsvetayev. I think, Comrade Khomutov, that it is your duty to take up the question with the Party group before the general meeting." "Don't try to scare me,'" Tsvetayev shouted defiantly. "I can go to the Party group myself, and what's more I have something to tell them about you. If you don't want to work yourself, don't interfere with those who do."

Pavel closed the door behind him. He passed his hand over his burning forehead and went through the empty office to the exit. Outside on the street he took a deep breath of air, lit a cigarette and set out for the little house on Batyeva Hill where Tokarev lived. He found the old mechanic at supper.

"Come on, let's hear the news. Darya, bring the lad a plate of gruel," said Tokarev, inviting Pavel to the table. Darya Fominichna, Tokarev's wife, as tall and buxom as her husband was short and spare, placed a plate of millet gruel before Pavel and wiping her moist lips with the edge of her white apron said kindly: "Set to, dearie."

* * * *

PAVEL HAD BEEN A FREQUENT visitor at the Tokarevs' in the days when the old man worked in the car-shops, and had spent many a pleasant evening with the old couple, but this was his first visit since his return to the city.

The old mechanic listened attentively to Pavel's story, working busily with his spoon and making no comment apart from an occasional grunt. When he had finished his porridge he wiped his moustache with his handkerchief and cleared his throat.

"You're right, of course," he said. "It's high time the question was put properly. There are more Communists down at the workshops than anywhere else in the district and that's where we ought to start. So you and Tsvetayev have come to blows after all, eh? Too bad. He's a bit of an upstart, of course, but you used to get on with the lads, didn't you? By the way, what exactly is your job at the workshops?" "I'm working in one of the departments. And generally I'm in on everything that's doing. In my own nucleus I lead a political study circle."

"What about the bureau?"

Korchagin hesitated. "I thought that while I still felt a bit shaky on my legs, and since I wanted to do some studying, I wouldn't take part officially in the leadership for a while."

"So that's it!" Tokarev cried in disapproval. "Now, my boy, if it weren't for your health I'd give you a good talking to. How do you feel now, by the way? Stronger?"

"Yes."

"Good, and now get to work in earnest. Stop beating about the bush. No good will come of sitting on the sidelines! You're just trying to evade responsibility and you know it. Now, you must put things to rights tomorrow. Okunev will hear from me about this." Tokarev's tone betrayed his annoyance. "No, dad, you leave him alone," Pavel hastened to object. "I asked him not to give me any work myself."

Tokarev whistled in scorn. "You did, eh, and he let you off? Oh well, what can we do with you, Komsomols. Will you read me the paper, son, the way you used to? My eyes aren't as good as they might be."

· · · ·

THE PARTY BUREAU AT the workshops upheld the decision of the majority in the Komsomol bureau, and the Party and Komsomol groups undertook the important and difficult task of setting an example of labour discipline. Tsvetayev was given a thorough dressing down at the bureau. He tried to bluster at first but pinned to the wall by Lopakhin, the secretary, an elderly man whose waxen pallor bore testimony to the tuberculosis that was wasting him, Tsvetayev gave in and partly admitted his error.

The following day the wall newspapers carried a series of articles that caused something of a sensation at the railway shops. The articles were read aloud and hotly discussed, and the unusually well-attended youth meeting held that same evening dealt exclusively with the problems they raised. Fidin was expelled from the Komsomol, and a new member was added to the bureau in charge of political education—Korchagin. Unusual quiet reigned in the hall as the meeting listened to Nezhdanov outline the new tasks confronting the railway workshops at this new stage.

After the meeting Tsvetayev found Korchagin waiting for him outside. "Let's go together, I have something to say to you," Pavel said. "What about?" Tsvetayev asked sourly.

Pavel took him by the arm and after they had gone a few yards paused at a bench. "Shall we sit down for a moment?" he suggested and set the example. The burning tip of Tsvetayev's cigarette now glowed red, now faded. "What have you got against me, Tsvetayev?"

There was silence for a few minutes. "Oh, so that's it? I thought you wanted to talk business," Tsvetayev said feigning surprise, but his voice was unsteady.

Pavel laid his hand firmly on the other's knee. "Get off your high horse, Dimka. That sort of talk is only for diplomats. You tell me this: why have you taken such a dislike to me?"

Tsvetayev shifted uneasily in his seat. "What are you talking about? Why should I have anything against you? I offered you work myself, didn't I? You refused, and now you're accusing me of trying to keep you out."

But his words carried no conviction, and Pavel, his hand still on Tsvetayev's knee, went on with feeling: "If you won't say it, I will. You think I want to cramp your style, you think it's your job I'm after. If you didn't, we wouldn't have quarrelled over the Kostya affair. Relations like these can ruin our work. If this concerned only the two of us it wouldn't matter a damn, I wouldn't care what you thought of me. But from tomorrow we'll be working together. How can we carry on like this? Now listen. There must be no rift between us. You and I are both workingmen. If our cause is dearer to you than everything else you'll give me your hand on it, and tomorrow we'll start as friends. But unless you throw all this nonsense out of your head and steer clear of intrigues, you and I will fight like blazes over every setback in the work that results. Now here's my hand, take it, while it is still proffered to you in friendship."

A deep sense of satisfaction swept Korchagin as Tsvetayev's rough fingers closed over his palm.

$$\cdot\ \cdot\ \cdot\ \cdot$$

A WEEK PASSED. THE workday was coming to an end in the District Committee of the Party. Quiet settled over the offices. But Tokarev was still at his desk. He was sitting in his armchair studying the latest reports, when a knock came at the door. "Come in!"

Korchagin entered and placed two filled out questionnaire blanks on the Secretary's desk. "What's this?"

"It's an end to irresponsibility, dad. And high time, if you ask me. If you are of the same opinion I would be grateful for your support."

Tokarev glanced at the heading, looked up quickly at the young man, then picked up his pen. Under the head: "party standing of comrades recommending Pavel Andreyevich Korchagin for candidate membership in the Russian Communist Party (Bolsheviks)" he wrote "nineteen-oh-three" with a firm hand, and signed his name. "There, my son. I know that you will never bring disgrace upon my old grey head."

$$\cdot\ \cdot\ \cdot\ \cdot$$

THE ROOM WAS SUFFOCATINGLY hot. One thought was uppermost in everyone's mind: to get away to the cool shade of the chestnut trees of Solomenka as quickly as possible. "Wind up, Pavka,

I can't stand another minute of this," implored Tsvetayev, who was sweating profusely. Katyusha and the others supported him.

Pavel Korchagin closed the book and the study circle broke up. As they rose in a body the old-fashioned Ericsson telephone on the wall jangled. Tsvetayev, who answered its summons, had to shout to make himself heard above the clamour of voices in the room. He hung up the receiver and turned to Korchagin. "There are two diplomatic railway cars down at the station belonging to the Polish consulate. Their lights are out, something's gone wrong with the wiring. The train leaves in an hour. Get some tools together and take a run down there, Pavel. It's urgent."

The two sleeping cars gleaming with polished brass and plate glass stood at the first platform. The parlour car with its wide windows was brightly lit. But the neighbouring car was in darkness. Pavel went up to the steps of the luxurious Pullman and gripped the handrail with the intention of entering the car.

A figure hastily detached itself from the station wall and seized him by the shoulder. "Where are you going, citizen?" The voice was familiar. Pavel turned and took in the leather jacket, wide-peaked cap, the thin, hooked nose and the guarded suspicious look in the eyes.

It was Artyukhin. He had not recognised Pavel at first, but now his hand fell from Pavel's shoulder, and his grim features relaxed although his glance paused questioningly on the instrument case. "Where were you heading for?" he said in a less formal tone. Pavel briefly explained. Another figure appeared from behind the car. "Just a moment, I'll call their conductor."

Several people faultlessly attired in travelling clothes were sitting in the saloon carriage when Korchagin entered on the heels of the conductor. A woman was sitting with her back to the door at a table covered with a damask cloth. When Pavel entered she was chatting with a tall officer who stood opposite her. They stopped talking as soon as the electrician appeared.

Korchagin made a rapid examination of the wiring which ran from the last lamp into the corridor, and finding it in order, left the car to continue his search for the damage. The stout bullnecked conductor in a uniform resplendent with large brass buttons bearing the Polish eagle kept close at his heels. "Let's try the next car, everything is in order here. The battery is working. The trouble must be there."

The conductor turned the key in the door and they passed into the darkened corridor. Training his flashlight on the wiring Pavel soon found the spot where the short circuit had occurred. A few minutes later the first lamp went on in the corridor suffusing it with opaque light. "The bulbs inside the compartment will have to be changed. They have burned out," Korchagin said to his guide. "In that case I'll have to call the lady, she has the key." Not wishing to leave the electrician alone in the car, the conductor bade him to follow.

The woman entered the compartment first, Korchagin followed. The conductor remained standing in the doorway blocking the entrance. Pavel noted the two elegant leather travelling bags, a silken cloak flung carelessly on the seat, a bottle of perfume and a tiny malachite vanity case on the table under the window. The woman sat down in a corner of the couch, patted her fair hair and watched the electrician at work. "Will madam permit me to leave for a moment?" the conductor said obsequiously, inclining his bull neck with some difficulty. "The Major has asked for some cold beer."

"You may go," replied the woman in an affected voice. The exchange had been in Polish. A shaft of light from the corridor fell on the woman's shoulder. Her exquisite gown of the finest Lyons silk made by the best Paris dress designers left her shoulders and arms bare. In the lobe of each delicate ear a diamond drop blazed and sparkled. Korchagin could only see one ivory shoulder and arm. The face was in shadow. Working swiftly with his screwdriver Pavel changed the outlet in the ceiling and a moment later the lights went on in the compartment. Now he had only to examine the other bulb over the sofa on which the woman sat.

"I need to test that bulb," Korchagin said, pausing in front of her. "Oh yes, I am in your way," the lady replied in perfect Russian. She rose lightly and stood close beside him. Now he had a full view of her. The arched eyebrows and the pursed, disdainful lips were familiar. There could be no doubt of it: it was Nelly Leszczinski, the lawyer's daughter. She could not fail to notice his look of astonishment. But though Pavel had recognised her, he had altered too much in these four years for Leszczinski to realise that this electrician was her troublesome neighbour.

With a frown of displeasure at his surprised stare, she went over to the door of the compartment and stood there tapping the heel of her patent leather shoe impatiently. Pavel turned his attention to the second bulb. He unscrewed it, raised it to the light and almost as much to his own surprise as hers he asked in Polish: "is Victor here as well?"

Pavel had not turned when he spoke. He did not see Nelly's face, but the long silence that followed his query bore testimony to her confusion. "Why, do you mean you know him?"

"Yes, and very well too. We were neighbours, you know." Pavel turned to look at her. "You're...you're Pavel, the son..." Nelly broke off in confusion. "...Of your cook," Korchagin came to her assistance. "But how you have grown! You were a wild youngster when I knew you."

Nelly examined him coolly from head to foot. "Why do you ask about Victor? As far as I remember you and he were not exactly friends," she said in her cooing voice. This unexpected encounter promised to be a pleasant relief to her boredom.

The screw swiftly sank into the wall.

"There is a certain debt Victor hasn't paid yet. Tell him when you see him that I haven't lost hope of seeing it settled." "Tell me how much he owes you and I shall pay you on his account." She knew very well what debt Korchagin had in mind. She knew about Pavel's betrayal to the Petlyura men, but the desire to make fun of this "ragamuffin" impelled her to adopt an insulting tone. Korchagin said nothing. "Tell me, is it true that our house has been looted and is now falling into decay? I daresay the summer house and the bushes have all been torn up," Nelly inquired wistfully.

"The house is not yours any more, it is ours, and we are not likely to destroy our own property." Nelly gave a mocking little laugh. "Oh, I see you have been well schooled! Incidentally, this car belongs to the Polish mission and here I am the mistress and you are the servant just as you always were. You see, you are working now to give me light so that I may lie comfortably on the sofa and read. Your mother used to wash clothes for us and you used to carry water. We meet again under precisely the same circumstances."

Her voice rang with malicious triumph. Scraping the insulation off the end of the wire with his pen knife, Pavel threw the Polish woman a look of undisguised scorn.

"I wouldn't hammer a single rusty nail for you, but since the bourgeoisie have invented diplomats we can play the same game. We don't cut off their heads, in fact we're even polite to them, which is more than can be said of yourself." Nelly's cheeks crimsoned. "What would you do with me if you succeeded in taking Warsaw? I suppose you would make mincemeat out of me, or perhaps take me for your mistress?" She stood in the doorway in a graceful pose; her sensitive nostrils that were no strangers to cocaine quivered. The light went on over the sofa. Pavel straightened up.

"You? Who would bother to kill the likes of you! You'll croak from too much cocaine without us. As for a mistress, I'd sooner take a streetwalker!"

He picked up his tool case and strode to the door. Nelly moved aside to let him pass. He was halfway down the corridor when he heard the curse she spat after him: "Damned Bolshevik!"

. . . .

THE FOLLOWING EVENING as he was on his way to the library Pavel met Katyusha Zeienova. She caught hold of his sleeve with her tiny hand and laughingly barred his path.

"Where are you dashing off to, old politics-and-enlightenment?"

"To the library, auntie, let me pass," Pavel replied in the same bantering tone. He took her gently by the shoulders and shifted her aside. Katyusha shook herself free and walked along beside him.

"Listen here, Pavlusha! You can't study all the time, you know. I'll tell you what – let's go to a party tonight. The crowd is meeting at Zina Gladysh's. The girls keep on asking me to bring you. But you never think of anything but political study nowadays. Don't you ever want to have some fun? It will do you good to miss your reading for once," Katyusha coaxed.

"What sort of a party is it? What are we going to do there?"

"What are we going to do!" Katyusha smilingly mocked him.

"We're not going to say prayers, we're going to have a good time, that's all. You play the accordion, don't you? I've never once heard you play! Do come and play for us this evening, won't you? Just to please me? Zina's uncle has an accordion but he can't play for anything. The girls are very much interested about you, you old bookworm. Who said Komsomols mustn't enjoy themselves? Come along, before I get sick of persuading you or else we'll quarrel and then I shan't talk to you for a month."

Katya, the house painter, was a good comrade and a first-rate Komsomol member. Pavel did not want to hurt the girl's feelings, and so he agreed, although he felt awkward and out of place at such parties.

A noisy crowd of young people had gathered at engine-driver Gladysh's home. The adults had retired to another room, leaving some fifteen lads and girls in possession of the large living room and porch which gave onto a small front garden. A game called "feeding the pigeons" was in progress when Katyusha led Pavel through the garden onto the porch. In the middle of the porch stood two chairs back to back. At a call from the hostess who was leading the game, a boy and girl seated themselves on the chairs with their backs to each other, and when she cried "Now feed the pigeons!" the couple leaned back until their lips met, much to the delight of the onlookers. After that they played "the ring" and "postman's knock," both kissing games, although in "postman's knock" the players avoided publicity by doing their kissing not on the brightly lit porch but in the room with the lights out. For those who did not care for these two games, there was a pack of "flower flirt" cards on a small round table in the corner. Pavel's neighbour, a girl of about sixteen with pale blue eyes who introduced herself as Mura, handed him one of the cards with a coy glance and said softly: "violet."

A few years back Pavel had attended parties of this kind, and if he had not taken a direct part in the frivolities he had not thought them anything out of the ordinary. But now that he had broken for ever with petty-bourgeois small-town life, the party struck him as disgusting and rather ridiculous.

Yet here he was with the "flower'" card in his hands. Opposite the "violet" he read the words: "I like you very much." Pavel looked up at the girl. She returned his look without a trace of embarrassment. "Why?" His question sounded rather flat. But Mura had her answer ready. "Rose," she murmured and handed him another card.

The card with the "rose" bore the legend: "You are my ideal." Korchagin turned to the girl and making a conscious effort to soften his tone, asked: "why do you go in for this nonsense?"

Mura was so taken aback that she did not know what to say. "Have I offended you?" she said with a capricious pout. Pavel ignored the question. Yet he was curious to know more about her. He asked her a number of questions which she willingly answered. Within a few minutes he had learned that she attended secondary school, that her father worked at the car-shops and that she had known Pavel for a long time and had wanted to make his acquaintance.

"What is your surname?" Pavel asked. "Volyntseva." "Your brother is secretary of the Komsomol nucleus at the yards, isn't he?" "Yes." Now Korchagin was on familiar ground. It was clear to him that Volyntsev, one of the most active Komsomols in the district, was allowing his own sister to grow up an ignorant little philistine. She and her friends had attended innumerable kissing parties like these in the past year. She told Pavel she had seen him several times at her brother's place.

Mura felt that her neighbour did not approve of her behaviour. Catching sight of the scornful smile on Korchagin's face she flatly refused to obey the summons to come and "feed the pigeons." They sat talking for another few minutes while Mura told him more about herself, until Zelenova came over to them.

"Shall I bring you the accordion?" she asked, adding with a mischievous glance at Mura, "I see you've made friends?" Pavel made Katyusha sit down beside them, and taking advantage of the noise and laughter around them, he said: "I'm not going to play. Mura and I are leaving." "Oho! So you've been bitten, eh?" Zelenova taunted. "That's right. Tell me, Katyusha, are there any other Komsomols here besides ourselves? Or are we the only 'pigeon fanciers'?" "We've stopped fooling about," Katyusha said placatingly. "Now we're going to dance."

Korchagin rose. "All right, old girl, you dance, but Mura and I are pushing off."

• • • •

ONE EVENING ANNA BORHART dropped in to Okunev's place and found Korchagin there alone. "Are you very busy, Pavel? Would you care to come with me to the plenary session of the City Soviet? I would rather not go alone, especially since we'll be returning late."

Korchagin was ready to go at once. He was about to take the Mauser that hung over his bed but decided it was too heavy. Instead he pulled Okunev's revolver out of the drawer and slipped it into his pocket. He left a note for Okunev and put the key where his roommate would find it.

At the theatre where the plenum was being held they met Pankratov and Olga Yureneva. They all sat together in the hall and during the intermissions strolled in a group on the square. As Anna had expected, the meeting ended very late. "Perhaps you'd better come to my place for the night?" Olga suggested. "It's late and you've a long way to go." But Anna declined. "Pavel has agreed to see me home," she said. Pankratov and Olga set off down the main street and the other two took the road up the hill to Solomenka.

It was a dark, stuffy night. The city was asleep as the plenum participants took their various ways home. Gradually the sound of their steps and voices died down. Pavel and Anna walked at a brisk pace away from the central section of the town. At the deserted market place they were stopped by a patrol who examined their papers and let them pass. They crossed the boulevard and came out onto a dark silent street which cut across a vacant lot. Turning left, they continued along the highway parallel to the main railway warehouses, a long row of gloomy and forbidding concrete buildings. Anna was seized by a vague feeling of apprehension. She peered anxiously into the darkness, giving nervous jerky answers to her companion's questions. When a sinister shadow turned out to be nothing more terrible than a telephone pole, she laughed aloud and confided her nervousness to Pavel. She took him by the arm and the pressure of his shoulder against hers reassured her. "I am only twenty-three but I'm as nervous as an old woman. If you think I'm a coward, you are mistaken. But somehow my nerves are all on edge tonight. With you here though I feel quite safe, and I'm really ashamed of my fears."

And indeed Pavel's calmness, the warm glow of his cigarette end which for an instant lit up a corner of his face, revealing the courageous sweep of his brows – all this drove away the terrors evoked by the dark night, the loneliness of the spot and the story they had just heard at the meeting about a horrible murder committed the night before on the outskirts of town.

The warehouses were left behind. They crossed the bridge spanning a small creek and continued along the main road to the tunnel which ran under the railway line and connected this section of the town with the railway district.

The station building was now far behind them to the right. The road ended in a blind alley beyond the depot. They were already on home-ground. Up above on the railway track the coloured lights of switches and semaphores twinkled in the darkness, and over by the depot a yard engine on its way home for the night sighed wearily.

Above the mouth of the tunnel a street lamp hung from a rusty hook. The wind swayed it gently, causing its murky yellow light to move from one wall of the tunnel to the other.

A small cottage stood solitary by the side of the highway some ten yards from the tunnel entrance. Two years ago it had been hit by a heavy shell which had destroyed the interior and reduced the facade to ruins, so that it was now one huge gaping hole, and it stood there like a beggar on the roadside exhibiting its wretchedness. A train roared over the embankment above. "We're nearly home now," Anna said with a sigh of relief. Pavel made a furtive attempt to extricate his arm. But Anna would not release it. They walked past the ruined house.

Suddenly something crashed behind them. There was a sound of running feet, hoarse breathing. They were overtaken. Korchagin jerked his arm but Anna, petrified with fear clung wildly to it. And by the time he was able to tear it loose, it was too late; his neck was caught in an iron grip. Another moment and he was swung round to face his assailant. The hand crept up to his throat and, twisting his tunic collar until it all but choked him, held him facing the muzzle of a revolver that slowly described an arc before his eyes.

Pavel's fascinated eyes followed the arc with superhuman tension. Death stared at him through the muzzle of the revolver, and he had neither the strength nor the will to tear his eyes from that muzzle for even the fraction of a second. He waited for the end: But his assailant did not fire, and Pavel's dilated eyes saw the bandit's face, saw the huge skull, the heavy jaw, the black shadow of unshaven beard and moustache. But the eyes under the wide peak of the cap were invisible.

Out of the corner of his eye Korchagin had one brief and stark glimpse of the chalk-white face of Anna whom one of the three dragged into the gaping hole in the wall at that moment. Twisting her arms cruelly he flung her onto the ground. Another shadow leapt toward Pavel; he only saw its reflection on the tunnel wall. He heard the scuffle within the ruined house behind him. Anna was fighting desperately; her choking cry broke off abruptly as a cap was stuffed against her mouth. The large-skulled ruffian who had Korchagin at his mercy was drawn to the scene of the rape like a beast to its prey. He was evidently the leader of the gang and the role of passive observer under the circumstances did not suit him. This youngster he had covered was just a greenhorn, looked like one of those "depot softies." Nothing to fear from a snot-nose like him.

"Give 'im a couple of good knocks on the head and tell him to cut along over the field and he'll run all the way to town without looking back." He relaxed his hold. "Leg it, you...clear out the way you came, but no squealin' mind, or you'll get a bullet in your neck." He pressed the barrel of the gun against Korchagin's forehead. "Leg it, now," he said in a hoarse whisper and lowered his gun to show that his victim need not fear a bullet in the back.

Korchagin staggered back and began to run sideways keeping his eyes on his assailant. The ruffian, seeing that the youngster was still afraid that he would shoot, turned and made for the ruined house.

Korchagin's hand flew to his pocket. If only he could be quick enough! He swung round, thrust his left hand forward, took swift aim and fired.

The bandit realised his mistake too late. The bullet tore into his side before he had time to raise his hand.

The blow sent him reeling against the tunnel wall with a low howl, and clawing at the wall he slowly sank to the ground. A shadow slid out of the house and made for the gully below. Korchagin sent another bullet in pursuit. A second shadow bent double darted toward the inky depths of the tunnel. A shot rang out. The dark shape, covered with the dust from the bullet-shattered concrete, leapt aside and vanished into the blackness. Once again the Browning rent the night's stillness. Beside the wall the large-headed bandit writhed in his death agony.

Korchagin helped Anna to her feet. Stunned by the horror of what she had just experienced she stared at the bandit's convulsions, as yet unable to believe that she was safe.

Korchagin dragged her away into the darkness back toward the town and away from the circle of light. As they ran toward the railway station, lights were already twinkling on the embankment near the tunnel and a rifle shot rang out on the track. By the lime they reached Anna's flat, on Batyeva Hill the cocks were crowing. Anna lay down on the bed. Korchagin sat by the table, smoking a cigarette and watching the grey spiral of smoke floating upward. He had just killed for the fourth time in his life.

Is there such a thing as courage, he wondered. Something that manifests itself always in its most perfect form? Reliving all his sensations he admitted that in those first few seconds with the black sinister eye of the gun muzzle upon him terror had laid its icy grip on his heart. And was it due solely to his weak eyesight and the fact that he had had to shoot with his left hand that those two shadows had been able to escape? No. At the distance of a few paces his bullets would have found their mark, but tension and haste, unmistakable signs of nervousness, had made him waver.

The light from the table lamp threw his head into relief. Anna, watching him, followed every movement of his features. His eyes were calm; the furrowed brow alone betrayed his mental concentration. "What are you thinking about, Pavel?"

His thoughts, startled by the sudden question, floated away like smoke beyond the circle of light, and he said the first thing that came into his head: "I must go over to the Commandant's Office. This business must be reported at once." He rose with reluctance, conscious of a great weariness.

She clung to his hand for she shrank from being left alone. Then she saw him to the door and stood on the threshold until the youth to whom she now owed so much, had vanished into the night.

Korchagin's report cleared up the mystery of the murder that had puzzled the railway guards. The body was identified at once as that of a notorious criminal named Fimka Death Skull, a murderer and bandit with a prison record.

The next day everybody was talking about the incident by the tunnel. It was indeed the cause of an unexpected clash between Pavel and Tsvetayev. The latter came into the workshop in the middle of the shift and asked Korchagin to step outside. Tsvetayev led the way in silence to a remote corner of the corridor. He was extremely agitated, and did not seem to know how to begin. At last he blurted out: "Tell me what happened yesterday." "I thought you knew?"

Tsvetayev jerked his shoulders uneasily. Pavel was unaware that the tunnel incident affected Tsvetayev more keenly than the others. He did not know that, for all his outward indifference, the blacksmith had formed a deep attachment for Anna Borhart. He was. not the only one who was attracted to the girl, but he was seriously smitten. Lagutina had just told him what had happened the night before at the tunnel and he was now tormented by one question that had remained unanswered. He could not put the question bluntly to the electrician, yet he had to know the answer. His better self told him that his fears were selfish and base, yet in the conflict of emotions that seethed within him the savage and primitive prevailed.

"Listen, Korchagin," he said hoarsely. "This is strictly between ourselves. I know you don't want to talk about it for Anna's sake, but you can surely trust me. Tell me this, while that bandit had you covered did the others rape Anna?" Covered with confusion he lowered his eyes before he finished speaking.

Dimly Korchagin began to perceive what was troubling the other. "If he cared nothing for Anna he would not be so upset. But if Anna is dear to him, then...." And Pavel burned at the insult to Anna the question implied. "Why do you ask?" Tsvetayev mumbled something incoherent. He felt that Pavel understood what was in question and he lost his temper: "don't try to wriggle out of it by questioning me. All I want is a straight answer. Do you love Anna?"

There was a long silence. At last Tsvetayev forced himself to reply: "Yes."

Korchagin, suppressing his anger with an effort, turned on his heel and strode down the corridor without looking back.

* * * *

ONE NIGHT OKUNEV, WHO had been hovering uncertainly around his friend's bed for some time, finally sat down on the edge and laid his hand on the book Pavel was reading.

"Listen, Pavlushka, there's something I've got to get off my chest. On the one hand, it mightn't seem important, but on the other, it's quite the reverse. There's been a misunderstanding between me and Talya Lagutina. You see, at first, I liked her quite a bit." Okunev scratched his head sheepishly, but seeing no sign of laughter on his friend's face, he took courage. "But then, Talya... well, you know. All right, I won't give you all the lurid details, it's clear enough without that. Yesterday she and I decided to hitch up and see how it works out. I'm twenty-two, we both have a vote. We want to live together on an equality basis. What do you think?"

Korchagin pondered the question. "What can I say, Kolya? You are both friends of mine, we're all members of the same clan, and we have everything else in common. Talya's a very nice girl. It's all plain sailing."

The next day Korchagin moved over to the depot workers' hostel, and a few days later Anna gave a party, a modest Communist party without food and drink, in honour of Talya and Nikolai. It was an evening of reminiscences, and readings of excerpts from favourite books. They sang many songs and sang them well; the rousing melodies echoed far and wide. Later on, Katyusha Zeienova and Volyntseva brought an accordion, and the rich rolling basses and silvery cadences filled the room. That evening Pavel played even better than usual, and when to everyone's delight the hulking Pankratov flung himself into the dance, Pavel forgot the new melancholy style he had adopted and played with abandon.

When Denikin gets to know
Of old Kolchak's overthrow,
Oh, how crazy he will go!

The accordion sang of the past, of the years of storm and stress and of today's friendship, struggles and joys. But when the instrument was handed over to Volyntsev and the mechanic tore into the whirling rhythm of the "Yablochko" dance, who should take to the floor but Korchagin with a wild tap dance – the third and last time he was to dance in his life.

CHAPTER FOUR

This is the frontier – two posts facing one another in silent hostility, each standing for a world of its own. One of them is planed and polished and painted black and white like a police box, and topped by a single-headed eagle nailed in place with sturdy spikes. Wings outspread, claws gripping the striped pole, hooked beak tensely outstretched, the bird of prey stares with malicious eyes at the cast-iron shield with the sickle and hammer emblem on the opposite pole – a sturdy, round, rough-hewn oak post planted firmly in the ground. The two poles stand on level ground, yet there is a deep gulf between them and the two worlds they stand for. You cannot cross the intervening six paces except at the risk of your life.

This is the frontier.

From the Black Sea over thousands of kilometres to the Arctic Ocean in the Far North stands the motionless file of these silent sentinels of the Soviet Socialist Republics bearing the great emblem of labour on their iron shields. The post with the rapacious bird marks the beginning of the border between Soviet Ukraine and bourgeois Poland. It stands ten kilometres from the small town of Berezdov tucked away in the Ukrainian hinterland, and opposite it is the Polish townlet of Korec. From Slavuta to Anapol the border area is guarded by the N Border Battalion.

The frontier posts march across the snowbound fields, push through clearings cut in forests, plunge down valleys and, heaving themselves up hillsides, disappear behind the crests only to pause on the high bank of a river to survey the hibernal plains of an alien land.

It is biting cold, one of those days when the frost makes the snow crunch under the soles of felt boots. A giant of a Red Army man in a helmet fit for the titans of old moves away from a post with the sickle-and-hammer shield and with heavy tread sets out on his beat. He is wearing a grey greatcoat with green facings, and felt boots. On top of the greatcoat he has a sheepskin coat reaching down to his heels with a collar of generous proportions to match – a coat that will keep a man warm in the cruellest blizzard. On his head he wears a cloth helmet and his hands are encased in sheepskin mittens. His rifle he has slung on his shoulder, and as he proceeds along the sentry path wearing a groove in the snow with the hem of his outer garment he pulls at a cigarette of home-grown tobacco with obvious relish. On open stretches the Soviet border guards are posted a kilometre apart so that each man can always see his neighbour. On the Polish side there are two sentries to the kilometre.

A Polish infantryman plods along his sentry path toward the Red Army man. He is wearing rough army issue boots, a greenish grey uniform and on top a black coat with two rows of shining buttons. On his head he has the square-topped uniform cap with the white eagle emblem; there are more white eagles on his cloth shoulder straps and the collar facings, but they do not make him feel any warmer. The severe frost has chilled him to the marrow, and he rubs his numb ears and knocks his heels together as he walks, while his hands in the thin gloves are stiff with cold. The Pole cannot risk stopping his pacing for a moment, and sometimes he trots, for otherwise the frost would stiffen his joints in a moment. When the two sentries draw together, the Ïoánierz turns around to walk alongside the Red Army man.

Conversation on the frontier is forbidden, but when there is no one around but the distant figures a kilometre away – who can tell whether the two are patrolling their beats in silence or violating international laws.

The Pole wants a smoke very badly, but he has forgotten his matches in the barracks, and here as if out of spite the breeze wafts over from the Soviet side the tantalising fragrance of tobacco. The Pole stops rubbing his ear and glances back over his shoulder, for who knows but that the captain, or maybe Pan the lieutenant, might not pop into sight from behind a knoll with a mounted patrol on one of those inspection rounds they are wont to make. But he sees nothing save the dazzling whiteness of the snow in the sun. In the sky there is not so much as a fleck of a cloud.

"Got a light, Comrade?" The Pole was the first to violate the sanctity of the law. And shifting his French magazine rifle with the sword bayonet back on his shoulder he laboriously extracted with stiff fingers a packet of cheap cigarettes from the depths of his coat pocket.

The Red Army man heard him, but the frontier service regulations forbid one from entering into any conversation across the border. Besides, he could not quite catch what the soldier wanted to say. So he continued on his way, firmly treading down on the crunching snow with his warm, soft felt boots.

"Comrade Bolshevik, got a light? Maybe you'll throw a box of matches across?" This time the Pole went over to Russian.

The Red Army man subjected his neighbour to a scrutinising glance. "The frost has nipped the Pan good and proper," he thought to himself. "The poor beggar may be a bourgeois soldier but he's got a hell of a life. Imagine being chased out into this cold in that miserable outfit, no wonder he jumps about like a rabbit, and with nothing to smoke either." Without turning around, the Red Army man threw a box of matches across to the other. The soldier caught it on the fly, and getting his cigarette going after several unsuccessful attempts, promptly sent the box back across the border the way it had come.

Whereupon the Red Army man willy-nilly found himself breaking the regulations: "keep it. I've got some more." From beyond the frontier came the response: "thanks, I'd better not. If they found that box on me I'd get a couple of years in jail."

The Red Army man examined the match box. On the label was an aeroplane with a sinewy fist instead of a propeller and the word "Ultimatum." "Right enough, it won't do for them."

The soldier continued walking alongside the Red Army man. He felt lonely in the midst of this deserted plain.

· · · ·

THE SADDLES CREAKED rhythmically as the horses trotted along at an even, soothing pace. The horses' breath congealed into momentary plumes of white vapour in the frosty air. A hoary rime stood out around the nostrils of the black stallion. Stepping gracefully, her fine neck arched, the Battalion Commander's dappled mare was playing with her bit. Both horsemen wore army greatcoats belted in at the waist and with three red squares on the sleeves; the only difference was that Battalion Commander Gavrilov's facings were green, while his companion's were red. Gavrilov was with the border guards; it was his battalion that manned the frontier posts on this seventy-kilometre stretch, he was the man in charge of this border belt. His companion was a visitor from Berezdov – Battalion Commissar Korchagin of the universal military training system.

It had snowed during the night and the fresh white fluff covered the countryside in a virginal blanket untouched by either man or beast. The two men cantered out from the woods and were about to cross an open stretch some forty paces from where the paired poles marked the border when Gavrilov suddenly reined in his horse. Korchagin wheeled, around to see Gavrilov leaning over from his saddle and inspecting a curious trail in the snow that looked as if someone had been running a tiny cogwheel over the surface. Some cunning little beast had passed here leaving behind the intricate, confusing pattern. It was hard to make out which way the creature had been travelling, but that was not what caused the Battalion Commander to halt. Two paces away lay another trail under a powdery sprinkling of snow—the footsteps of a human being. There was nothing uncertain about these footprints – they led straight toward the woods, and there was not the slightest doubt that the interloper had come from the Polish side. The Battalion Commander urged on his horse and followed the tracks to the sentry path.

The footprints showed distinctly for a dozen paces or so on the Polish side. "Somebody crossed the border last night," muttered the Battalion Commander. "The third platoon has been napping again – no mention of it in the morning report. Damn them!" Gavrilov's greying moustache silvered by his congealed breath hung grimly over his lip.

In the distance two figures were approaching the mounted men—one a slight man garbed in black and with the blade of a French bayonet gleaming in the sun, the other a giant in a yellow sheepskin coat. The dapple mare responded to a jab in her flanks and briskly the two riders bore down on the approaching pair. As they came, the Red Army man hitched up the rifle slung on his shoulder and spat out the butt of his cigarette into the snow.

"Good day, Comrade. How's everything on your beat?" The Battalion Commander stretched out his hand to the Red Army man, who hurriedly removed a mitt to return the handclasp. So tall was the border guard that the Commander hardly had to bend forward in his saddle to reach him.

The Pole looked on from a distance. Here were two Red officers greeting a soldier as they would a close friend. For a moment he pictured himself shaking hands with Major Zakrzewski, but the very thought was so absurd that he looked around him startled. "Just took over, Comrade Battalion Commander," reported the Red Army man. "Seen the track over there?" "No, not yet." "Who was on duty here from two to six at night?" "Surotenko, Comrade Battalion Commander." "All right, but keep your eyes open."

As the commander was about to ride on he added a stern word of warning: "and you'd better do a little less walking with those fellows." "You have to keep your eyes open on the border," the Commander said to his companion as their horses cantered along the broad

road leading from the frontier to Berezdov. "The slightest lapse and you're bound to rue it bitterly. Can't afford to take a nap on a job like ours. In broad daylight it's not so easy to skip the border, but at night you've got to be on the alert. Now judge for yourself. Comrade Korchagin. On my sector the frontier cuts right through four villages, which complicates things considerably. No matter how close you place your guards you'll find all the relatives from the one side of the line attending every wedding or feast held on the other. And no wonder—it's only a couple of dozen paces from between the cottages and the creek's shallow enough for a chicken to wade across. And there's some smuggling being done, too. True, much of it on a petty scale—an old woman carting across a bottle or two of Polish vodka and that sort of thing. But there is quite a bit of large-scale contraband traffic—people with big money to operate with. Have you heard that the Poles have opened shops in all the border villages where you can get practically everything you want? Those shops aren't intended for their own pauperised peasants, you may be sure."

As he listened to the Battalion Commander, Korchagin reflected that life on the border must resemble an endless scouting mission. "Probably there's something more serious than smuggling going on. What do you say. Comrade Gavrilov?" "That's just the trouble," the Battalion Commander replied gloomily.

Berezdov was a small backwoods town that had been within the Jewish pale of residence. It had two or three hundred small houses scattered haphazardly, and a huge market square with a couple of dozen shops in the middle. The square was filthy with manure. Around the town proper were the peasant huts. In the Jewish central section, on the road to the slaughter house, stood an old synagogue—a rickety, depressing building. Although the synagogue still drew crowds on Saturdays, its heyday had gone, and the rabbi lived a life that was by no means to his liking. What happened in nineteen-seventeen must have been evil indeed if even in this Godforsaken corner the youngsters no longer accorded him the respect due his position. True, the old folk would still eat only kosher food, but how many of the youngsters indulged in the pork sausage which God had cursed. The very thought was revolting! And Rabbi Borukh in a fit of temper kicked viciously at a pig that was assiduously digging in a heap of manure in search of something edible. The rabbi was not at all pleased that Berezdov had been made a district centre, nor did he approve of these Communists who had descended on the place from the devil knows where and were now turning things upside down. Each day brought some fresh unpleasantness. Yesterday, for instance, he had seen a new sign over the gate of the priest's house: "Berezdov District Committee, Young Communist League of the Ukraine," it had read.

To expect this sign to augur anything but ill would be useless, mused the rabbi. So engrossed was he in his thoughts that he did not notice the small announcement pasted on the door of his synagogue before he actually bumped into it.

A public meeting of working youth will he held today at the club. The speakers will be Lisitsyn, Chairman of the Executive Committee, and Korchagin, Acting Secretary of the Y.C.L. District Committee. After the meeting a concert will be given by the pupils of the nine-year school. In a fury the rabbi tore down the sheet of paper. "So they've begun already!"

In the centre of a large garden adjoining the local church stood a big old house that had once belonged to the priest. A deadly air of boredom filled the musty emptiness of the rooms in which the priest and his wife had lived, two people as old and as dull as the house itself and long bored with one another. The dreariness was swept away as soon as the new masters of the place moved in. The big hall in which the former pious residents had entertained guests only on church holidays was now always full of people, for the house was now the headquarters of the Berezdov Communist Party Committee. On the door leading into a small room to the right just inside the front hall the words "Komsomol District Committee" had been written in chalk. Here Korchagin, who besides being Military Commissar of the Second Universal Military Training Battalion was also Acting Secretary of the newly organised Komsomol District Committee, spent part of his working day.

Eight months had passed since he had been at that gathering at Anna's, yet it seemed that it had been only yesterday. Korchagin pushed the stack of papers aside and leaning back in his chair gave himself up to his thoughts...

The house was still. It was late at night and the Party Committee office was deserted. Trofimov, the Committee's Secretary, had gone home some time ago, leaving Korchagin alone in the building. Frost had woven a fantastic pattern on the window, but the room was warm. A kerosene lamp was burning on the table. Korchagin was recalling the recent past. He remembered how in August the car-shop Komsomol organisation had sent him as a youth organiser with a repair train to Yekaterinoslav. Until late autumn he had travelled with the train's crew of a hundred and fifty from station to station bringing order into the chaotic aftermath of war, repairing damage and clearing away the remnants of smashed and burnt-out railway cars. Their route took them from Sinelnikovo to Pologi, through country where the bandit Makhno had once operated leaving behind him a trail of wreckage and wanton destruction. In Gulyai-Polye a whole week went into repairing the brick structure of the water tower and patching the sides of the dynamited water tank with iron sheets. Though lacking the skill of a fitter and unaccustomed to the heavy work, the electrician wielded a wrench along with the others and tightened more thousands of rusty bolts than he could remember.

Late in the autumn the train returned home and the car-shops again were the richer for a hundred and fifty pairs of hands.

The electrician was now a more frequent visitor at Anna's place. The crease on his forehead smoothed out and his infectious laughter could again be heard.

Once again the grimy-faced fraternity from the railway shops gathered to hear him talk of bygone years of struggle, of the attempts made by rebellious but enslaved peasant Russia to overthrow the crowned monster that sat heavy on her shoulders, of the insurrections of Stepan Razin and Pugachov.

One evening at Anna's, when even more young people than usual had gathered there, Pavel announced that he was going to give up smoking, which unhealthy habit he had acquired practically in his childhood. "I'm not smoking any more," he declared with a note of unbending resolve. It all came about unexpectedly. One of the young people present had said that habit—smoking, for instance—was stronger than will power. Opinions were divided. At first the electrician said nothing, but drawn in by Talya, he finally joined the debate.

"Man governs his habits, and not the other way around. Otherwise what would we get?"

"Sounds fine, doesn't it?" Tsvetayev put in from his corner. "Korchagin likes to talk big. But why doesn't he apply his wisdom to himself? He smokes, doesn't he? He knows it's a rotten habit. Of course he does. But he isn't man enough to drop it." Then, changing his tone, Tsvetayev went on with a cold sneer; "He was busy 'spreading culture' in the study circles not so long ago. But did this prevent him from using foul language? Anyone who knows Pavka will tell you that he doesn't swear very often, but when he does he certainly lets himself go. It's much easier to lecture others than to be virtuous yourself."

There was a strained silence. The sharpness of Tsvetayev's tone had laid a chill on the gathering. Korchagin did not reply at once. Slowly he removed the cigarette from between his lips and said quietly: "I'm not smoking any more." Then, after a pause, he added: "I'm doing this more for myself than for Dimka. A man who can't break himself of a bad habit isn't worth anything. That leaves only the swearing to be taken care of. I know I haven't quite overcome that shameful habit, but even Dimka admits that he doesn't hear bad language from me very often. It's harder to stop a bad word from slipping out than to stop smoking, so I can't say at the moment that I've finished with that too. But I will."

• • • •

JUST BEFORE THE FROSTS set in, rafts of firewood drifting down the river jammed the channel. Then the autumn floods broke them up and the much-needed fuel was swept away by the rushing waters. And again Solomenka sent its people to the rescue, this time to save the precious wood.

Unwilling to drop behind the others, Korchagin concealed the fact that he had caught a bad chill until a week later, when the wood had been piled high on shore. The icy water and the chill dankness of autumn had awakened the enemy lying low in his blood and he came down with a high fever. For two weeks acute rheumatism racked his body, and when he returned from hospital, he was able to work at the vice only by straddling the bench. The foreman would look at him and shake his head sadly. A few days later a medical board declared him unfit for work and he was given his discharge pay and papers certifying his right to a pension. This, however, he indignantly refused to accept.

With a heavy heart he left the carshops. He moved about slowly, leaning on his stick, but every step caused excruciating pain. There were several letters from his mother asking him to come home for a visit, and each time he thought of her, her parting words came back to his mind: "I never see you unless you're crippled!"

At the Gubernia Committee he was handed his Komsomol and Party registration cards and, with as few leave-takings as possible to evade the pain of parting, he slipped out of town to go to his mother. For two weeks the old woman steamed and massaged his swollen legs, and a month later he was already able to walk without the cane. Joy again filled his heart as the twilight was supplanted by a new day. Once again the train brought him to the Gubernia centre; three days there and the organisational department issued him a paper directing him to the regional military commissariat to be used as a political worker in a military training unit.

Another week passed and Pavel arrived in a small snowbound town as Military Commissar assigned to Battalion Two. The area committee of the Komsomol too gave him an assignment: to rally the scattered Komsomol members in the locality and set up a youth league organisation in the district. Thus life got into a new stride.

· · · ·

OUTSIDE IT WAS STIFLING hot. The branch of a cherry tree peeped in through the open window of the Executive Committee Chairman's office. Across the way the gilded cross atop the gothic belfry of the Polish church blazed in the sun. And in the yard in front of the window tiny downy goslings as green as the grass around—the property of the caretaker of the Executive Committee premises—were busily searching for food.

The Chairman of the Executive Committee read the dispatch he had just received to the end. A shadow flitted across his face, and a huge gnarled hand strayed into his luxurious crop of hair and paused there. Nikolai Nikolayevich Lisitsyn, the Chairman of the Berezdov Executive Committee, was only twenty-four, but none of the members of his staff and the local Party workers would have believed it. A big, strong man stern and often formidable in appearance, he looked at least thirty-five. He had a powerful physique, a big head firmly planted on a thick neck, piercing brown eyes with a steely glint, and a strong, energetic jaw. He wore blue breeches and a grey tunic, somewhat the worse for wear, with the Order of the Red Banner pinned on the left breast pocket.

Like his father and grandfather before him Lisitsyn had been a metalworker practically from his childhood, and before the October Revolution he had "commanded" a lathe at a Tula gunworks.

Beginning with that autumn night when the Tula gunsmith shouldered a rifle and went out to fight for the workers' power, he had been caught up in the whirlwind of events. The revolution and the Party sent Kolya Lisitsyn from one tight spot to another along a glorious path that witnessed his rise from rank-and-file Red Army man to regimental commander and commissar.

The fire of battle and the thunder of guns had moved back into the past. Nikolai Lisitsyn was now working in a frontier district. Life went on at a measured, peaceful beat, and the Executive Committee Chairman sat in his office until late night after night poring over harvest reports. The dispatch he now had in hand, however, momentarily revived the recent past. It was a warning couched in terse telegraphic language:

Strictly confidential. To Lisitsyn, Chairman of the Berezdov Executive Committee.

Marked activity has been observed lately on the border where the Poles have been trying to send across a large band to terrorise the frontier districts. Take precautions. Suggest everything valuable at the finance department including collected taxes, be transferred to area centre.

From his window Lisitsyn could see everyone who entered the District Executive Committee building. Looking up he caught sight of Pavel Korchagin on the porch. A moment later there was a knock on the door. "Sit down, I've got something to tell you," Lisitsyn said returning Pavel's handshake. For a whole hour the two were closeted in the office.

By the time Korchagin emerged from the office it was noon. As he stepped out, Lisitsyn's little sister, a timid child far too serious for her years, ran toward him from the garden. She always had a warm smile for Korchagin, who used to address her by the endearing diminutive Anyutka, and now too she greeted him shyly, tossing a stray lock of her cropped hair back from her forehead. "Is Kolya busy?" she asked. "Maria Mikhailovna has had his dinner ready for a long time." "Go right in, Anyutka, he's alone."

Long before dawn the next morning three carts harnessed to well-fed horses pulled up in front of the Executive Committee. The men who came with them exchanged a few words in undertones, and several sealed sacks were then carried out of the Finance Department. These were loaded into the carts and a few minutes later the rumble of wheels receded along the highway. The carts were convoyed by a detail under Korchagin's command. The forty kilometres to the regional centre (twenty-five of them passed through forest) were covered safely and the valuables were transferred into safes at the Area Finance Department.

Some days after this a cavalryman riding a foaming mount galloped into Berezdov from the direction of the frontier. As he passed through the streets he was followed by the wondering stares of the local idlers.

At the gates of the Executive Committee the rider leapt to the ground and supporting his sabre with one hand stamped up the front stairs in his heavy boots. Lisitsyn with a worried frown took the missive he brought and signed for it on the envelope. The message delivered, the border guard mounted his horse and giving the animal no time to rest spurred it to a gallop and dashed back in the direction whence he had come.

• • • •

NO ONE BUT THE CHAIRMAN of the Executive Committee knew the contents of the dispatch, and he had just read it. But the local townsfolk had a keen nose for maturing events – two out of three petty traders here were smugglers in a small way, and plying this trade they had developed an instinctive ability to sense impending danger.

Two men walked briskly along the pavement leading to the headquarters of the Military Training Battalion. One of them was Pavel Korchagin. He was armed but this excited no surprise in the onlookers. That was his habit. But the fact that the second of the men, Party Committee Secretary Trofimov, had strapped on a revolver looked ominous.

Several minutes later a dozen men ran out of the headquarters carrying rifles with bayonets fixed and marched briskly to the mill standing at the crossroads. The rest of the local Communist Party and Komsomol members were being issued arms at the Party Committee offices. The Chairman of the Executive Committee galloped past, wearing a Cossack cap and the customary Mauser at his belt. Something was obviously afoot. The main square and sidestreets grew deserted. Not a soul was in sight. In a flash huge medieval padlocks appeared at the doors of the tiny shops and shutters were clamped down over windows. Only the fearless hens and the hogs tormented by the heat continued to rummage among piles of refuse.

The pickets took cover in the gardens at the edge of the town whence they had a good view of the open fields and the straight ribbon of road reaching into the distance.

The dispatch received by Lisitsyn had been brief:

A mounted band of about one hundred effectives with two light machine guns broke through to Soviet territory after an action fought in the area of Poddubtsy last night. Take precautionary measures. The trail of the band has been lost in the Slavuta woods. A Red Cossack company has been sent in pursuit of the band. The company will pass through Berezdov during the day. Do not mistake them for the enemy.

Gavrilov, Commander,

Separate Frontier Battalion.

No more than an hour had passed when a mounted man appeared on the road leading to the town, followed by a group of horsemen moving about a kilo-metre behind. Korchagin's keen eyes followed their movements. The lone rider was a young Red Army man from the Seventh Red Cossack Regiment, a novice at reconnaissance, and hence, though he picked his way cautiously enough, he failed to spot the pickets in ambuscade in the roadside gardens. Before he knew it he was surrounded by armed men who poured onto the road from the greenery, and when he saw the Komsomol emblem on their tunics, he smiled sheepishly. Following brief explanations, he turned his horse around and galloped back to the mounted force now coming up at the trot. The pickets let the Red Cossacks through and resumed their watch in the gardens.

Several anxious days passed before Lisitsyn received word that the diversionist band had failed to carry out its assignment. Pursued by the Red cavalry, the raiders had had to beat a hasty retreat behind the frontier cordon.

A handful of Bolsheviks, numbering nineteen in all, applied themselves energetically to the job of building up Soviet life in the district. This was a new administrative unit and hence everything had to be created from bottom up. Besides, the proximity of the border called for unflagging vigilance on the part of everyone.

Lisitsyn, Trofimov, Korchagin and the small group of active workers they had rallied toiled from dawn till dusk arranging for re-elections of Soviets, fighting the bandits, organising cultural work, putting down smuggling, in addition to Party and Komsomol work to strengthen defence.

From saddle to desk, and from desk to the common where squads of young military trainees diligently drilled, then the club and the school and two or three committee meetings – such was the daily round of the Military Commissar of Battalion Two. Often enough his nights were spent on horseback, Mauser strapped to his side, nights whose stillness was broken by a sharp "Halt, who goes there?" and the pounding of the wheels of a fleeing cart laden with smuggled goods from beyond the border.

The Berezdov District Committee of the Komsomol consisted of Korchagin, Lida Polevykh, a sloe-eyed girl from the Volga who headed the Women's Department, and Zhenka Razvalikhin, a tall, handsome young man who had been a Gymnasium student only a short time before. Razvalikhin had a weakness for thrilling adventures and was an authority on Sherlock Holmes and Louis Boussenard. Previously he had been office manager for the District Committee of the Party, and though he had joined the Komsomol only four months before, posed before the youth as an "old Bolshevik." The Area Committee had sent him after some hesitation to Berezdov to take charge of political education work for the simple reason that there was no one else to send.

· · · ·

THE SUN HAD REACHED its zenith. The heat penetrated everywhere and all living creatures sought refuge in the shade. Even the dogs crawled under sheds and lay there panting, inert and sleepy. The only sign of life in the village was a hog revelling in a puddle of mud next to the well.

Korchagin untethered his horse, and biting his lip from the pain in his knee, climbed into the saddle. The teacher was standing on the steps of the schoolhouse, shading her eyes from the sun with the palm of her hand. "I hope to see you soon again, Comrade Military Commissar," she smiled. The horse stamped impatiently, stretched its neck and pulled at the reins. "Goodbye, Comrade Rakitina. So it's settled: you'll give the first lesson tomorrow."

Feeling the pressure of the bit relax, the horse was off at a brisk trot. Suddenly wild cries reached Pavel's ears. It sounded like the shrieking of women when villages catch fire. Wheeling his mount sharply around, the Military Commissar saw a young peasant woman running breathlessly into the village. Rakitina rushed forward and stopped her. From the nearby cottages the inhabitants, mostly old men and women, for the able-bodied peasants were working in the fields, looked out.

"O-o-oh! Good people! Come quickly! Come quickly! They're murdering each other over there!" When Korchagin galloped up people were crowding around the woman, pulling at her white blouse and showering her with anxious questions, but they could make nothing of her incoherent cries. "It's murder! They're cutting them up..." was all she could say. An old man with a tousled beard came up at an awkward trot, supporting his homespun trousers with one hand as he ran.

"Now you stop squawking," he shouted at the hysterical woman. "Who's being murdered? What's it all about? Stop your squealing, damn you!" "It's our men and the Poddubtsy crowd...fighting over balks. They're slaughtering our men!" That told them all. Women wailed and the old men bellowed in fury. The message swept through the village and eddied in the backyards: "The Poddubtsy crowd's cutting up our fellows with scythes ... It's those boundaries again!" Only the bedridden remained indoors, all the rest poured into the village street and arming themselves with pitchforks, axes or sticks pulled from wattle fences ran toward the fields where the two villages were engaged in their bloody annual contest over the boundaries between their fields.

Korchagin struck his horse and the animal was off at a gallop. Urged forward by the cries of the rider, the animal flew past the running village folk and ears pressed back and hooves furiously pounding the ground, steadily increased its breakneck pace. On a hillock ahead a windmill spread out its arms as if to bar the way. To the right, by the river bank, were the low meadows, and to the left a rye field rose and dipped all the way to the horizon. The wind rippled the ears of the ripe grain. Poppies sprinkled the roadside with bright red. It was quiet here, and unbearably hot. But from the distance, where the silvery ribbon of the river basked in the sun, came the cries of battle.

The horse continued its wild career down toward the meadows. "If he stumbles, it's the end of both of us," flashed in Pavel's mind. But there was no stop-ping now, and all he could do was to listen to the wind whistle in his ears as he bent low in the saddle.

Like a whirlwind he galloped into the field where men blinded by fury were engaged in brute combat. Several already lay bleeding on the ground. The horse ran down a bearded peasant armed with the stub of a scythe handle who was pursuing a young man with blood streaming down his face. Nearby a sun-tanned giant of a man was aiming vicious kicks with his big heavy boots at the solar plexus of a prostrate adversary.

Charging into the mass of struggling men at full speed, Korchagin sent them flying in all directions. Before they could recover from the surprise, he whirled madly now upon one, now on another, realising that he could disperse this bleeding knot of brutalised humanity only by terrorising them. "Scatter, you vermin!" he shouted in a fury. "Or I'll shoot every last man of you, you blasted bandits!"

And pulling out his pistol he fired over an upturned face twisted with savage rage. Again the horse whirled around and again the pistol spoke. Some of the combatants dropped their scythes and turned back. Dashing up and down the field and firing incessantly, the Commissar finally got the situation in hand. The peasants took to their heels and scattered in all directions to seek escape both from responsibility for the bloody brawl and from the mounted man so terrible in his fury who was shooting without stop.

Luckily no one was killed and the wounded recovered. Nevertheless soon afterward a session of the district court was held in Poddubtsy to hear the case, but all the judge's efforts to discover the ringleaders were unavailing. With the persistence and patience of the true

Bolshevik, the judge sought to make the sullen peasants before him see how barbarous their actions had been, and to impress upon them that such violence would not be tolerated.

"It's the boundaries that are to blame, comrade judge," they said. "They've a way of getting mixed up – every year we've got to fight over them." Nevertheless some of the peasants had to answer for the fight.

A week later a commission came to the hay lands in question and began staking out the disputed strips. "This is the thirtieth year I've been working as land surveyor, and always it's been the dividing lines that caused trouble," the old surveyor with the commission said to Korchagin as he rolled up his tape.

Exhausted by the heat and the considerable walking he had done, the old man was sweating profusely. "Looking at the way the meadows are divided you'd hardly believe your eyes. A drunkard could draw straighter lines. And the fields are even worse. Strips three paces wide and one crossing into the other – to try and separate them is enough to drive you mad. And they're being cut up more and more what with sons growing up and fathers splitting up their land with them. Believe me, twenty years from now there won't be any land left to till, it'll all be balks. As it is, ten per cent of the land is being wasted in this way."

Korchagin smiled. "Twenty years from now we won't have a single balk left, comrade surveyor."

The old man gave him an indulgent look. "The Communist society, you mean? Well, now, that's pretty much in the future, isn't it?"

"Have you heard about the Budanovka Kolkhoz?"

"Oh, I see what you mean."

"Well?"

"I've been in Budanovka. But that's the exception, Comrade Korchagin."

The commission went on measuring strips of land. Two young men hammered in stakes. And on both sides stood the peasants watching closely to make sure that they went down where the half-rotten sticks barely visible in the grass marked the previous dividing lines.

· · · ·

WHIPPING UP HIS WRETCHED nag, the garrulous driver turned to his passengers. "Where all these Komsomol lads have come from beats me!" he said. "I don't remember anything like it before. It's that schoolteacher woman who's started it, for sure. Rakitina's her name, maybe you know her? She's a young wench, but not much good. Stirs up all the womenfolk in the village, puts all kinds of silly notions into their heads and that's how the trouble begins. It's got so a man can't beat his wife any more! In the old days you'd give the old woman a clout whenever you felt out of sorts and she'd slink away and sulk, but now she kicks up such a row you wished you hadn't touched her. She'll threaten you with the people's court, and as for the younger ones, they'll talk about divorce and reel off all the laws to you. Look at my Ganka, the quietest wench you ever saw, now she's gone and got herself made a delegate; the elder among the women-folk, I think that means. The women come to her from all over the village. I nearly let her have a taste of the whip when I heard about it, but I spat on the whole business. They can go to the devil! She isn't a bad wench when it comes to housework and such things."

The driver scratched his hairy chest visible through the opening in his homespun shirt and flicked his whip under the horse's belly. The two in the cart were Razvalikhin and Lida. They both had business in Poddubtsy. Lida planned to call a conference of women's delegates, and Razvalikhin had been sent to help the local nucleus organise its work. "So you don't like the Komsomols?" Lida jokingly asked the driver.

He plucked at his little beard for a while before replying. "Oh I don't mind them...I believe in letting the youngsters enjoy themselves, putting on plays and such like. I'm fond of a comedy myself if it's good. We did think at the beginning the young folk would get out of hand, but it turned out just the opposite. I've heard folks say they're very strict about drinking and rowing and such like. They go in more for book learning. But they won't leave God be, and they're always trying to take the church away and use it for a club. Now that's no good, it's turned the old folks against them. But on the whole they're not so bad. If you ask me, though, they make a big mistake taking in all the down-and-outs in the village, the ones who hire out, or who can't make a go of their farms. They won't have anything to do with the rich peasants' sons."

The cart clattered down the hill and pulled up outside the school building. The janitor had put up the new arrivals and gone off to sleep in the hay. Lida and Razvalikhin had just returned from a meeting which had ended rather late. It was dark inside the cottage. Lida undressed quickly, climbed into bed and fell asleep almost at once. She was rudely awakened by Razvalikhin's hands travelling over her in a manner that left no doubt as to his intentions.

"What do you want?" "Shush, Lida, don't make so much noise. I'm sick of lying there all by myself. Can't you find anything more exciting to do than snooze?" "Stop pawing me and get off my bed at once!" Lida said, pushing him away. Razvalikhin's oily smile had always sickened her and she wanted to say some-thing insulting and humiliating, but sleep overpowered her and she closed her eyes.

"Aw, come on! What's all this fancy behaviour about? You weren't brought up in a nunnery by any chance? Stop playing the little innocent, you can't fool this lad. If you were really an advanced woman, you'd satisfy my desire and then go to sleep as much as you want." Considering the matter settled, he went over and sat on the edge of the bed again, laying a possessive hand on Lida's shoulder.

"Go to hell!" Lida was now wide awake. "I'm going to tell Korchagin about this tomorrow." Razvalikhin seized her hand and whispered testily: "I don't care a damn about your Korchagin, and you'd better not try to resist or I'll take you by force." There was a brief scuffle and then two resounding slaps rang out in the silence of the night. Razvalikhin leapt aside. Lida groped her way to the door, pushed it open and rushed out into the yard. She stood there in the moonlight, seething with wrath and indignation.

"Get inside, you fool!" Razvalikhin called to her viciously. He carried his own bed out under the eaves and spent the rest of the night there. Lida fastened the door on the latch, curled up on the bed and went to sleep again.

In the morning they set out for home. Razvalikhin sat beside the old driver smoking one cigarette after another. "That touch-me-not may really go and spill the beans to Korchagin, blast her! Who'd have thought she'd turn out to be such a prig? You'd think she was a raving beauty by the way she acts, but she's nothing to look at. But I'd better make it up with her or there may be trouble. Korchagin has his eye on me as it is." He moved over to Lida. He pretended to be ashamed of himself, put on a downcast air and mum-bled a few words of apology.

That did the trick. Before they had reached the edge of the village. Lida had given him her promise not to tell anyone what had happened that night.

· · · ·

KOMSOMOL NUCLEI SPRANG up one after another in the border villages. The District Committee members carefully tended these first young shoots of the Communist movement. Korchagin and Lida Polevykh spent much time in the various localities working with the local League members.

Razvalikhin did not like making trips to the countryside. He did not know how to win the confidence of the peasant lads and only succeeded in bungling things. Lida and Pavel had no difficulty in making friends with the peasant youth. The girls took to Lida at once, they accepted her as one of themselves and gradually she awakened their interest in the Komsomol movement. As for Korchagin, all the young folk in the district knew him. One thousand six hundred of the young men due to be called up for military service went through preliminary training in his battalion. Never before had his accordion played such an important role in propaganda as here in the village. The instrument made Pavel tremendously popular with the young folk, who gathered of an evening on the village lane to enjoy themselves, and for many a tousle-haired youngster the road to the Komsomol began here as he listened to the enchanting music of the accordion, now passionate and stirring, now strident and brave, now tender and caressing as only the sad, wistful songs of the Ukraine can be. They listened to the accordion, and they listened to the young man who played it, a railway worker who was now Military Commissar and Komsomol secretary. And the music of the accordion seemed to mingle harmoniously with what the young Commissar told them. Soon new songs rang out in the villages, and new books appeared in the cottages beside the Psalters and bibles.

The smugglers now had more than the border guards to reckon with; in the Komsomol members the Soviet Government had acquired staunch friends and zealous assistants. Sometimes the Komsomol nuclei in the border towns allowed themselves to be carried away by their enthusiasm in hunting down enemies and then Korchagin would have to come to the aid of his young comrades. Once Grishutka Khorovodko, the blue-eyed secretary of the Poddubtsy nucleus, a hot-headed lad fond of an argument and very active in the anti-religious movement, learned from private sources of information that some smuggled goods were to be brought that night to the village mill. He roused all the Komsomol members and, armed with a training rifle and two bayonets, they set out at dead of night, quietly laid an ambush at the mill and waited for their quarry to appear. The GPU border post, which had been informed of the smugglers' move, sent out a detail of its own. In the dark the two sides met and clashed, and had it not been for the vigilance displayed by the border guards, the young men might have suffered heavy casualties in the skirmish. As it was the youngsters were merely disarmed, taken to a village four kilometres away and locked up.

Korchagin happened to be at Gavrilov's place at the time. When the Battalion Commander told him the news the following morning, Pavel mounted his horse and galloped off to rescue his boys. The GPU man in charge laughed as he told him the story. "I'll tell you what we'll do, Comrade Korchagin," he said. "They're fine lads and we shan't make trouble for them. But you had better give them a good talking to so that they won't try to do our work for us in the future."

The sentry opened the door of the shed and the eleven lads got up and stood sheepishly shifting their weight from one foot to the other. "Look at them," the CPU man said with studied severity. "They've gone and made a mess of things, and now I'll have to send them on to area headquarters." Then Grishutka spoke up. "But Comrade Sakharov," he said agitatedly, "what crime have we committed? We've had our eye on those ruffians for a long time. We only wanted to help the Soviet authorities, and you go and lock us up like bandits." He turned away with an injured air.

After a solemn consultation, during which Korchagin and Sakharov had difficulty in preserving their gravity, they decided the boys had had enough of a fright. "If you will vouch for them and promise us that they won't go taking walks over to the frontier any more I'll let them go," Sakharov said to Pavel. "They can help us in other ways."

"Very well, I'll vouch for them. I hope they won't let me down any more." The youngsters marched back to Poddubtsy singing. The incident was hushed up. And it was not long before the miller was caught, this time by the law.

· · · ·

IN THE MAIDAN-VILIA woods there lived a colony of rich German farmers. The kulak farms stood within half a kilometre of each other, as sturdily built as miniature fortresses. It was from Maidan-Vilia that Antonyuk and his band operated. Antonyuk, a one-time tsarist army sergeant major, had recruited a band of seven cut-throats from among his kith and kin and, armed with pistols, staged hold-ups on the country roads. He did not hesitate to spill blood, he was not averse to robbing wealthy speculators, but neither did he stop at molesting Soviet workers. Speed was Antonyuk's watchword. One day he would rob a couple of co-operative store clerks and the next day he would disarm a postal employee in a village a good twenty kilometres away, stealing everything the man had on him, down to the last kopeck. Antonyuk competed with his fellow-brigand Gordei, one was no better than the other, and between them the two kept the area militia and GPU authorities very busy. Antonyuk operated just outside Berezdov, and it grew dangerous to appear on the roads leading to the town. The bandit eluded capture; when things grew too hot for him he would withdraw beyond the border and lie low only to turn up again when he was least expected. His very elusiveness made him a menace. Every report of some fresh outrage committed by this brigand caused Lisitsyn to gnaw his lips with rage.

"When will that rattlesnake stop biting us? He'd better take care, the scoundrel, or I'll have to settle his hash myself," he muttered through clenched teeth. Twice the District Executive Chairman, taking Korchagin and three other Communists with him, set out hot on the bandit's trail, but each time Antonyuk got away.

A special detail was sent to Berezdov from the area centre to fight the bandits. The detachment commander was a dapper youth named Filatov. Instead of reporting to the Chairman of the Executive Committee, as frontier regulations demanded, this conceited young fool went straight to the nearest village, Semaki, and arriving at the dead of night, put up with his men in a house on the outskirts. The mysterious arrival of these armed men was observed by a Komsomol member living next door who hurried off at once to report to the chairman of the Village Soviet. The latter, knowing nothing about the detachment, took them for bandits and dispatched the Young Communist at once to the district centre for help. Filatov's foolhardiness very nearly cost many lives. Lisitsyn roused the militia in the middle of the night and hurried off with a dozen men to tackle the "bandits" in Semaki. They galloped up to the house, dismounted and climbing over the fence closed in on the house. The sentry on duty at the door was knocked down by a blow on the head with a revolver butt, Lisitsyn broke in the door with his shoulder and he and his men rushed into a room dimly lighted by an oil lamp hanging from the ceiling. With a grenade in one hand and his revolver in the other Lisitsyn roared so that the windowpanes rattled:

"Surrender, or I'll blow you to bits!"

Another second and the sleepy men leaping to their feet from the floor might have been cut down by a hail of bullets. But the sight of the man with the grenade poised for the throw was so awe-inspiring that they put up their hands. A few minutes later, when the "bandits" were herded outside in their underwear, Filatov noticed the decoration on Lisitsyn's tunic and hastened to explain. Lisitsyn was furious. "You fool!" he spat out with withering contempt.

Tidings of the German revolution, dim echoes of the rifle fire on the Hamburg barricades reached the border area. An atmosphere of tension hung over the frontier. Newspapers were read with eager expectation. The wind of revolution blew from the West. Applications poured in to the Komsomol District Committee from Young Communists volunteering for service in the Red Army. Korchagin was kept busy explaining to the youngsters from the nuclei that the Soviet Land was pursuing a policy of peace and that it had no intentions of going to war with its neighbours. But this had little effect. Every Sunday Komsomol members from the entire district held meetings in the big garden of the priest's house, and one day at noon the Poddubtsy nucleus turned up in proper marching order in the yard of the District Committee. Korchagin saw them through the window and went out onto the porch. Eleven lads, with Khorovodko at their head, all wearing top boots, and with large canvas kitbags over their shoulders, halted at the entrance.

"What's this, Grisha?" Korchagin asked in surprise. Instead of replying, Khorovodko signed to Pavel with his eyes and went inside the building with him. Lida, Razvalikhin and two other Komsomol members pressed around the newcomer demanding an explanation. Khorovodko closed the door and wrinkling his bleached eyebrows announced:

"This is a sort of test mobilisation, Comrades. My own idea. I told the boys this morning a telegram had come from the district, strictly confidential of course, that we're going to war with the German bourgeoisie, and we'll soon be fighting the Polish Pany as well. All Young Communists are called up, on orders from Moscow, I told them. Anyone who's scared can file an application and he'll be allowed to stay home. I ordered them not to say a word about the war to anyone, just to take a loaf of bread and a hunk of fatback apiece, and those who didn't have any fatback could bring garlic or onions. We were to meet secretly outside the village and go to the district centre and from there to the area centre where arms would be issued. You ought to see what an effect that had on the boys! They tried hard to pump me, but I told them to get busy and cut out the questions. Those who wanted to stay behind should say so. We only wanted volunteers. Well, my boys dispersed and I began to get properly worried. Supposing nobody turned up? If that happened I would disband the whole nucleus and move to some other place. I sat there outside the village waiting with my heart in my boots. After a while they began coming, one by one. Some of them had been blubbering, you could see by their faces, though they tried to hide it. All ten of them turned up, not a single deserter. That's our Poddubtsy nucleus for you!" he wound up triumphantly.

When the shocked Lida Polevykh began to scold him, he stared at her in amazement. "What do you mean? This is the best way to test them, I tell you. You can see right through each one of them. There's no fraud there. I was going to drag them to the area centre just to keep up appearances, but the poor beggars are dog-tired. You'll have to make a little speech to them, Korchagin. You will, won't you? It wouldn't be right without a speech. Tell them the mobilisation has been called off or something, but say that we're proud of them just the same."

• • • •

KORCHAGIN SELDOM VISITED the area centre, for the journey took several days and pressure of work demanded his constant presence in the district. Razvalikhin, on the other hand, was ready to ride off to town on any pretext. He would set out on the journey armed from head to foot, fancying himself one of Fenimore Cooper's heroes. As he drove through the woods he would take pot shots at crows or at some fleet-footed squirrel, stop lone passers-by and question them sternly as to who they were, where they had come from and whither they were bound. On approaching the town he would remove his weapons, stick his rifle under the hay in the cart and, hiding his revolver in his pocket, stroll into the office of the Komsomol Area Committee looking his usual self.

"Well what's the news in Berezdov?" Fedotov, Secretary of the Area Committee, inquired as Razvalikhin entered his office one day. Fedotov's office was always crowded with people all talking at once. It was not easy to work under such conditions, listening to four different people, while replying to a fifth and writing something at the same time. Although Fedotov was very young he had been a Party member since nineteen-nineteen; it was only in those stormy times that a fifteen-year-old lad could have been admitted into the Party.

"Oh, there's plenty of news," answered Razvalikhin nonchalantly. "Too much to tell all at once. It's one long grind from morning till night. There's so much to attend to. We've had to start from the very beginning, you know. I set up two new nuclei. Now, tell me what you called me here for?" And he sat down in an armchair with a businesslike air. Krymsky, the head of the economic department, looked up from the heap of papers on his desk for a moment. "We asked for Korchagin, not you," he said.

Razvalikhin blew out a thick cloud of tobacco smoke. "Korchagin doesn't like coming here, so I have to do it on top of everything else...In general, some secretaries have a fine time of it. They don't do anything themselves. It's the donkeys like me who have to carry the load. Whenever Korchagin goes to the border he's gone for two or three weeks and all the work is left to me."

Razvalikhin's broad hint that he was the better man for the job of district secretary was not lost on his hearers. "That fellow doesn't appeal to me much," Fedotov remarked to the others when Razvalikhin had gone.

Razvalikhin's trickery was exposed quite by chance. Lisitsyn dropped into Fedotov's office one day to pick up the mail, which was the custom for anyone coming from the district, and in the course of a conversation between the two men Razvalikhin was exposed.

"Send Korchagin to us anyway," said Fedotov in parting. "We hardly know him here."

* * * *

"VERY WELL. BUT DON't try to take him away from us, mind. We shan't allow that." This year the anniversary of the October Revolution was celebrated on the border with even greater enthusiasm than usual. Korchagin was elected chairman of the committee or-

ganising the celebrations in the border villages. After the meeting in
Poddubtsy, five thousand peasants from three neighbouring villages
marched to the frontier in a procession half a kilometre long, carrying scarlet banners and with a military band and the training battalion at the head. They marched in perfect order on the Soviet side
of the frontier, parallel to the border posts, bound for the villages
that had been cut in two by the demarcation line. Never before had
the Poles witnessed the like on their frontier. Battalion Commander
Gavrilov and Korchagin rode ahead of the column on horseback, and
behind them the band played, the banners rustled in the breeze and
the singing of the people resounded far and wide. The peasant youth
clad in their holiday best were in high spirits, the village girls twit-
tered and laughed gaily, the adults marched along gravely, the old folk
with an air of solemn triumph. The human stream stretched as far
as eye could see. One of its banks was the frontier, but no one so
much as stepped across that forbidden line. Korchagin watched the
sea of people march past. The strains of the Komsomol song "From
the forests dense to Britain's seas, the Red Army is strongest of all!"
gave way to a girls' chorus singing "Up on yonder hillside the girls are
a-mowing..."

The Soviet sentries greeted the procession with happy smiles. The
Polish guards looked on bewildered. This demonstration on the frontier caused no little consternation on the other side, although the Polish command had been warned of it in advance. Mounted gendarme
patrols moved restlessly back and forth, the frontier guard had been
strengthened fivefold and reserves were hidden behind the nearby
hills ready for any emergency. But the procession kept to its own territory, marching along gaily, filling the air with its singing.

A Polish sentry stood on a knoll. The column approached with
measured tread. The first notes of a march rang out. The Pole brought
his rifle smartly to his side and then presented arms, and Korchagin
distinctly heard the words: "Long live the Commune!" The soldier's

eyes told Pavel that it was he who had uttered the words. Pavel stared at him fascinated.

A friend! Beneath the soldier's uniform a heart beat in sympathy with the demonstrators. Pavel replied softly in Polish: "greetings, Comrade!" The sentry stood in the same position while the demonstration marched past. Pavel turned round several times to look at the dark little figure. Here was another Pole. His whiskers were touched with grey and the eyes under the shiny peak of his cap expressed nothing. Pavel, still under the impression of what he had just heard, murmured in Polish as if to himself: "greetings, Comrade!" But there was no reply.

Gavrilov smiled. He had overheard what had passed. "You expect too much," he observed. "They aren't all plain infantrymen, you know. Some of them are gendarmes. Didn't you notice the chevron on his sleeve? That one was a gendarme for sure."

The head of the column was already descending the hill toward a village cut in two by the frontier. The Soviet half of the village had prepared to meet the guests in grand style. All the inhabitants were waiting at the frontier bridge on the bank of the stream. The young folk were lined up on either side of the road. The roofs of cottages and sheds on the Polish side were covered with people who were watching the proceedings on the opposite bank with tense interest. There were crowds of peasants on the cottage porches and by the garden fences. When the procession entered the human corridor the band struck up the Internationale. Later stirring speeches were delivered from a platform decorated with greenery. Young men and white-headed veterans addressed the crowd. Korchagin too spoke in his native Ukrainian. His words flew over the border and were heard on the other side of the river, whereupon the gendarmes over there began to disperse the villagers for fear that those fiery words might inflame the hearts of those who listened. Whips whistled and shots were fired into the air.

The streets emptied out. The young folk, scared off the roofs by gendarme bullets, disappeared. Those on the Soviet side looked on and their faces grew grave. Filled with wrath by what he had just witnessed, an aged shepherd climbed onto the platform with the help of some village lads and addressed the crowd in great agitation.

"You have seen, my children! That was how we used to be dealt with once. But now the peasant is the master in the village, and there is no more whip. The rule of the gentry has ended and our backs no longer smart under the whiplash. It is for you, my sons, to make sure the gentry never return. I am an old man and not much good at making speeches. But there is much I would tell you if I could. All our lives under the tsars we toiled like oxen in misery and hunger...like those poor things over there!" He pointed a bony hand toward the other side of the river and broke down and wept as only the very young and the very old can weep.

Then Grishulka Khorovodko spoke. Gavrilov, listening to his wrathful speech, turned his horse around and scanned the opposite bank to see whether anyone there was taking notes. But the river bank was deserted. Even the sentry by the brigade had been removed.

"Well, it looks as if there won't be any protest note to the Foreign Affairs Commissariat after all," he laughed.

* * * *

ONE RAINY NIGHT IN late autumn the bloody trail of Antonyuk and his seven men ended. The bandit was caught at a wedding party in the house of a wealthy farmer in the German colony in Maidan-Villa. It was the peasants from the Khrolinsky Commune who nabbed him.

The local women had spread the news about these guests at the colony wedding, and the Komsomols got together at once, twelve of them, and armed with whatever they could lay their hands on, set out for Maidan-Villa by cart, sending a messenger post-haste to

Berezdov. At Semaki the messenger chanced to meet Filatov's detachment, which rushed off hot on the trail. The Khrolinsky men surrounded the farm and began to exchange rifle fire with the Antonyuk band. The latter entrenched themselves in a small wing of the farmhouse and opened fire at anyone who came within range. They tried to make a dash for it, but were driven back inside the building after losing one of their number. Antonyuk had been in many a tight corner like this and had fought his way out with the aid of hand grenades and darkness. He might have escaped this time too, for the Khrolinsky Komsomols had already lost two men, but Filatov arrived in the nick of time. Antonyuk saw that the game was up. He continued firing back till morning from all the windows, but at dawn they took him. Not one of the seven surrendered. It cost four lives to stamp out the viper's nest. Three of the casualties were lads from the newly-organised Khrolinsky Komsomol group.

· · · ·

KORCHAGIN'S BATTALION was called up for the autumn manoeuvres of the territorial forces. The battalion covered the forty kilometres to the divisional camp in a single day's march under a driving rain. They set out early in the morning and reached their destination late at night. Gusev, the Battalion Commander, and his commissar rode on horseback. The eight hundred trainees reached the barracks exhausted and went to sleep at once. The manoeuvres were due to begin the following morning; the headquarters of the territorial division had been late in summoning the battalion. Lined up for inspection, the battalion, now in uniform and carrying rifles, presented an entirely different appearance. Both Gusev and Korchagin had invested much time and effort in training these young men and they were confident that the unit would pass muster. After the official inspection had ended and the battalion had shown its skill on the drill ground, one of the commanders, a man with a handsome though flaccid face, turned to Korchagin and demanded sharply: "why are you mounted? The commanders and commissars of our training battalions are not entitled to horses. Turn your mount over to the stables and report for manoeuvres on foot."

Korchagin knew that if he dismounted he would be unable to take part in the manoeuvres, for his legs would not carry him a single kilometre. But how could he explain the situation to this loudmouth festooned with leather straps? "I shall not be able to take part in the manoeuvres on foot." "Why not?"

Realising that he would have to give some explanation, Korchagin replied in a low voice: "my legs are swollen and I will not be able to stand a whole week of running and walking. But perhaps you will tell me who you are, Comrade?"

"In the first place I am the Chief of Staff of your regiment. Secondly, I order you once more to get off that horse. If you are an invalid you ought not to be in the army."

Pavel felt as if he had been struck on the face with a whip. He clutched convulsively at the reins, but Gusev's strong hand checked him. For a few moments injured pride and self-restraint fought for supremacy in Pavel. But Pavel Korchagin was no longer the Red Army man who could shift light-heartedly from unit to unit. He was a Battalion Commissar now, and his battalion stood there behind him. What a poor example of discipline he would be showing his men if he disobeyed the order! It was not for this conceited ass that he had reared his battalion. He slipped his feet out of the stirrups, dismounted and, fighting the excruciating pain in his joints, walked over to the right flank.

. . . .

FOR SEVERAL DAYS THE weather had been unusually fine. The manoeuvres were drawing to a close. On the fifth day the troops were in the vicinity of Shepetovka, Where the exercises were to end. The

Berezdov Battalion had been given the assignment of capturing the station from the direction of Klimentovichi village.

Korchagin, who was now on homeground, showed Gusev all the approaches. The battalion, divided into two parts, made a wide detour and emerging in the enemy rear broke into the station building with loud cheers. The operation was given the highest appraisal.

The Berezdov men remained in possession of the station while the battalion that had defended it withdrew to the woods having been judged to have "lost" fifty per cent of its effectives.

Korchagin was in command of one half of the battalion. He had ordered his men to deploy and was standing in the middle of the street with the commander and political instructor of the third company when a Red Army man came running up to him.

"Comrade Commissar," he panted, "the battalion commander wants to know whether the machine gunners are holding the railway crossings. The commission's on its way here."

Pavel and the commanders with him went over to one of the crossings. The Regimental Commander and his aides were there. Gusev was congratulated on the successful operation. Representatives from the routed battalion looked sheepish and did not even try to justify themselves.

Gusev said: "I can't take the credit for it. It was Korchagin here who showed us the way. He hails from these parts." The chief of staff rode up to Pavel and said with a sneer: "So you can run quite well after all, Comrade. The horse was only intended for effect, I suppose?" He was about to say something else, but the look on Korchagin's face stopped him.

"You don't happen to know his name, do you?" Korchagin asked Gusev when the higher commanders had gone. Gusev slapped him on the shoulder. "Now then, don't you pay any attention to that upstart. His name is Chuzhanin. A former ensign, I believe."

Several times that day Pavel racked his brains in an effort to recall where he had heard that name before, but he could not remember. Soon, the manoeuvres were over. The battalion, having been highly commended, went back to Berezdov. Korchagin remained behind for a day or two to pay a visit to his mother who was very poorly. For two days he slept twelve hours on end, and on the third day he went to see Artem down at the yards. Here in this grimy, smoke-blackened building Pavel felt at home. Hungrily he inhaled the coal smoke. This was where he really belonged and it was here he wished to be. He felt as if he had lost something infinitely dear to him. It was months since he had heard a locomotive whistle, and the one-time stoker and electrician yearned as much for the familiar surroundings as the sail-or yearns for the boundless sea expanse after a pro-longed stay on shore. It was a long time before he could get over this feeling. He spoke little to his brother, who now worked at a portable forge. He noticed a new furrow on Artem's brow. He was the father of two children now. Evidently Artem was having a hard time of it. He did not complain, but Pavel could see for himself.

They worked side by side for an hour or two. Then they parted. At the railway crossing Pavel reined in his horse and gazed for a long while at the station. Then he struck his mount and galloped down the road through the woods.

The forest roads were now quite safe. All the bandits, big and small, had been stamped out by the Bolsheviks, and the villages in the area now lived in peace.

. . . .

PAVEL REACHED BEREZDOV around noon. Lida Polevykh ran out onto the porch of the District Committee to meet him. "Welcome home!" she said with a warm smile. "We have missed you here!" She put her arm around him and the two went indoors.

"Where is Razvalikhin?" he asked her as he took off his coat. "I don't know," Lida replied rather reluctantly. "Oh yes, I remember now. He said this morning he was going to the school to take the class in sociology instead of you. He says it's his job not yours."

This was an unpleasant surprise for Pavel. He had never liked Razvalikhin. "That fellow may make a hash of things at the school," he thought in annoyance. "Never mind him," he said to Lida. "Tell me, what's the good news here. Have you been to Grushevka? How are things with the youngsters over there?"

While Lida gave him the news, Pavel relaxed on the couch resting his aching limbs. "The day before yesterday Rakitina was accepted as candidate member of the Party. That makes our Poddubtsy nucleus much stronger. Rakitina is a good girl, I like her very much. The teachers are beginning to come over to our side, some of them are with us already."

· · · ·

KORCHAGIN AND LYCHIKOV, the new Secretary of the Party District Committee, often met at Lisitsyn's place of an evening and the three would sit studying at the big desk until the early hours of the morning.

The door leading to the bedroom where Lisitsyn's wife and sister slept would be tightly closed and the three bending over a small volume would converse in low tones. Lisitsyn had time to study only at night. Even so whenever Pavel returned from his frequent trips to the villages he would find to his chagrin that his comrades had gone far ahead of him.

· · · ·

ONE DAY A MESSENGER from Poddubtsy brought the news that Grishutka Khorovodko had been murdered the night before by unknown assailants. Pavel rushed off at once to the Executive Committee stables, forgetting the pain in his legs, saddled a horse with feverish haste and galloped off toward the frontier.

Grishutka lay amid spruce branches on a table in the Village Soviet cottage, the red banner of the Soviet draped over him. A border guard and a Komsomol stood on guard at the door admitting no one until the authorities arrived. Korchagin entered the cottage, went over to the table and turned back the banner.

Grishutka, his face waxen, his dilated eyes transfixed in agony of death, lay with his head to one side. A spruce branch covered the spot where the back of his head had been cut open by some sharp weapon. Who had taken the life of this young man, only son of widow Khorovodko whose husband, a mill hand and later member of the Poor Peasants' Committee, had died fighting for the revolution?

The shock of her son's death had brought the old woman to her bed and neighbours were trying to comfort her. And her son lay cold and still, preserving the secret of his untimely end.

Grishutka's murder had aroused the indignation of the whole village. The young Komsomol leader and champion of the poor peasants turned out to have far more friends in the village than enemies. Rakitina, greatly upset by the news, sat in her room weeping bitterly. She did not even look up when Korchagin came in.

"Who do you think killed him, Rakitina?" Korchagin asked hoarsely, dropping heavily into a chair.

"It must be that gang from the mill. Grisha had always been a thorn in the side of those smugglers."

* * * *

TWO VILLAGES TURNED up for Grisha Khorovodko's funeral. Korchagin brought his battalion, and the whole Komsomol organisation came to pay its last respects to their comrade. Gavrilov mustered a company of two hundred and fifty border guards on the square in front of the Village Soviet. To the accompaniment of the mournful strains of the funeral march the coffin swathed in red bunting was brought out and placed on the square where a fresh grave had been dug beside the graves of the Bolshevik partisans who had fallen in the Civil War.

Grishutka's death united all those whose interests he had so staunchly upheld. The young agricultural labourers and the poor peasants vowed to support the Komsomol, and all who spoke at the graveside wrathfully demanded that the murderers be brought to book, that they be found arid tried here on the square beside the grave of their victim, so that everyone might see who the enemies were.

Three volleys thundered forth, and fresh spruce branches were laid on the grave. That evening the nucleus elected a new secretary—Rakitina. A message came for Korchagin from the GPU border post with the news that they were on the trail of the murderers.

A week later, when the second District Congress of Soviets opened in the town theatre, Lisitsyn, gravely triumphant, announced: "Comrades, I am happy to be able to report to this congress that we have accomplished a great deal in the past year. Soviet power is firmly established in the district, banditism has been uprooted and smuggling has been all but wiped out. Strong organisations of peasant poor have come into being in the villages, the Komsomol organisations are ten times as strong as they were and the Party organisations have expanded. The last kulak provocation in Poddubtsy, which cost us the life of our comrade Khorovodko, has been exposed. The murderers, the miller and his son-in-law, have been arrested and will be tried in a few days by the Gubernia assizes. Several delegations from the villages have demanded that this congress pass a resolution demanding the supreme penalty for these bandits and terrorists."

A storm of approval shook the hall. "Hear, hear! Death to the enemies of Soviet power!" Lida Polevykh appeared at one of the side doors. She beckoned to Pavel.

Outside in the corridor she handed him an envelope marked "urgent." He opened it and read:

To the Berezdov District Committee of the Komsomol.

Copy to the District Committee of the Party.

By decision of the Gubernia Committee Comrade Korchagin is recalled from the district to the Gubernia Committee for appointment to responsible Komsomol work.

Pavel took leave of the district where he had worked for the past year. There were two items on the agenda of the last meeting of the Party District Committee held before his departure: one, Transfer of Comrade Korchagin to membership in the Communist Party, and two, Endorsement of his testimonial upon his release from the post of Secretary of the Komsomol District Committee.

Lisitsyn and Lida wrung Pavel's hand on parting and embraced him affectionately, and when his horse turned out of the courtyard onto the road, a dozen revolvers fired a parting salute.

CHAPTER FIVE

The tramcar crawled laboriously up Fundukleyev hill, its motors groaning with the effort. At the opera house it stopped and a group of young people alighted. The car continued the climb. "We'd better get a move on," Pankratov urged the others, "or we'll be late for sure." Okunev caught up with him at the theatre entrance. "We came here under similar circumstances three years ago, you remember, Genka? That was when Dubava came back to us with the 'Workers' Opposition.' A grand meeting! And tonight we've got to grapple with him again!"

They had presented their passes and been admitted into the hall before Pankratov replied. "Yes, history is repeating itself on the very same spot." They were hissed to silence. The evening session of the conference had already begun and they had to take the first seats they could find. A young woman was addressing the gathering from the rostrum.

"We're just in time. Now sit quiet and pay close attention to what your wife has to say," Pankratov whispered, giving Okunev a dig in the ribs.

"...It's true that we have spent much time and energy on this discussion, but I think that we have all learned a great deal from it. Today we are very glad to note that in our organisation Trotsky's followers have been defeated. They cannot complain that they were not given a hearing. On the contrary: they have had every opportunity to express their point of view. As a matter of fact they have abused the freedom we gave them and committed a number of gross violations. of Party discipline."

Talya was excited; you could tell by the way she kept tossing back a lock of hair that fell forward over her eyes as she spoke.

"Many comrades from the districts have spoken here and they have all had something to say about the methods the Trotskyites have been using. There are quite a number of Trotskyites at this conference. The districts deliberately sent them here to give us another opportunity to hear them out at this city Party conference. It is not our fault if they are not making full use of this opportunity. Evidently their complete defeat in the districts and nuclei has taught them something. They could hardly get up at this conference and repeat what they were saying only yesterday."

A harsh voice from the right-hand corner of the hall interrupted Talya at this point: "we haven't had our say yet!" Talya turned in the direction of the voice: "all right, Dubava, come up here now and speak, we'll listen to you." Dubava stared gloomily back at her and his lips twisted in anger. "We'll talk when the time comes!" he shouted back. He thought of the crushing defeat he had sustained the day before in his own district. The memory still rankled.

A low murmur passed over the hall. Pankratov, unable to restrain himself, cried out: "going to try shaking up the Party again, eh?" Dubava recognised the voice, but did not turn round. He merely dug his teeth into his lower lip and bent his head. "Dubava himself offers a striking example of how the Trotskyites are violating Party discipline." Talya went on. "He has worked in the Komsomol for a long time, many of us know him, the arsenal workers in particular. He is a student of the Kharkov Communist University, yet we all know that he has been here with Shumsky for the past three weeks. What has brought them here in the middle of the university term? There isn't a single district in town where they haven't addressed meetings. True, during the past few days Shumsky has shown signs of coming to his senses. Who sent them here? Besides them, there are a good number of other Trotskyites from various organisations. They all worked here before at one time or another and now they have come back to stir up trouble within the Party. Do their Party organisations know where they are? Of course not."

The conference was expecting the Trotskyites to come forward and admit their mistakes. Talya, hoping to persuade them to take this step, appealed to them earnestly. She addressed herself directly to them as if in comradely, informal debate: "three years ago in this very theatre Dubava came back to us with the former 'Workers' Opposition.' Remember? And do you remember what he said then: 'Never shall we let the Party banner fall from our hands.' But hardly three years have passed and Dubava has done just that. Yes, I repeat, he has let the Party banner fall. 'We haven't had our say yet!' he just said. That shows that he and his fellow Trotskyites intend to go still further."

"Let Tufta tell us about the barometer," came a voice from the back rows. "He's their weather expert." To which indignant voices responded: "this is no time for silly jokes!" "Are they going to stop fighting the Party or not? Let them answer that!" "Let them tell us who wrote that anti-Party declaration!"

Indignation rose higher and higher and the chairman rang his bell long and insistently for silence. Talya's voice was drowned out by the din, and it was some time before the storm subsided and she was able to continue. "The letters we receive from our comrades in the outlying localities show that they are with us in this and that is very encouraging. Permit me to read part of one letter we have received. It is from Olga Yureneva. Many of you here know her. She is in charge of the organisational department of an area committee of the Komsomol."

Talya drew a sheet of paper out of a pile before her, ran her eye over it and began:

All practical work has been neglected. For the past four days all bureau members have been out in the districts where the Trotskyites have launched a more vicious campaign than ever. An incident occurred yesterday which aroused the indignation of the entire organisation. Failing to get a majority in a single nucleus in town, the opposition decided to rally their forces and put up a fight in the nucleus of the Area Military Commissariat, which also includes the Communists working in the Area Planning Commission and Educational Department. The nucleus has forty-two members, but all the Trotskyites banded together there. Never had we heard such anti-Party speeches as were made at that meeting.

One of the Military Commissariat members got up and said outright: 'If the Party apparatus doesn't give in, we will smash it by force.' The oppositionists applauded that statement. Then Korchagin took the floor. 'How can you applaud that fascist and call yourselves Party members?' he said, but they raised such a commotion, shouting and banging their chairs, that he could not go on. The nucleus members who were disgusted by this outrageous behaviour demanded that Korchagin be given a hearing, but the uproar was repeated as soon as he tried to make himself heard. 'So this is what you call democracy!' he shouted above the din. 'I'm going to speak just the same!' At that point several of them fell on him and tried to drag him off the platform.

There was wild confusion. Pavel fought back and went on speaking, but they dragged him off the stage, opened a side door and threw him onto the stairway.

Some scoundrel cut open his face. After that, nearly all the nucleus members left the meeting. That incident was an eye-opener for many...

Talya left the platform.

· · · ·

SEGAL, WHO HAD BEEN in charge of the agitation and propaganda department of the Gubernia Party Committee for two months now, sat in the presidium next to Tokarev and listened attentively to the speeches of the delegates. So far the conference had been addressed exclusively by young people who were still in the Komsomol. "How they have matured these past few years!" Segal was thinking. "The opposition is already getting it hot," he remarked to Tokarev, "and the heavy artillery has not yet been brought into action. It's the youth who are routing the Trotskyites."

Just then Tufta leapt onto the platform. He was met by a loud buzz of disapproval and a brief outburst of laughter. Tufta turned to the presidium to protest against his reception, but the hall had already quietened down. "Someone here called me a weather expert. So that is how you mock at my political views, comrades of the majority!" he burst out in one breath. A roar of laughter greeted his words. Tufta appealed indignantly to the chairman. "You can laugh, but I tell you once again, the youth is a barometer. Lenin has said so time and again."

In an instant silence reigned in the hall. "What did Lenin say?" came voices from the audience. Tufta livened up. "When preparations were being made for the October uprising Lenin issued instructions to muster the resolute working-class youth, arm them and send them together with the sailors to the most important sectors. Do you want me to read you that passage? I have all the quotations down on cards." Tufta dug into his portfolio. "Never mind, we know it!" "But what did Lenin write about unity? ' "And about Party discipline?" "When did Lenin ever set up the youth in opposition to the old guard?" Tufta lost the thread of his thoughts and switched over to another theme: "Lagutina here read a letter from Yureneva. We cannot be expected to answer for certain excesses that might occur in the course of debate."

Tsvetayev, sitting next to Shumsky, hissed in fury; "Fools barge in..." "Yes," Shumsky whispered back. "That idiot will ruin us completely." Tufta's shrill, high-pitched voice continued to grate on the ears of his hearers: "if you have organised a majority faction, we have the right to organise a minority faction."

A commotion arose in the hall. Angry cries rained down on Tufta from all sides: "What's that? Again Bolsheviks and Mensheviks!" "The Russian Communist Party isn't a parliament!" "They're working for everybody, from Myasnikov to Martov!" Tufta threw up his arms as if about to plunge into a river, and returned an excited rapid-fire: "yes, we must have freedom to form groups. Otherwise how can we who hold different views fight for our opinions against such an organised, well-disciplined majority?"

The uproar increased. Pankratov got up and shouted: "let him speak. We might as well hear what he has to say. Tufta will blurt out what the others prefer to keep to themselves." The hall quieted down. Tufta realised that he had gone too far. Perhaps he ought not to have said that now. His thoughts went off at a tangent and he wound up his speech in a rush of words: "of course you can expel us and shove us overboard. That sort of thing is beginning already. You've already eased me out of the Gubernia Committee of the Komsomol. But never mind, we'll soon see who was right." And with that he jumped off the stage into the hall.

Tsvetayev passed a note down to Dubava. "Mityai, you take the floor next. Of course it won't alter the situation, we are obviously getting the worst of it here. We must put Tufta right. He's a blockhead and a gasbag." Dubava asked for the floor and his request was granted immediately.

An expectant hush fell over the hall as he mounted the platform. It was the usual silence that precedes a speech, but to Dubava it was pregnant with hostility. The ardour with which he had addressed the nuclei meetings had cooled off by now. From da y to day his passion had waned, and after the crushing defeat and the stern rebuff from his former comrades, it was like a fire doused with water, and now he was enveloped by the bitter smoke of wounded vanity made bitterer still by his stubborn refusal to admit himself in the wrong. He resolved to plunge straight in although he knew that he would only be alienating himself still further from the majority. His voice when he spoke was toneless, yet distinct.

"Please do not interrupt me or annoy me by heckling. I want to set forth our position in full, although I know in advance that it is no use. You have the majority." When at last he finished speaking it was as if a bombshell had burst in the hall. A hurricane of angry shouts descended upon him, stinging him like whiplashes. "Shame!" "Down with the splitters!" "Enough mudslinging!"

To the accompaniment of mocking laughter Dubava went back to his seat, and that laughter destroyed him. Had they stormed and railed at him he would have been gratified, but instead he was being jeered at like a third-rate actor whose voice had cracked on a false note. "Shumsky has the floor." announced the chairman. Shumsky got up. "I decline to speak." Then Pankratov's bass boomed from the back rows.

"Let me speak!" Dubava could tell by his voice that Pankratov was seething inwardly. The docker's deep voice always boomed thus when he was mortally insulted, and a deep uneasiness seized Dubava as he gloomily watched the tall, slightly bent figure stride swiftly over to the rostrum. He knew what Pankratov was going to say. He thought of the meeting he had had the day before with his old friends at Solomenka and how they had pleaded with him to break with the opposition. Tsvetayev and Shumsky had been with him. They had met at Tokarev's place. Pankratov, Okunev, Talya, Volyntsev, Zeienova, Staroverov and Artyukhin had been present. Dubava had remained deaf to this attempt to restore unity. In the middle of the discussion he had walked out with Tsvetayev, thereby emphasising his unwillingness to admit his mistakes. Shumsky had remained. And now he had refused to take the floor. "Spineless intellectual! Of course they've won him over," Dubava thought with bitter resentment. He was losing all his friends in this frenzied struggle. At the university there had been a rupture in his friendship with Zharky, who had sharply censured the declaration of the "forty-six" at a meeting of the Party bureau. And later, when the clash grew sharper, he had ceased to be on speaking terms. Several times after that Zharky had come to his place to visit Anna. It was a year since Dubava and Anna had been married. They occupied separate rooms, and Dubava believed that his strained relations with Anna, who did not share his views, had been aggravated by Zharky's frequent visits. It was not jealousy on his part, he assured himself, but under the circumstances her friendship with Zharky irritated him. He had spoken to Anna about it and the result had been a scene which had by no means improved their relations. He had left for the conference without telling her where he was going.

The swift flight of his thoughts was cut short by Pankratov. "Comrades!" the word rang out as the speaker took up a position at the very edge of the platform. "'Comrades! For nine days we have listened to the speeches of the opposition, and I must say quite frankly that they spoke here not as fellow fighters, revolutionaries. our comrades in the class struggle. Their speeches were hostile, implacable, malicious and slanderous. Yes. Comrades, slanderous! They have tried to represent us Bolsheviks as supporters of a mailed-fist regime in the Party, as people who are betraying the interests of their class and the revolution. They have attempted to brand as Party bureaucrats the best, the most tried and trusty section of our Party, the glorious old guard of Bolsheviks, men who built up the Russian Communist Party, men who suffered in tsarist prisons, men who with Comrade Lenin at their head have waged a relentless struggle against world Menshevism and Trotsky. Could anyone but an enemy make such statements? Is the Party and its functionaries not one single whole? Then what is this all about, I want to know? What would we say of men who would try to incite young Red Army men against their commanders and commissars, against army headquarters – and at a time when the unit was surrounded by the enemy? According to the Trotskyites, so long as I am a mechanic I'm 'all right', but if tomorrow I should become the secretary of a Party Committee I would be a 'bureaucrat' and a 'chair-warmer'! Isn't it a bit strange, Comrades, that among the oppositionists who are fighting against bureaucracy and for democracy there should be men like Tufta, for example, who was recently removed from his job for being a bureaucrat? Or Tsvetayev, who is well known to the Solomenka folks for his 'democracy'; or Afanasyev, who was taken off the job three times by the Gubernia Committee for his highhanded way of running things in Podolsk District? It turns out that all those whom the Party has punished have united to fight the Party. Let the old Bolsheviks tell us about Trotsky's 'Bolshevism.' It is very important for the youth to know the history of Trotsky's struggle against the Bolsheviks, about his constant shifting from one camp to another. The struggle against the opposition has welded our ranks and it has strengthened the youth ideologically. The Bolshevik Party and the Komsomol have become steeled in the fight against petty-bourgeois trends. The hysterical panic-mongers of the opposition are predicting complete economic and political collapse. Our tomorrow will show how much these prophecies are worth. They are demanding that we send old Bolsheviks like Tokarev, for instance, back to the bench and replace him by some weathervane like Dubava who imagines his struggle against the Party to be a sort of heroic feat. No, Comrades, we won't agree to that. The old Bolsheviks will get replacement, but not from among those who violently attack the Party line whenever we are up against some difficulty. We shall not permit the unity of our great Party to be disrupted. Never will the old and young guard be split. Under the banner of Lenin, in unrelenting struggle against petty-bourgeois trends, we shall march to victory!"

Pankratov descended the platform amid thunderous applause.

• • • •

THE FOLLOWING DAY A group of ten met at Tufta's place. "Shumsky and I are leaving today for Kharkov," Dubava said. "There is nothing more for us to do here. You must try to keep together. All we can do now is to wait and see what happens. It is obvious that the All-Russian Conference will condemn us, but it seems to me that it is too soon to expect any repressive measures to be taken against us. The majority has decided to give us another chance. To carry on the struggle openly now, especially after the conference, means getting kicked out of the Party, and that does not enter into our plans. It is hard to say what the future will bring. I think that's all there is to be said." Dubava got up to go.

The gaunt, thin-lipped Staroverov also rose. "I don't understand you, Mityai," he said, rolling his r's and slightly stammering. "Does that mean that the conference decision is not binding on us?"

"Formally, it is," Tsvetayev cut in abruptly. "Otherwise you'll lose your Party card. But we'll wait and see which way the wind blows and in the meantime we'll disperse."

Tufta stirred uneasily in his chair. Shumsky, pale and downcast, with dark circles under his eyes, sat by the window biting his nails. At Tsvetayev's words he abandoned his depressing occupation and turned to the meeting. "I am opposed to such manoeuvres," he said in sudden anger. "I personally consider that the decision of the conference is binding on us. We have fought for our convictions, but now we must submit to the decision that has been taken."

Staroverov looked at him with approval. "That is what I wanted to say," he lisped. Dubava fixed Shumsky with his eyes and said with a sneer: "nobody's suggesting that you do anything. You still have a chance to 'repent' at the Gubernia Conference."

Shumsky leapt to his feet. "I resent your tone, Dmitri! And to be quite frank, what you say disgusts me and forces me to reconsider my position."

Dubava waved him away. "That's exactly what I thought you'd do. Run along and repent before it is too late". With that Dubava shook hands with Tufta and the others and left. Shumsky and Staroverov followed soon after.

.... 1924

CRUEL COLD MARKED THE advent in history of the year one thousand nine hundred and twenty-four. January fastened its icy grip on the snowbound land, and from the second half of the month howling storms and blizzards raged.

The South-western railways were snowed up. Men fought the maddened elements. The steel screws of snowploughs cut into the drifts, clearing a path for the trains. Telegraph wires weighted down with ice snapped under the impact of frost and blizzard, and of the twelve lines only three functioned—the Indo-European and two government lines.

In the telegraph office at Shepetovka station three machines continued their unceasing chatter understandable only to the trained ear. The girl operators were still young; the length of the tape they had tapped out would not have exceeded twenty kilometres, but the old telegrapher who worked beside them had already passed the two-hundred-kilometre mark. Unlike his younger colleagues he did not need to read the tape in order to make out the message, nor did he puzzle with wrinkled brow over difficult words or phrases. Instead he wrote down the words one after the other as the apparatus ticked them out. Now his ear caught the words: "To all, to all, to all!"

"Must be another of those circulars about clearing away the snow," the old telegrapher thought to himself as he wrote down the words. Outside, the blizzard raged, hurling the hard snow against the window. The telegrapher thought someone was knocking at the window, his eyes strayed in the direction of the sound and for a moment were arrested by the intricate pattern the frost had traced on the panes. No engraver could ever match that exquisite leaf-and-stalk design! His thoughts wandered and for a while he stopped listening to the telegraph. But presently he looked down and reached for the tape to read the words he had missed.

The telegraph had tapped out these words: "At six-fifty in the afternoon of January Twenty-first..." Quickly writing down the words, the telegrapher dropped the tape and resting his head on his hand returned to listening.

"Yesterday in Gorki the death occurred..." Slowly he put the letters down on paper. How many messages had he taken down in his long life, joyous messages as well as tragic ones, how often had he been the first to hear of the sorrows or happiness of others! He had long since ceased to ponder over the meaning of the terse, clipped phrases, he merely caught the sounds and mechanically set them down on paper.

Now too someone had died, and someone was being notified of the fact. The telegrapher had forgotten the initial words: "To all, to all, to all". The apparatus clicked out the letters "V-L-A-D-M-I-R-I-L-Y-I-C-H", and the old telegrapher translated the hammer taps into words. He sat there unperturbed, a trifle weary. Someone named Vladimir Ilyich had died somewhere, someone would receive the message with the tragic tidings, a cry of grief and anguish would be wrung from someone, but it was no concern of his, for he was only a chance witness. The apparatus tapped out a dot, a dash, more dots, another dash, and out of the familiar sounds he caught the first letter and set it down on the telegraph form. It was the letter "L." Then came the second letter, "E"; next to it he inscribed a neat "N," drawing a heavy slanting line between the two uprights, hastily added an "I" and absently picked up the last letter – "N."

The apparatus tapped out a pause, and for the fraction of a second the telegrapher's eye rested on the word he had written: "LENIN." The apparatus went on tapping, but the familiar name now pierced the telegrapher's consciousness. He glanced once more at the last words of the message – "LENIN." What? Lenin? The entire text of the telegram flashed before his mind's eye. He stared at the telegraph form, and for the first time in all his thirty-two years of work he could not believe what he had written.

He ran his eye swiftly thrice over the lines, but the words obstinately refused to change: "the death occurred of Vladimir Ilyich Lenin." The old man leapt to his feet, snatched up the spiral of tape and bored it with his eyes. The two-metre strip confirmed that which he refused to believe! He turned a deathlike face to his fellow workers, and his frightened cry fell on their ears: "Lenin is dead!"

* * * *

THE NEWS OF THE TERRIBLE bereavement slipped through the wide open door of the telegraph office and with the speed of a hurricane swept over the station and into the blizzard, whipped over the tracks and switches and along with the icy blast tore through the ironbound gates of the railway shops.

A current repair crew was busy overhauling a locomotive standing over the first pot. Old Polentovsky himself had crawled down under the belly of his engine and was pointing out the ailing spots to the mechanics. Zakhar Bruzzhak and Artem were straightening out the bent bars of the fire grate. Zakhar held the grating on the anvil and Artem wielded the hammer.

Zakhar had aged. The past few years had left a deep furrow on his forehead and touched his temples with silver. His back was bent and there were shadows in his sunken eyes. The figure of a man was silhouetted for a moment in the doorway, and then the evening shadows swallowed him up. The blows of the hammer on iron drowned out his first cry, but when he reached the men working at the engine Artem paused with his hammer poised to strike.

"Comrades! Lenin is dead!" The hammer slid slowly from Artem's shoulder and his hands lowered it noiselessly onto the concrete floor. "What's that? What did you say?" Artem's hand clutched convulsively at the leather jacket of the man who had brought the fearful tidings.

And he, gasping for breath, covered with snow, repeated in a low, broken voice: "yes, Comrades, Lenin is dead." And because the man did not shout, Artem realised that the terrible news was true. Only now did he recognise the man—it was the secretary of the local Party organisation.

Men climbed out of the pit and heard in silence of the death of the man with whose name the whole world had rung. Somewhere outside the gates an engine shrieked. sending a shudder through the group of men. The anguished sound was echoed by another engine at the far side of the station, then by a third. Their mighty chorus was joined by the siren of the power station, high—pitched and piercing like the flight of shrapnel. Then all was drowned out by the deep sonorous voice of the handsome "S" locomotive of the passenger train about to leave for Kiev.

A GPU agent started in surprise when the driver of the Polish locomotive of the Shepetovka-Warsaw express, on learning the reason for the alarming whistles, listened for a moment, then slowly raised his hand and pulled at the whistle cord. He knew that this was the last time he would do so, that he would never be allowed to drive this train again, but his hand did not let go of the cord. and the shriek of his engine roused the startled Polish couriers and diplomats from their soft couches.

People crowded into the railway yards. They poured through all the gates and when the vast building was filled to overflowing the funeral meeting opened amid heavy silence. The old Bolshevik Sharabrin. Secretary of the Shepetovka Area Committee of the Party, addressed the gathering.

"Comrades! Lenin, the leader of the world proletariat, is dead. The Party has suffered an irremediable loss, for the man who created the Bolshevik Party and taught it to be implacable to its enemies is no more... The death of the leader of our Party and our class is a summons to the best sons of the proletariat to join our ranks..."

The strains of the funeral march rang out, the hundreds bared their heads, and Artem, who had not wept for fifteen years, felt a spasm constricting his throat and his powerful shoulders shook.

The very walls of the railwaymen's club seemed to groan under the pressure of the human mass. Outside it was bitterly cold, the two tall fir trees at the entrance to the hall were garbed in snow and icicles, but inside it was suffocating from the heated stoves and the breath of six hundred people who had flocked to the memorial meeting arranged by the Party organisation.

The usual hum of conversation was stilled. Overpowering grief muffled men's voices and they spoke in whispers, and there was sorrow and anxiety in the eyes of many a hundred. They were like the crew of a ship that had lost her helmsman in a storm.

Silently the members of the bureau took their seats on the platform. The stocky Sirotenko carefully lifted the bell, rang it gently and replaced it on the table. This was enough for an oppressive hush to settle over the hall.

• • • •

WHEN THE MAIN SPEECH had been delivered, Sirotenko the secretary of the Party organisation, rose to speak. And although the announcement he made was unusual for a memorial meeting, it surprised no one.

"A number of workers," he said. "have asked this meeting to consider an application for membership in the Party. The application is signed by thirty-seven comrades." And he read out the application:

To the railway organisation of the Bolshevik Party at Shepetovka Station. South-western Railway.

The death of our leader is a summons to us to join the ranks of the Bolsheviks, and we ask that this meeting judge of our worthiness to join the Party of Lenin.

Two columns of signatures were affixed to this brief statement. Sirotenko read them aloud, pausing a few seconds after each name to allow the meeting to memorise them. "Stanislav Zigmundovich Polentovsky, engine driver, thirty-six years of service." A murmur of approval rippled over the hall. "Artem Andreyevich Korchagin, mechanic, seventeen years of service. Zakhar Filippovich Bruzzhak, engine driver, twenty-one years of service."

The murmur increased in volume as the man on the platform continued to call out the names of veteran members of the callous-handed fraternity of railroaders.

Silence again reigned when Polentovsky, whose name headed the list, stood before the meeting.

The old engine driver could not but betray his agitation as he told the story of his life. "...What can I tell you, Comrades? You all know what the life of a workingman was like in the old days. Worked like a slave all my life and remained a beggar in my old age. When the revolution came, I confess I considered myself an old man burdened down by family cares, and I did not see my way into the Party. And although I never sided with the enemy I rarely took part in the struggle myself. In nineteen hundred and five I was a member of the strike committee in the Warsaw carshops and I was on the side of the Bolsheviks. I was young then and full of fight. But what's the use of recalling the past! Ilyich's death has struck right at my heart; we've lost our friend and champion, and it's the last time I'll ever speak about being old. I don't know how to put it, for I never was much good at speechmaking. But let me say this: my road is the Bolsheviks' road and no other."

The engine driver tossed his grey head and his eyes under his white brows looked out steadily and resolutely at the audience as if awaiting its decisive word. Not a single voice was raised in opposition to the little grey-haired man's application, and no one abstained during the voting in which the non-Party people too were invited to take part.

Polentovsky walked away from the presidium table a member of the Communist Party.

Everyone was conscious that something momentous was taking place. Now Artem's great bulk loomed where the engine driver had just stood. The mechanic did not know what to do with his hands, and he nervously gripped his shaggy fur cap. His sheepskin jacket, threadbare at the edges, was open, but the high-necked collar of his grey army tunic was fastened on two brass buttons lending his whole figure a holiday neatness. Artem turned to face the hall and caught a fleeting glimpse of a familiar woman's face. It was Galina, the stonemason's daughter, sitting with her work-mates from the tailor shop.

She was gazing at him with a forgiving smile, and in that smile he read approval and something he could not have put into words.

"Tell them about yourself, Artem!" he heard Sirotenko say. But it was not easy for Artem to begin his tale. He was not accustomed to addressing such a large audience, and he suddenly felt that to express all that life had stored within him was beyond his powers. He fumbled painfully for words, and his nervousness made it all the harder for him to speak. Never had he experienced the like. He was acutely conscious that he stood on the threshold of a great change, that he was about to take a step that would bring warmth and meaning into his harsh, warped life.

"There were four of us," Artem began. The hall was hushed. Six hundred people listened eagerly to this tall worker with the beaked nose and the eyes hidden under the dark fringe of eyebrows. "My mother worked as cook for the rich folk. I hardly remember my father; he and mother didn't get along. He drank too much. So mother had to take care of us kids. It was hard for her with so many mouths to feed. She slaved from morning till night and got four rubles a month and her meals. I was lucky enough to get two winters of school. They taught me to read and write, but when I turned nine my mother had no way out but to get me taken on as an apprentice in a machine shop. I worked for three years for nothing but my food..."

"The owner of the shop was a German by the name of Foerster. He didn't want to take me at first, because I was too young, but I was a sturdy lad, and my mother added on a couple of years. I worked three years for that German, but instead of learning a trade I had to do odd jobs around the house and run for vodka. The boss drank like a fish..."

"He would send me to fetch coal and iron too...The mistress made a regular slave out of me: I had to peel potatoes and scour pots. I was always getting kicked and cuffed, most times for no reason, just out of habit. If I didn't please the mistress – and she was always on the rampage on account of her husband's drinking – she would slap my face hard. I'd run away from her out into the street, but where could I go, who was there to complain to? My mother was seventy kilometres away. and she couldn't keep me anyway...And in the shop it wasn't any better. The master's brother was in charge, a swine of a man who used to enjoy playing tricks on me. ?Here boy,' he'd say, 'fetch me that washer from over there,' and he'd point to the corner by the forge. I'd run over and grab the washer and let out a yell. It had just come out of the forge; and though it looked black lying there on the ground, when you touched it, it burned right through the flesh. I would stand there screaming with the pain and he would burst his sides laughing. I couldn't stand any more of this misery and I ran away home to mother. But she didn't know what to do with me, so she brought me back to the German. She cried all the way there, I remember. In my third year they began to teach me something about the trade, but the beatings continued. I ran away again, this time to Starokonstantinov. I found work in a sausage factory and wasted more than a year and a half washing casings. Then our boss gambled away his factory. didn't pay us a kopeck for four months and disappeared. I got out of that hole. I took a train to Zhmerinka and went to look for work. I was lucky enough to meet a railwayman there who took pity on me. When I told him I was a mechanic of sorts, he took me to his boss and said I was his nephew and asked him to find some work for me. By my size they took me for seventeen, and so I got a job as a mechanic's helper. As for my present job, I've been working here for more than eight years. That is all I can tell you about my past. You all know about my present life here."

Artem wiped his brow with his cap and heaved a deep sigh. He had not yet said the chief thing. This was the hardest thing of all to say, but he had to say it before anyone asked the inevitable question. And knitting his bushy eyebrows, he went on with his story: "why did I not join the Bolsheviks when the flames of revolution first flared up? That is a question you all have the right to ask me. And how can

I answer? After all, I'm not an old man yet. How is it I didn't find the road here until today? I'll tell you straight, for I have nothing to hide. We missed that road, we ought to have taken it back in nineteen eighteen when we rose against the Germans. Zhukhrai, the sailor, told us so many a time. It wasn't until nineteen-twenty that I took up a rifle. When the storm was over and we had driven the Whites into the Black Sea, we came back home. Then came the family, children... I got all tied up in family life. But now that our Comrade Lenin is gone and the Party has issued its call, I have looked back at my life and seen what was lacking. It's not enough to defend your own power, we have to stick together like one big family, in Lenin's place, so that the Soviet power should stand solid like a mountain of steel. We must become Bolsheviks. It's our Party, isn't it?"

Thus, simply but with deep sincerity spoke the mechanic. And when he finished, somewhat abashed by the unaccustomed flow of words, he felt as though a great weight had been lifted from his shoulders and pulling himself up to his full height he stood waiting for the questions to come. "Any questions?" Sirotenko's voice broke the ensuing silence. A stir ran over the gathering, but no one responded at first to the chairman's call. Then a stoker, straight from his engine and black as a beetle, said with finality: "what's there to ask? Don't we know him? Give him his running orders and be done with it!"

Gilyaka, the smith, his face scarlet from the heat and the excitement, cried out hoarsely: "this comrade's the right sort, he won't jump the rails, you can depend on him. Put it to the vote, Sirotenko!"

At the very back of the hall where the Komsomols were sitting, someone, invisible in the semidarkness, rose and said: "let Comrade Korchagin explain why he has settled on the land and how he reconciles his peasant status with his proletarian psychology."

A light rustle of disapproval passed over the hall and a voice rose in protest: "why don't you talk so plain folks can understand? A fine time to show off...." But Artem was already replying: "that's all right.

Comrade. The lad is right about my having settled on the land. That's true, but I haven't betrayed my working-class conscience. Anyhow, that's over and done with from today. I'm moving my family closer to the yards. It's better here. That cursed land has been sticking in my throat for a long time."

Once again Artem's heart trembled when he saw the forest of hands raised in his favour, and with head held high he walked back to his seat, feeling miraculously light on his feet. Behind him he heard Sirotenko announce: "Unanimous."

The third to take his place at the presidium table was Zakhar Bruzzhak, Polentovsky's former helper. The taciturn old man had been an engine driver himself now for some time. When he finished his account of a lifetime of labour and brought his story up to the present, his voice dropped and he spoke softly but loud enough for all to hear: "it is my duty to finish what my children began – they wouldn't have wanted me to hide away in a corner with my grief. That isn't what they died for, I haven't tried to fill the gap left by their death, but now the death of the leader has opened my eyes. Don't ask me to answer for the past. From today our life starts anew."

As painful memories stirred within him Zakhar's face clouded and looked stern. But when a sea of hands swept up, voting for his acceptance into the Party, his eyes lit up and his greying head was no longer bowed.

Far into the night continued this review of the new Party replacements. Only the best were admitted, those whom everyone knew well. Whose lives were without blemish.

The death of Lenin made Bolsheviks of hundreds of thousands of workers. The leader was gone, but the Party's ranks were not shaken. A tree which has thrust its mighty roots deep into the ground does not perish if its crown is severed.

CHAPTER SIX

Two men stood at the entrance to the hotel concert hall. The taller of the two wore pince-nez and a red armband marked "Commandant."

"Is the Ukrainian delegation meeting here?" Rita inquired. "Yes," the tall man replied in a tone of chill formality. "Your business. Comrade?" The tall man blocked the entrance and examined Rita from head to foot. "Have you a delegate's mandate?" Rita produced her card with the gilt-embossed words "Member of the Central Committee" and the man's manner changed instantly to one of politeness and affability. "Pass in, Comrade, you'll find some empty seats over to the left." Rita walked down the aisle, saw an unoccupied seat and sat down.

The meeting was evidently drawing to a close, for the chairman was summing up. His voice struck Rita as familiar. "The council of the All-Russian Congress has now been elected. The Congress opens in two hours' time. In the meantime permit me to go over the list of delegates once more." It was Akim! Rita listened with rapt attention as he hurriedly read out the list. As his name was called each delegate raised his hand showing his red or white pass.

Suddenly Rita caught a familiar name: Pankratov. She glanced round as a hand shot up but through the intervening rows she could not glimpse the docker's face. The names ran on, and again Rita heard one she knew – Okunev, and immediately after that another, Zharky. Scanning the faces of the delegates she caught sight of Zharky. He was sitting not far away with his face half turned toward her. Yes, it was Vanya all right. She had almost forgotten that profile. After all, she had not seen him for several years.

The roll-call continued. And then Akim read out a name that caused Rita to start violently: "Korchagin.'" Far away in one of the front rows a hand rose and fell, and, strange to say, Rita Ustinovich was seized with a painful longing to see the face of the man who bore the same name as her lost comrade. She could not tear her eyes away from the spot where the hand had risen, but all the heads in the rows before her seemed all alike. Rita got up and went down the aisle toward the front rows. At that moment Akim finished reading. Chairs were pushed back noisily and the hall was filled with the hum of voices and young laughter.

Akim, trying to make himself heard above the din, shouted: "Bolshoi Theatre... seven o'clock. Don't be late!" The delegates crowded to the single exit. Rita saw that she would never be able to find any of her old friends in this throng. She must try to catch Akim before he left; he would help her find the others. Just then a group of delegates passed her in the aisle on their way to the exit and she heard someone say: "well, Korchagin old man, we'd better be pushing off too!" And a voice, so familiar, so memorable, replied: "good, let's go."

Rita turned quickly. Before her stood a tall, dark-complexioned young man in a khaki tunic with a slender Caucasian belt, and blue riding breeches. Rita stared at him with dilated eyes. Then she felt his arms around her and heard his trembling voice say softly: "Rita," and she knew that it was Pavel Korchagin. "So you're alive?" These words told him all. So she had not known that his reported death was a mistake.

The hall had emptied out long since, and the din and bustle of Tverskaya, that mighty artery of the city, poured through the open window. The clock struck six, but to both of them it seemed that they had met only a moment ago. But the clock summoned them to the Bolshoi Theatre. As they walked down the broad staircase to the exit she surveyed Pavel once more. He was a head taller than her now and more mature and self-possessed. But otherwise he was the Pavel she had always known. "I haven't even asked you where you are working," she said.

"I am Secretary of the Area Committee of the Komsomol, what Dubava would call a pen pusher," Pavel replied with a smile. "Have you seen him?" "Yes, and I have the most unpleasant memories of that meeting." They stepped onto the street. Automobiles tooted past, noisy bustling throngs filled the pavements. They hardly exchanged a word on the way to the theatre, their minds full of the same thoughts. They found the theatre besieged by a surging, tempestuous sea of people which tossed itself against the stone bulk of the theatre building in an effort to break through the chain of Red Army men guarding the entrances. But the sentries gave admittance only to delegates, who passed through the cordon, their credentials proudly displayed.

It was a Komsomol sea that surrounded the theatre, a sea of young people who had been unable to obtain tickets to the opening of the Congress but who were determined to get in at all costs. Some of the more agile youngsters managed to work their way into the midst of groups of delegates and by presenting some slip of red paper sometimes contrived to get as far as the entrance. A few even managed to slip through the doors only to fall foul of the Central Committee man on duty, or the commandant who directed the guests and delegates to their appointed places. And then to the infinite satisfaction of all the rest of the "ticket-less" fraternity, they were unceremoniously ejected.

The theatre could not hold a fraction of all who wished to be present. Rita and Pavel pushed their way with difficulty to the entrance. The delegates continued to pour in, some arriving by tram, others by car. A large knot of them gathered at the entrance and the Red Army men, Komsomols themselves, were pressed back against the wall. At that moment a mighty shout arose from the crowd near the entrance: "Bauman Institute, here goes!" "Come on, lads, our side's winning!" "Hooray!"

Through the doorway along with Pavel and Rita slipped a sharp-eyed youngster wearing a Komsomol badge, and eluding the commandant, made a beeline for the foyer. A moment later he was swallowed up by the crowd. "Let's sit here," Rita said, indicating two seats in a corner at the back of the stalls. "There is one question I must ask you," said Rita when they were seated. "It concerns bygone days, but I am sure you will not refuse to answer it. Why did you break off our studies and our friendship that time?"

And though Pavel had been expecting this question ever since they had met, it disconcerted him. Their eyes met and Pavel saw that she knew. "I think you know the answer yourself, Rita. That happened three years ago, and now I can only condemn Pavka for what he did. As a matter of fact Korchagin has committed many a blunder, big and small, in his life. That was one of them."

Rita smiled. "An excellent preamble. Now for the answer!" "It is not only I who was to blame," Pavel began in a low voice. "It was the Gadfly's fault too, that revolutionary romanticism of his. In those days I was very much influenced by books with vivid descriptions of staunch, courageous, revolutionaries consecrated to our cause. Those men made a deep impression on me and I longed to be like them. I allowed The Gadfly to influence my feeling for you. It seems absurd to me now, and I regret it more than I can say."

"Then you have changed your mind about The Gadfly?". "No Rita, not fundamentally. I have only discarded the needless tragedy of that painful process of testing one's will. I still stand for what is most important in The Gadfly, for his courage, his supreme endurance, for the type of man who is capable of enduring suffering without exhibiting his pain to all and sundry. I stand for the type of revolutionary whose personal life is nothing as compared with the life of society as a whole."

"It is a pity, Pavel, that you did not tell me this three years ago," said Rita with a smile that showed her thoughts to be far away. "A pity, you mean, because I have never been more to you than a com-

rade, Rita?" "No, Pavel, you might have been more." "But surely that
can be remedied." "No, Comrade Gadfly, it is too late for that."

"You see, I have a little daughter now," Rita smilingly explained.
"I am very fond of her father. In general, the three of us are very good
friends, and so far our trio is inseparable." Her fingers brushed Pavel's
hand. The gesture was prompted by anxiety for him, but she realised
at once that it was unnecessary. Yes, he had matured in these three
years, and not only physically. She could tell by his eyes that he was
deeply hurt by her confession, but all he said was: "what I have left is
still incomparably more than what I have just lost." And Rita knew
that this was not merely an empty phrase, it was the simple truth.

It was time to take their places nearer to the stage. They got up
and went forward to the row occupied by the Ukrainian delegation.
The band struck up. Scarlet streamers flung across the hall were em-
blazoned with the words: "The Future Is Ours!" Thousands filled the
stalls, the boxes and the tiers of the great theatre. These thousands
merged here in one mighty organism throbbing with inexhaustible
energy. The flower of the young guard of the country's great industrial brotherhood was gathered here. Thousands of pairs of eyes reflected the glow of those words traced in burning letters over the heavy
curtain: "The Future Is Ours!" And still the human tide rolled in. Another few moments and the heavy velvet curtain would move aside,
and the Secretary of the Central Committee of the Russian Communist Youth League, his self-possession deserting him for an instant at
this solemn moment, would announce: "I declare the Sixth Congress
of the Russian Communist Youth League open."

Never before had Pavel Korchagin been so profoundly, so stir-
ringly conscious of the grandeur and might of the Revolution, and
an indescribable surge of pride and joy swept over him at the thought
that life had brought him, a fighter and builder, to this triumphant
rally of the young guard of Bolshevism.

• • • •

THE CONGRESS CLAIMED all of his time from early morning until late at night, so that it was not until one of the final sessions that Pavel met Rita again. She was with a group of Ukrainians.

"I am leaving tomorrow as soon as the Congress closes," she told him. "I don't know whether we will have another chance for a talk, and so I have prepared two old notebooks of my diary for you, and a short note. Read them and send them back to me by post. They will tell you all that I have not told you."

He pressed her hand and gazed long at her features as if committing them to memory. They met as agreed the following day at the main entrance and Rita handed him a package and a sealed letter. They were not alone and so their leave-taking was restrained, but in her slightly misted eyes Pavel read a deep tenderness tinged with sorrow.

The next day their trains bore them away in different directions. The Ukrainian delegation occupied several cars of the train in which Pavel travelled. He shared a compartment with some delegates from Kiev. In the evening, when the other passengers had retired and Okunev on the neighbouring berth was snoring peacefully, Pavel moved the lamp closer and opened the letter.

Pavel, my darling!

I might have told you all this when we were together, but it is better this way. I wish only one thing: that what we spoke of before the Congress should leave no scar on your life. I know you are strong and

I believe that you meant what you said. I do not take a formal attitude to life, I feel that one may make exceptions—though rarely—in one's personal relationships, provided they are founded on a genuine and deep attachment. For you I would have made that exception, but I rejected my impulse to pay tribute to our youth. I feel that there would be no true happiness in it for either of us. Still, you ought not to be so harsh to yourself, Pavel. Our life is not all struggle, there is room in it for the happiness that real love brings.

*As for the rest, the main purport of your life, I have no fears for you.
I press your hand warmly.*

Rita.

Pavel tore up the letter reflectively; he thrust his hand out of the
window and felt the wind tearing the scraps of paper out of his hand.
By morning he had read both notebooks of Rita's diary, wrapped
them up and tied them ready for posting. At Kharkov he left the train
with Okunev and Pankratov and several other delegates. Okunev was
going to Kiev to fetch Talya, who was staying with Anna. Pankratov, who had been elected member of the Central Committee of the
Ukrainian Komsomol, also had business in Kiev. Pavel decided to go
on with them to Kiev and pay a visit to Dubava and Anna.

By the time he emerged from the post office at the Kiev station
after sending off the parcel to Rita, the others had gone, so he set off
alone. The tram stopped outside the house where Anna and Dubava lived. Pavel climbed the stairs to the second floor and knocked at
the door on the left, Anna's room. No one answered. It was too early for her to have gone to work. "She must be sleeping," he thought.
The door of the neighbouring room opened and a sleepy-eyed Dubava came out on the landing. His face was ashen-hued and there were
dark circles under his eyes. He exuded a strong smell of onions and
Pavel's sharp nose caught a whiff of alcohol. Through the half-open
door he caught a glimpse of the fleshy leg and shoulders of some
woman on the bed.

Dubava, noticing the direction of his glance, kicked the door
shut. "You've come to see Comrade Borhart, I suppose?" he inquired
hoarsely, evading Pavel's eyes. "She doesn't live here anymore. Didn't
you know that?" Korchagin, his face stern, looked searchingly at
Dubava. "No, I didn't. Where has she gone?" Dubava suddenly lost
his temper.

"That's no concern of mine!" he shouted. He belched and added
with suppressed malice: "Come to console her, eh? You're just in time

to fill the vacancy. Here's your chance. Don't worry, she won't refuse you. She told me many a time how much she liked you or however those silly women put it. Go on, strike the iron while it's hot. It will be a true communion of soul and body." Pavel felt the blood rising to his cheeks. Restraining himself with difficulty, he said in a low voice: "what are you doing to yourself, Mityai! I never thought you'd fall so low. You weren't a bad fellow once. Why are you letting yourself go to the dogs?"

Dubava leaned back against the wall. The cement floor evidently felt cold to his bare feet, for he shivered.

The door opened and a woman's face with swollen eyes and puffy cheeks appeared. "Come back in, darlin', what're you standing out there for?" Before she could say any more, Dubava slammed the door to and stood against it. "A fine beginning," Pavel observed. "Look at the company you're keeping. Where will it all end?" But Dubava would hear no more.

"Are you going to tell me who I should sleep with?" he shouted. "I've had enough of your preaching. Now get back where you came from! Run along and tell them all that Dubava has taken to drink and sleeping with loose women." Pavel went up to him and said in a voice of suppressed emotion: "Mityai, get rid of that woman. I want to talk to you, for the last time..."

Dubava's face darkened. He turned on his heel and went back into the room without another word.

"The swine!" Pavel muttered and walked slowly down the stairs.

• • • •

TWO YEARS WENT BY. Inexorable time counted off the days and months, but the swift colourful pageant of life filled its seeming monotony with novelty, so that no two days were alike. The great nation of one hundred and sixty million people, the first people in the world to have taken the destiny of their vast land with its untold riches into their own hands, were engaged in the herculean task of reviving their war-ravaged economy. The country grew stronger, new vigour flowed into its veins, and the dismal spectacle of smokeless abandoned factories was no longer to be seen.

For Pavel those two years fled by in ceaseless activity. He was not one to take life calmly, to greet each day with a leisurely yawn and retire at the stroke of ten. He lived at a swift tempo, grudging himself and others every wasted moment. He allowed a bare minimum of time for sleep. Often the light burned in his window late into the night, and within one would see a group of people gathered around the table engrossed in study. They had made a thorough study of Volume III of Capital in these two years and the subtle mechanics of capitalist exploitation were now revealed to them.

Razvalikhin had turned up in the area where Korchagin now worked. He had been sent by the Gubernia Committee with the recommendation that he be appointed secretary of a district Komsomol organisation. Pavel happened to be away when Razvalikhin arrived and in his absence the Bureau had sent the newcomer to one of the districts. Pavel received the intelligence on his return without comment

A month later Pavel made an unexpected visit to Razvalikhin's district. There was not much evidence, but what there was turned out to be sufficiently damning: the new secretary drank, he had surrounded himself with toadies and was suppressing the initiative of the conscientious members. Pavel submitted the evidence to the Bureau, and when the meeting spoke in favour of administering Razvalikhin a severe reprimand, Pavel surprised everyone by getting up and saying: "I move that he be expelled and that his expulsion be final."

The others were taken aback by the motion. It seemed too stringent a measure under the circumstances. But Pavel insisted. "The scoundrel must be expelled. He had every chance to become a decent human being, but he has remained an outsider in the Komsomol." And Pavel told the Bureau about the Berezdov incident.

"I protest!" Razvalikhin shouted. "Korchagin is simply trying to settle personal scores. What he says is nothing but idle gossip. Let him back up his charges with facts and documents. Suppose I were to come to you with a story that Korchagin had gone in for smuggling, would you expel him on the strength of that? He's got to submit written proof."

"Don't worry, I'll submit all the proofs necessary," Korchagin replied. Razvalikhin left the room. Half an hour later Pavel had persuaded the Bureau to adopt a resolution expelling Razvalikhin from the Komsomol as an alien element.

* * * *

SUMMER CAME AND WITH it the vacation season. Pavel's fellow workers left for their well-earned holiday one after another. Those whose health demanded it went to the seaside and Pavel helped them to secure sanatorium accommodations and financial assistance. They went away pale and worn, but elated at the prospect of their coming holiday. The burden of their work fell on Pavel's shoulders and he bore the added load without a murmur. In due time they returned sunburned and full of life and energy, and others went off. Throughout the summer the office was short-handed. But life did not lessen its swift pace, and Pavel could not afford to miss a single day's work.

The summer passed. Pavel dreaded the approach of autumn and winter for they invariably brought him much physical distress. He had looked forward with particular eagerness to the coming of summer that year. For painful though it was for him to admit it even to himself he felt his strength waning from year to year. There were only two alternatives: to admit that he could not endure the intensive effort his work demanded of him and declare himself an invalid, or remain at his post as long as he could function. He chose the latter course

One day at a meeting of the Bureau of the Area Committee of the Party Dr. Bartelik, an old Party underground worker now in charge of public health in the area, came over and sat down beside him. "You're looking rather seedy, Korchagin. How is your health? Have you been examined by the medical commission? You haven't? I thought as much. But you look as if you were in need of an overhauling, my friend. Come over on Thursday evening and we'll have a look at you."

Pavel did not go. He was too busy. But Bartelik did not forget him and some time later he came for Pavel and took him to the commission in which he participated as neuropathologist. The Medical Commission recommended "an immediate vacation with prolonged treatment in the Crimea, to be followed by regular medical treatment. Unless this is done serious consequences are unavoidable."

From the long list of ailments in Latin that preceded this recommendation Pavel understood only one thing—the main trouble was not in his legs, but in his central nervous system, which was seriously impaired. Bartelik put the commission's decision before the Bureau, and the motion that Korchagin be released at once from work evoked no opposition. Korchagin himself, however, suggested that his vacation be postponed until the return of Sbitnev, Chief of the Organisational Department. He did not want to leave the Committee without leadership. The Bureau agreed, although Bartelik objected to the delay.

And so in three weeks' time Pavel was to leave for his holiday, the first in his life. Accommodation had already been reserved for him in a Eupatoria sanatorium and a paper to that effect lay in his desk drawer. He worked at even greater pressure in this period; he held a plenary meeting of the Area Komsomol and drove himself relentlessly to tie up all loose ends so as to be able to leave with his mind at rest.

And on the very eve of his departure for his first glimpse of the sea, a revolting, unbelievable thing happened. Pavel had gone to the Party agitprop section after work that day to attend a meeting. There was no one in the room when he arrived and so he had sat down on the window sill by the open window behind the bookcase to wait for the others to assemble. Before long several people came in. He could not see them from behind the bookcase but he recognised one voice. It belonged to Failo, the man in charge of the Area Economic Department, a tall, handsome fellow with a dashing military bearing, who had earned himself a reputation for drinking and running after women.

Failo had once been a partisan and never missed an opportunity to brag laughingly of the way he had sliced off the heads of Makhno men by the dozen. Pavel could not stand the man. One day a Komsomol girl had come weeping to Pavel with the story that Failo had promised to marry her but after living with her for a week had left her and now did not even greet her when they met. When the matter came up before the Control Commission, Failo wriggled out of it since the girl could give no proofs. But Pavel had believed her. He now listened while the others, unaware of his presence, talked freely. "Well, Failo, how goes it? What have you been up to lately?"

That was Gribov, one of Failo's boon companions. For some reason Gribov was considered a propagandist although he was ignorant, narrow-minded and stupid. Nevertheless he prided himself on being called a propaganda worker and made a point of reminding everyone of the fact on all and every occasion. "You can congratulate me, my boy. I made another conquest yesterday. Korotayeva. You said nothing would come of it. That's where you were mistaken, my lad. If I go after a woman you may be sure I'll get her sooner or later," Failo boasted, adding an obscene expression.

Pavel felt himself shaking all over with the nervous chill that always seized him when he was deeply roused. Korotayeva was in charge of the women's department and had come to the Area Committee at the same time as he had. Pavel knew her for a pleasant, earnest Party worker, kind and considerate to the women who came to her for help and advice, and respected by her fellow workers in the Committee. Pavel knew that she was not married, and he had no doubt that it was of her that Failo had spoken.

"Go on, Failo, you're making it up! It doesn't sound like her." "Me, making it up? What do you take me for? I've broken in harder cases than that. You only have to know how. Got to have the right approach to each one. Some of them will give in right away, but that kind aren't worth the trouble. Others take a whole month to come to heel. The important thing is to understand their psychology. The right approach, that's the thing. Why, man, it's a whole science, but I'm a regular professor in such matters. Ha! ha! ha!"

Failo was positively slobbering with self-satisfaction. His listeners egged him on, all agog for more juicy details. Korchagin got up. He clenched his fists, feeling his heart pounding wildly in his chest. "I knew there wasn't much hope of catching Korotayeva with the usual bait, but I didn't want to give up the game, especially since I'd wagered Gribov a dozen of port wine that I'd do it. So I tried subversive tactics, so to speak. I dropped in to see her once or twice. But I could see I wasn't making much of an impression. Besides, there's all sorts of silly talk going on about me and some of it must have reached her ears. ... Well, to cut a long story short, the frontal attack failed, so I tried flanking tactics. Pretty good that, eh? Well, I told her my sad story, how I'd fought at the front, wandered about the earth and had plenty of hard knocks, but I'd never been able to find the right sort of woman and so here I was a lonely cuss with nobody to love me... And plenty more of the same sort of tripe. I was striking at her weak spots, see? I must admit I had a lot of trouble with her. At one point I thought I'd send her to hell and drop the whole silly business. But by now it was a matter of principle, and so out of principle I had to stick it out. And finally I broke down her resistance, and what do you think? She turned out to be a virgin! Ha! Ha! What a lark!"

And Failo went on with his revolting story. Pavel, seething with rage, found himself beside Failo. "You swine!" he roared. "Oh, I'm a swine, am I, and what about you spying on other people?" Pavel evidently said something else, because Failo who was not quite sober seized him by the front of his tunic. "Insult me, eh?" He shouted and struck Pavel with his fist. Pavel picked up a heavy oak stool and knocked the other down with one blow. Fortunately for Failo, Pavel did not happen to have his revolver on him, or he would have been a dead man.

But the senseless, incredible thing had happened, and on the day scheduled for his departure to the Crimea, Pavel stood before a Party court. The whole Party organisation had assembled in the town theatre. The incident had aroused much feeling, and the hearing developed into a serious discussion of Party ethics, morals and personal relationships. The case served as a signal for the discussion of the general issues involved, and the incident itself was relegated to the back-

ground. Failo behaved in the most insolent manner, smiling sardon-
ically and declaring that he would take the case to the People's Court
and that Korchagin would get a hard labour sentence for bashing in
his head. He refused categorically to answer any questions.

"You want to have a nice little gossip at my expense? Nothing doing. You can accuse me of anything you like, but the fact remains that
the women here have their knife in me because I don't pay any attention to them. And this whole case of yours isn't worth a damn. If this
was nineteen-eighteen I'd settle scores with that madman Korchagin
in my own way. And now you can carry on without me." And he left
the hall. The chairman then asked Pavel to tell what had happened.
Pavel began calmly enough, though he restrained himself with difficulty.

"The whole thing happened because I was unable to control myself. But the days when I worked more with my hands than with my
head are long since gone. What happened this time was an accident.
I knocked Failo down before I knew what I was doing. This is the only instance of 'partisan' action I have been guilty of in the past few
years, and I condemn it, although I think that the blow was well deserved. Failo's type is a disgusting phenomenon. I cannot understand,
I shall never believe that a revolutionary, a Communist, can be at the
same time a dirty beast and a scoundrel. The only positive aspect of
the whole business is that it has focussed our attention on the behaviour of our fellow Communists in private life."

The overwhelming majority of the membership voted in favour
of expelling Failo from the Party. Gribov was administered a severe
reprimand for giving false evidence and a warning that the next of-
fence would mean expulsion. The others who had taken part in the
conversation admitted their mistake and got off with a word of cen-
sure.

Bartelik then told the gathering about the state of Pavel's nerves
and the meeting protested violently when the comrade who had been

appointed by the Party to investigate the case moved that Korchagin be reprimanded. The investigator withdrew his motion and Pavel was acquitted.

• • • •

A FEW DAYS LATER PAVEL was on his way to Kharkov. The Area Committee of the Party had finally granted his insistent request to be released from his job and placed at the disposal of the Central Committee of the Ukrainian Komsomol. He had been given a good testimonial. Akim was one of the secretaries of the Central Committee. Pavel went to see him as soon as he arrived in Kharkov and told him the whole story.

Akim looked over Pavel's testimonial. It declared him to be "boundlessly devoted to the Party," but added: "A level-headed Party worker, on the whole, he is, however, on rare occasions apt to lose his self-control. This is due to the serious condition of his nervous system."

"Spoiled a good testimonial with that fact, Pavel," said Akim. "But never mind, boy, such things happen to the strongest of us. Go south and build up your health and when you come back we'll talk about work."

And Akim gave him a hearty handshake.

• • • •

THE COMMUNARD SANATORIUM of the Central Committee. White buildings overgrown with vines set amid gardens of rose bushes and sparkling fountains, and vacationers in white summer suits and bathing costumes...

A young woman doctor entered his name in the register and he found himself in a spacious room in the comer building. Dazzling white bed linen, virginal cleanliness and peace, blessed undisturbed peace.

After a refreshing bath and a change of clothes, Pavel hurried down to the beach.

The sea lay before him calm, majestic, a blue-black expanse of polished marble spreading all the way to the horizon. Far away in the distance where sea met sky a bluish haze hovered and a molten sun was reflected in a ruddy glow on its surface. The massive contours of a mountain range were dimly seen through the morning mist. Pavel breathed the invigorating freshness of the sea breeze deep into his lungs and feasted his eyes on the infinite calm of the blue expanse.

A wave rolled lazily up to his feet, licking the golden sand of the beach.

CHAPTER SEVEN

The garden of the central polyclinic adjoined the grounds of the Central Committee Sanatorium whose patients used it as a short cut on their way home from the beach. Pavel loved to rest here in the shade of a spreading plane tree which grew beside a high limestone wall. From this quiet nook he could watch the lively movement of the crowd strolling along the garden paths and listen to the music of the band in the evenings without being jostled by the gay throngs of the large health resort.

Today too he had sought his favourite retreat. Drowsy from the sunshine and the seawater bath he had just taken, he stretched himself out luxuriously on the chaise-lounge and fell into a doze. His bath towel and the book he was reading, Furmanov's Insurrection, lay on the chair beside him. His first days in the sanatorium had brought no relief to his nerves and his headaches continued. His ailment had so far baffled the sanatorium doctors, who were still trying to get to the root of the trouble. Pavel was sick of the perpetual examinations. They wearied him and he did his best to avoid his ward doctor, a pleasant woman, a Party member, with the curious name of Yerusalimchik, who had a difficult time hunting for her unwilling patient and persuading him to let her take him to some specialist or other.

"I'm tired of the whole business," Pavel would plead with her. "Five times a day I have to tell the same story and answer all sorts of silly questions: was your grandmother insane, or did your great-grandfather suffer with rheumatism? How the devil should I know what he suffered from? I never saw him in my life! Every doctor tries to induce me to confess that I had gonorrhoea or something worse, until I swear I'm ready to punch their bald heads. Give me a chance to rest, that's all I want. If I'm going to let myself be diagnosed all the six weeks of my stay here I'll become a danger to society."

Yerusalimchik would laugh and joke with him, but a few minutes later she would take him gently by the arm and lead him to the surgeon, chattering volubly all the way.

But today there was no examination in the offing, and dinner was an hour away. Presently, through his doze. he heard steps approaching. He did not open his eyes. "They'll think I'm asleep and go away," he thought. Vain hope! He heard the chair beside him creak as someone sat down. A faint whiff of perfume told him it was a woman. He opened his eyes. The first thing he saw was a dazzling white dress and a pair of bronzed feet encased in soft leather slippers, then a boyish bob, two enormous eyes, and a row of white teeth as sharp as a mouse's. She gave him a shy smile.

"I haven't disturbed you, I hope?" Pavel made no reply, which was not very polite of him, but he still hoped that she would go. "Is this your book?" She was turning the pages of Insurrection. "It is." There was a moment of silence. "You're from the Communard Sanatorium, aren't you?"

Pavel stirred impatiently. Why couldn't she leave him in peace? A fine rest he'd had. Now she would start asking about his illness. She would have to go. "No," he replied curtly. "I was sure I had seen you there." Pavel was on the point of rising when a deep, pleasant woman's voice behind him said. "Why. Dora, what are you doing here?"

A plump, sunburned, fair- haired girl in a beach costume seated herself on the edge of a chair. She glanced quickly at Korchagin. "I've seen you somewhere, Comrade. You're from Kharkov, aren't you?" "Yes." "Where do you work?" Pavel decided to put an end to the conversation. "In the garbage disposal department," he replied. The laugh this sally evoked made him jump. "You're not very polite, are you, Comrade?"

That is how their friendship began, Dora Rodkina turned out to be a member of the Bureau of the Kharkov City Committee of the Party and later, when they came to know each other well, she often teased him about the amusing incident with which their acquaintance had started.

- - - -

ONE AFTERNOON AT AN open-air concert in the grounds of the Thalassa Sanatorium Pavel ran across his old friend Zharky. And curious to relate, it was a foxtrot that caused them to meet.

After the audience had been treated to a highly emotional rendering of Oh, Nights of Burning Passion by a buxom soprano, a couple sprang onto the stage. The man, naked but for a red top hat, some shiny spangles on his hips, a dazzling white shirt front and bow tie, presented a feeble imitation of a savage. His doll-faced partner was swathed in voluminous quantity of cloth. To the accompaniment of a delighted buzz from the crowd of beefy-necked traders standing behind the armchairs and cots occupied by the sanatorium patients, the couple gyrated about the stage in the intricate figures of a foxtrot. A more revolting spectacle could scarcely be imagined. The fleshy man in his idiotic top hat, with his partner pressed tightly to him, writhed on the stage in suggestive poses. Pavel heard the torturous breathing of some fat carcass at his back. He turned to go when someone in the front row got up and shouted: "enough of this brothel show! To hell with it!" It was Zharky.

The pianist stopped playing and the violin subsided with a squeak. The couple on the stage ceased writhing. The crowd at the back set up a vicious hissing. "What impudence to interrupt a number!" "All Europe is dancing!" "Outrageous!" But Seryozha Zhbanov, Secretary of the Cherepovets Komsomol organisation, and one of the Communard patients, put four fingers into his mouth and emitted a piercing whistle. Others followed his example and in an instant the couple vanished from the stage, as if swept off by a gust of wind. The obsequious master of ceremonies who looked like nothing so much as an old-time flunkey, announced that the concert troupe was leaving.

"Good riddance to bad rubbish!" a lad in a sanatorium bathrobe shouted amid general laughter. Pavel went over to the front rows and found Zharky. The two friends had a long chat in Pavel's room. Zharky told Pavel that he was working in the agitprop section of one of the Party's area committees. "You didn't know I was married, did you?" said Zharky. "I'm expecting a son or a daughter before long."

"Married, eh?" Pavel was surprised. "Who is your wife?" Zharky took a photograph out of his pocket and showed it to Pavel. "Recognise her?" It was a photo of himself and Anna Borhart. "And what happened to Dubava?" Pavel asked in still greater surprise. "He's in Moscow. He left the university after he was expelled from the Party. He's at the Bauman Technical Institute now. I hear he's been reinstated. Too bad, if it's true. He's rotten through and through...Guess what Pankratov is doing? He's assistant director of a shipyard. I don't know much about the others. We've lost touch lately. We all work in different corners of the country. But it's nice to get together occasionally and recall the old times."

Dora came in bringing several other people with her. She glanced at the decoration on Zharky's jacket and asked Pavel: "is your comrade a Party member? Where does he work?" Puzzled, Pavel told her briefly about Zharky. "Good," she said. "Then he can remain. These comrades have just come from Moscow. They are going to give us the latest Party news. We decided to come to your room and hold a sort of closed Party meeting," she explained.

With the exception of Pavel and Zharky all the newcomers were old Bolsheviks. Bartashev, a member of the Moscow Control Commission, told them about the new opposition headed by Trotsky, Zinoviev and Kamenev. "At this critical moment we ought to be at our posts," Bartashev said in conclusion. "I am leaving tomorrow."

Three days after that meeting in Pavel's room the sanatorium was deserted. Pavel too left shortly afterward, before his time was up. The Central Committee of the Komsomol did not detain him. He was given an appointment as Komsomol Secretary in one of the industrial regions, and within a week he was already addressing a meeting of the local city organisation.

Late that autumn the car in which Pavel was travelling with two other Party workers to one of the remote districts, skidded into a ditch and overturned.

All the occupants were injured. Pavel's right knee was crushed. A few days later he was taken to the surgical institute in Kharkov. After an examination and X-ray of the injured limb the medical commission advised an immediate operation. Pavel gave his consent. "Tomorrow morning then," said the stout professor, who headed the commission. He got up and the others filed out after him.

A small bright ward with a single cot. Impeccable cleanliness and the peculiar hospital smell he had long since forgotten. He glanced about him. Beside the cot stood a small table covered by a snow-white cloth and a white-painted stool. And that was all.

The nurse brought in his supper. Pavel sent it back. Half-sitting in his bed, he was writing letters. The pain in his knee interfered with his thoughts and robbed him of his appetite.

When the fourth letter had been written the door opened softly and a young woman in a white smock and cap came over to his bed.

In the twilight he made out a pair of slender brows and large eyes that seemed black. In one hand she held a portfolio, in the other, a sheet of paper and a pencil.

"I am your ward doctor," she said. "Now I am going to ask you a lot of questions and you will have to tell me all about yourself, whether you like it or not."

She smiled pleasantly and her smile took the edge off her "cross-examination." Pavel spent the better part of an hour telling her not only about himself but about all his relatives several generations back.

• • • •

THE OPERATING THEATRE. People with gauze masks over noses and mouths. Shining nickel instruments, a long narrow table with a huge basin beneath it.

The professor was still washing his hands when Pavel lay down on the operating table. Behind him swift preparations were being made for the operation. He turned his head. The nurse was laying out pincets and lancets. "Don't look, Comrade Korchagin," said Bazhanova, his ward doctor, who was removing the bandage from his leg. "It is bad for the nerves."

"For whose nerves, doctor?" Pavel asked with a mocking smile. A few minutes later a heavy mask covered his face and he heard the professor's voice saying: "we are going to give you an anaesthetic. Now breathe in deeply through your nose and begin counting."

"Very well," a calm voice muffled by the mask replied. "I apologise in advance for any unprintable remarks I am liable to make."

The professor could not suppress a smile.

• • • •

THE FIRST DROPS OF ether. The suffocating loathsome smell. Pavel took a deep breath and making an effort to speak distinctly began counting. The curtain had risen on the first act of his tragedy.

• • • •

ARTEM TORE OPEN THE envelope and trembling inwardly unfolded the letter. His eyes bored into the first few lines, then ran quickly over the rest of the page.

Artem!

We write to each other so seldom, once, or at best twice a year! But is it how often we write that matters? You write that you and your family have moved from Shepetovka to Kazatin railway yards because you wished to tear up your roots. I know that those roots lie in the backward, petty-proprietor psychology of Styosha and her relatives. It is hard to re-make people of Styosha's type, and I am very much afraid even you will not succeed. You say you are finding it hard to study 'in your old age,' yet you seem to be doing not so badly. You are wrong in your stubborn re-fusal to leave the factory and take up work as chairman of the City Sovi-et. You fought for the Power, didn't you? Then take it! Take over the City Soviet tomorrow and get to work!

Now about myself. Something is seriously wrong with me. I have be-come a far too frequent inmate in hospitals. They have cut me up twice, I have lost quite a bit of blood and strength, but nobody can tell me yet when it will all end.

I have been torn from my work and acquired a new profession, that of 'invalid.' I am enduring much pain, and the net result of all this is loss of movement in my right knee, several scars in various parts of my body, and now the latest medical discovery: seven years ago I injured my spine and now I am told that this injury may cost me dearly. But I am ready to endure anything so long as I can return to the ranks.

There is nothing more terrible to me in life than to fall out of the ranks. That is a possibility I refuse to contemplate. And that is why I let them do anything they like with me. But there is no improvement and the clouds get darker and thicker all the time. After the first operation I returned to work as soon as I could walk, but before long they brought me back again. Now I am being sent to a sanatorium in Eupatoria. I leave tomorrow. But don't be downhearted, Artem, you know I don't give up easily. I have life enough in me for three.

You and I will do good work yet, brother. Now take care of your health, don't try to overtax your strength, because health repairs cost the

*Party far too much. All the experience we gain in work, and the knowl-
edge we acquire by study is far too precious to be wasted in hospitals.*

I press your hand.

Pavel

While Artem, his heavy brows knitted, was reading his brother's
letter, Pavel was taking leave of Dr. Bazhanova in the hospital. "So
you are leaving for the Crimea tomorrow?" she said as she gave him
her hand. "How are you going to spend the rest of the day?"

"Comrade Rodkina is coming here soon," Pavel replied. "She is
taking me to her place to meet her family. I shall spend the night
there and tomorrow she will take me to the station." Bazhanova knew
Dora for she had often visited Pavel in the hospital. "But, Comrade
Korchagin, have you forgotten your promise to let my father see you
before you go? I have given him a detailed account of your illness and
I should like him to examine you. Perhaps you could manage it this
evening." Pavel agreed at once.

That evening Bazhanova showed Pavel into her father's spacious
office. The famous surgeon gave Pavel a careful examination. His
daughter had brought all the X-ray pictures and analyses from the
clinic. Pavel could not help noticing her sudden pallor when her father made some lengthy remark in Latin. Pavel stared at the professor's large bald head bent over him and searched his keen eyes, but
Bazhanov's expression was impenetrable.

When Pavel had dressed, the professor took leave of him cordial-
ly, explaining that he was due at a conference, and left his daughter to
inform Pavel of the result of his examination.

Pavel lay on the couch in Bazhanova's tastefully furnished room
waiting for the doctor to speak. But she did not know how to begin.
She could not bring herself to repeat what her father had told her –
that medicine was so far unable to check the disastrous inflammatory
process at work in Pavel's organism. The professor had been opposed

to an operation. "This young man is faced with the prospect of losing the use of his limbs and we are powerless to avert the tragedy."

She did not consider it wise either as doctor or friend to tell him the whole truth and so in carefully chosen words she told him only part of the truth. "I am certain, Comrade Korchagin, that the Eupatoria Mud will put you right and that by autumn you will be able to return to work." But she had forgotten that his sharp eye had been watching her all the time.

"From what you say, or rather from what you have not said, I see that the situation is grave. Remember I asked you always to be perfectly frank with me. You need not hide anything from me, I shan't faint or try to cut my throat. But I very much want to 'know what is in store for me." Bazhanova evaded a direct answer by making some cheerful remark and Pavel did not learn the truth about his future that night.

"Do not forget my friendship for you, Comrade Korchagin," the doctor said softly in parting. "Who knows what life has in store for us. If ever you need my help or my advice please write to me. I shall do everything in my power to help you."

Through the window she watched the tall leather-coated figure, leaning heavily on a stick, move painfully from the door to the waiting cab.

· · · ·

EUPATORIA AGAIN. THE hot southern sun. Noisy, sunburned people in embroidered skullcaps. A ten-minute drive brought the new arrivals to a two-story grey limestone building—the Mainak Sanatorium. The doctor on duty, learning that Pavel's accommodation had been reserved by the Central Committee of the Ukrainian Communist Party, took him up to room No. eleven.

"I shall put you in with Comrade Ebner. He is a German and he has asked for a Russian roommate," he explained as he knocked at the door. A voice with a heavy German accent sounded from within. "Come in." Pavel put down his travelling bag and turned to the fair-haired man with the lively blue eyes who was lying on the bed. The German met him with a warm smile. "Gutten Morgen, Genosse. I mean, gut day," he corrected himself, stretching a pale long-fingered hand to Pavel.

A few moments later Pavel was sitting by his bed and the two were engrossed in a lively conversation in that "international language" in which words play a minor role, and imagination, gestures and mimicry, all the media of the unwritten Esperanto, fill in the gaps. Pavel learned that Ebner was a German worker who had been wounded in the hip during the Hamburg uprising of nineteen-twenty-three. The old wound had reopened and he was confined to his bed. But he bore his sufferings cheerfully and that won Pavel's respect for him at once.

Pavel could not have wished for a better roommate. This one would not talk about his ailments from morning till night and bemoan his lot. On the contrary, with him one could forget one's own troubles. "Too bad I don't know any German, though," Pavel thought ruefully.

In a corner of the sanatorium grounds stood several rocking chairs, a bamboo table and two bath chairs. It was here that the five patients whom the others referred to as the "Executive of the Comintern"" were wont to spend their time after the day's medical treatments were over.

Ebner half reclined in one of the bath chairs. Pavel, who had also been forbidden to walk, in the other. The three other members of the group were Weiman, a thick-set Estonian, who worked at a Republican Commissariat of Trade, Marta Laurin, a young, brown-eyed Lettish woman who looked like a girl of eighteen, and Ledenev, a tall, powerfully-built Siberian with greying temples. This small group indeed represented five different nationalities –German, Estonian. Lettish, Russian and Ukrainian. Marta and Weiman spoke German and Ebner used them as interpreters. Pavel and Ebner were friends because they shared the same room; Marta, Weiman and Ebner, because they shared a common language. The bond between Ledenev and Korchagin was chess.

Before Ledenev arrived, Korchagin had been the sanatorium chess "champion." He had won the title from Weiman after a stiff struggle. The phlegmatic Estonian had been somewhat shaken by his defeat and for a long time he could not forgive Korchagin for having worsted him. But one day a tall man, looking remarkably young for his fifty years, turned up at the sanatorium and offered to play a game of chess with Korchagin. Pavel, having no inkling of danger, calmly began with a Queen's Gambit, which Ledenev countered by advancing his central pawns. As "champion" Pavel was obliged to play all new arrivals, and there was always a knot of interested spectators around the board. From the ninth move Pavel realized that his opponent was cramping him by steadily advancing his pawns. Pavel saw now that he had a dangerous opponent and began to regret that he had treated the game so lightly at the start.

After a three-hour tussle during which Pavel exerted all his skill and ingenuity he was obliged to give up. He foresaw his defeat long before any of the onlookers. He glanced up at his opponent and saw Ledenev looking at him with a kindly smile. It was clear that he too saw how the game would end. The Estonian, who was following the game tensely and making no secret of his desire to see Korchagin defeated, was still unaware of what was happening.

"I always hold out to my last pawn," Pavel said, and Ledenev nodded approvingly. Pavel played ten games with Ledenev in five days, losing seven, winning two and drawing one. Weiman was jubilant. "Thank you. Comrade Ledenev, thank you! That was a wonderful thrashing you gave him! He deserved it! He knocked out all of us old chess players and now he's been paid back by an old man himself. Ha!

Ha!" "How does it feel to be the loser, eh?" he teased the now van-
quished victor. Pavel lost the title of "champion" but won in Ledenev
a friend who was later to become very precious to him. He saw now
that his defeat on the chessboard was only to have been expected. His
knowledge of chess strategy had been purely superficial and he had
lost to an expert who knew all the secrets of the game.

Korchagin and Ledenev found that they had one important date
in common: Pavel was born the year Ledenev joined the Party. Both
were typical representatives of the young and old guard of Bolsheviks.
The one had behind him a long life of intensive political activity,
years of work in the underground movement and tsarist imprison-
ment, followed by important government work; the other had his
flaming youth and only eight years of struggle, but years that could
have burnt up more than one life. And both of them, the old man and
the young, were avid of life and broken in health.

In the evenings the room shared by Ebner and Korchagin became
a sort of club. All the political news emanated from here. The room
rang with laughter and talk. Weiman usually tried to insert a bawdy
anecdote into the conversation but invariably found himself attacked
from two sides, by Marta and Korchagin. As a rule Marta was able to
restrain him by some sharp sarcastic remark, but when this did not
help Korchagin would intervene. "Your particular brand of 'humour'
is not exactly to our taste, you know, Weiman," Marta would say.

"In general, I can't understand how you can stoop to that sort of
thing," Korchagin would begin with mounting anger. Weiman would
stick out his thick underlip and survey the gathering with a mocking
glint in his small eyes.

"We shall have to set up a department of morals under the Political Enlightenment Department and recommend Korchagin as chief
inspector. I can understand why Marta objects, she is the professional
feminine opposition, but Korchagin is just trying to pose as a young

innocent, a sort of Komsomol babe in the woods.... What's more, I object to the egg trying to teach the hen."

After one heated debate on the question of communist ethics, the matter of obscene jokes was discussed from the standpoint of principle. Marta translated to Ebner the various views expressed. "Die erotische Anekdote ," he said, "is no gut. I agree with Pavel." Weiman was obliged to retreat. He laughed the matter off as best he could, but told no more smutty stories.

Pavel had taken Marta for a Komsomol member, judging her to be no more than nineteen. What was his surprise when he learned that she had been in the Party since nineteen-seventeen, that she was thirty-one and an active member of the Latvian Communist Party. In nineteen-eighteen the Whites had sentenced her to be shot, but she had eventually been turned over to the Soviet Government along with some other comrades in an exchange of prisoners. She was now working on the editorial staff of Pravda and taking a university course at the same time. Before Pavel was aware of it a friendship sprang up between them, and the little Lettish woman who often dropped in to see Ebner, became an inseparable member of the "five."

Eglit, a Latvian underground worker, liked to tease her on this score. "What about poor Ozol pining away at home in Moscow? Oh Marta, how can you?"

One morning, just before the bell to rise sounded, a lusty cock crow rang out over the sanatorium. The puzzled attendants ran hither and thither in search of the errant bird. It never occurred to them that Ebner, who could give a perfect imitation of a cock crow, was having a little joke at their expense. This was repeated for several mornings and Ebner enjoyed himself immensely.

Toward the end of his month's stay in the sanatorium Pavel's condition took a turn for the worse. The doctors ordered him to bed. Ebner was much upset. He had grown very fond of this courageous young Bolshevik, so full of life and energy, who had lost his health so early in life. And when Marta told him of the tragic future the doctors predicted for Korchagin, Ebner was deeply distressed.

Pavel was confined to his bed for the remainder of his stay in the sanatorium. He managed to hide his suffering from those around him, and Marta alone guessed by his ghastly pallor that he must be in pain. A week before his departure Pavel received a letter from the Ukrainian Central Committee informing him that his leave had been prolonged for two months on the advice of the sanatorium doctors who declared him unfit for work. Money to cover his expenses arrived along with the letter.

Pavel took this first blow as years before during his boxing lessons he had taken Zhukhrai's punches. Then too he had fallen only to rise again at once.

A letter came from his mother asking him to go and see an old friend of hers, Albina Kyutsam, who lived in a small port town not far from Eupatoria. Pavel's mother had not seen her friend for fifteen years and she begged him to pay her a visit while he was in the Crimea. This letter was to play an important role in Pavel's life.

· · · ·

A WEEK LATER HIS SANATORIUM friends gave him a warm send-off at the pier. Ebner embraced him and kissed him like a brother. Marta was away at the time and Pavel left without saying goodbye to her. The next morning the horse cab which brought Pavel from the pier drove up to a little house fronted by a small garden.

The Kyutsam family consisted of five people: Albina the mother, a plump elderly woman with dark, mournful eyes and traces of beauty on her aging face, her two daughters, Lola and Taya, Lola's little son, and old Kyutsam, the head of the house, a burly, unpleasant old man resembling a boar.

Old Kyutsam worked in a co-operative store. Taya, the younger girl, did any odd job that came along, and Lola, who had been a typist, had recently separated from her husband, a drunkard and a bully, and now stayed at home to look after her little boy and help her mother with the housework.

Besides the two daughters, there was a son named George, who was away in Leningrad at the time of Pavel's arrival. The family gave Pavel a warm welcome. Only the old man eyed the visitor with hostility and suspicion. Pavel patiently told Albina all the family news, and in his turn learned a good deal about life in the Kyutsam menage.

Lola was twenty-two. A simple girl, with bobbed brown hair and a broad-featured, open face, she at once took Pavel into her confidence and initiated him into all the family secrets. She told him that the old man ruled the whole family with a despotic hand, suppressing the slightest manifestation of independence on the part of the others. Narrow-minded, bigoted and captious, he kept the family in a permanent state of terror. This had earned him the deep dislike of his children and the hatred of his wife who had fought vainly against his despotism for twenty-five years. The girls always took their mother's side. These incessant family quarrels were poisoning their lives.

Days passed in endless bickering and strife. Another bane of the family existence, Lola told Pavel, was her brother George, a typical good-for-nothing, boastful, arrogant, caring for nothing but good food, strong drink and smart clothes. When he finished school, George, who had been his mother's favourite, announced that he was going to the capital and demanded money for the trip. "I'm going to university. Lola can sell her ring and you've got some things you can raise money on too. I need the money and I don't care how you get it."

George knew very well that his mother would refuse him nothing and he shamelessly took advantage of her affection for him. He treated his sisters with lofty condescension, considering them his inferiors. The mother sent her son all the money she could wheedle out of her husband, and whatever Taya earned besides. In the meantime

George, having flunked the entrance examinations, had a pleasant time in Leningrad staying with his uncle and terrorizing his mother by frequent telegraphic demands for more money.

Pavel did not meet Taya until late in the evening of his arrival. Her mother hurried out to meet her in the hallway and Pavel heard her whispering the news of his coming. The girl shook hands shyly with the strange young man, blushing to the tips of her small ears, and Pavel held her strong, calloused little hand for a few moments before releasing it.

Taya was in her nineteenth year. She was not beautiful, yet with her large brown eyes, and her slanting, Mongolian brows, fine nose and full fresh lips she was very attractive. Her firm young breasts stood out under her striped blouse.

The sisters had two tiny rooms to themselves. In Taya's room there was a narrow iron cot, a chest of drawers covered with knick-knacks, a small mirror, and dozens of photographs and postcards on the walls. On the window sill stood two flower pots with scarlet geraniums and pale pink asters. The lace curtain was caught up by a pale blue ribbon.

"Taya does not usually admit members of the male sex to her room. She is making an exception for you," Lola teased her sister.

The next evening the family was seated at tea in the old couple's half of the house. Kyutsam stirred his tea busily, glancing up now and again over his spectacles at the visitor seated opposite him. "I don't think much of the marriage laws nowadays," he said. "Married one day, unmarried the next. Just as you please. Complete freedom."

The old man choked and spluttered. When he recovered his breath he pointed to Lola. "Look at her, she and that fine fellow of hers got married without asking anyone's permission and separated the same way. And now it's me who's got to feed her and her brat. An outrage I call it!" Lola blushed painfully and hid her tear-filled eyes from Pavel. "So you think she ought to live with that scoundrel?" Pavel asked and there was a wild gleam in his eye.

"She should have known whom she was marrying." Albina intervened. Barely repressing her wrath, she said quickly: "why must you discuss such things before a stranger? Can't you find anything else to talk about?" The old man turned and pounced on her: "I know what I'm talking about! Since when have you begun to tell me what to do!"

That night Pavel lay awake for long time thinking about the Kyutsams. Brought here by chance, he had unwittingly become a participant in this family drama. He wondered how he could help the mother and daughters to free themselves from this bondage. His own life was far from settled, many problems remained to be solved and it was harder than ever before to take resolute action.

There was clearly but one way out: the family had to break up, the mother and daughters must leave the old man. But this was not so simple. Pavel was in no position to undertake this family revolution, for he was due to leave in a few days and he might never see these people again. Was it not better to let things take their course instead of trying to stir these turbid backwaters? But the repulsive image of the old man gave him no rest. Several plans occurred to Pavel but on second thoughts he discarded them all as impracticable.

The next day was Sunday and when Pavel returned from a walk in town he found Taya alone at home. The others were out visiting relatives. Pavel went to her room and dropped wearily onto a chair. "Why don't you ever go out and enjoy yourself?" he asked her. "I don't want to go anywhere," she replied in a low voice. He remembered the plans he had thought of during the night and decided to put them before her. Speaking quickly so as to finish before the others returned, he went straight to the point. "Listen, Taya, you and I are good friends. Why should we stand on ceremony with each other? I am going away soon. It is a pity that I should have come to know your family just at the time when I myself am in trouble, otherwise things might have turned out differently. If this happened a year ago we could all leave here together. There is plenty of work everywhere for people like you and Lola. The old man is another matter, you can't make him see reason. But there is nothing to be done at present in any case. I don't know yet what is going to happen to me. I am helpless at the moment. But that can't be helped. I am going to insist on being sent back to work. The doctors have written all sorts of nonsense about me and the comrades are trying to make me cure myself endlessly. But we'll see about that... I shall write to mother and get her advice about your trouble here. I can't let things go on this way. But you must realize, Taya, that this will mean wrenching yourselves loose from your present life. Would you want that, and would you have the strength to go through with it?"

Taya looked up. "I want it," she said softly. "As for the strength, I don't know." Pavel could understand her uncertainty. "Never mind, Taya! So long as the desire is there everything will be all right. Tell me, are you very much attached to your family?"

The question took Taya by surprise and she hesitated for a moment. "I am very sorry for mother," she said at last. "Father has made her life miserable and now George is torturing her. I'm terribly sorry for her, although she never loved me as much as she does George..."

They had a long heart to heart talk. Shortly before the rest of the family returned, Pavel remarked jokingly: "it's surprising the old man hasn't married you off to someone by now."

Taya threw up her hands in horror at the thought. "Oh no, I'll never marry. I've seen what poor Lola has been through. I shan't get married for anything."

Pavel laughed. "So you've settled the matter for the rest of your life? And what if some fine, handsome young fellow comes along, what then?"

"No, I won't. They're all fine, while they're courting." Pavel laid a conciliatory hand on her shoulder. "That's all right, Taya. You can get along quite well without a husband. But you needn't be so hard on the young men. It's a good thing you don't suspect me of trying to court you, or there'd be trouble," and he patted her arm in brotherly fashion.

"Men like you marry girls of a different sort," she said softly.

. . . .

A FEW DAYS LATER PAVEL left for Kharkov. Taya, Lola and Albina with her sister Rosa came to the station to see him off. Albina made him promise not to forget her daughters and to help them all to find some way out of their plight. They took leave of him as of someone near and dear to them, and there were tears in Taya's eyes. From the window of his car Pavel watched Lola's white kerchief and Taya's striped blouse grow smaller and smaller until they finally disappeared.

On arrival in Kharkov he went straight to his friend Petya Novikov's place, for he did not want to disturb Dora. As soon as he had rested from the journey he went to the Central Committee. There he waited for Akim, and when at last the two were alone, he asked to be sent at once to work. Akim shook his head. "Can't be done, Pavel! We have the decision of the medical commission and the Central Committee which says that in view of the serious condition of your health you're to be sent to the Neuropathological Institute for treatment and not to be permitted to work."

"What do I care what they say, Akim! I am appealing to you. Give me a chance to work! This moving about from clinic to clinic does me no good." Akim tried to refuse. "We can't go against the decision. Don't you see it's for your own good, Pavlusha?" he argued. But Pavel pleaded his cause so fervently that Akim finally gave in.

The very next day Pavel was working in the Special Department of the Central Committee Secretariat. He believed that he had only to begin working for his lost strength to return to him. But he soon saw that he had been mistaken. He sat at his desk for eight hours at a stretch without pausing for lunch simply because the effort of going down three flights of stairs to the public dining room across the way was too much for him. Very often his hand or his leg would suddenly go numb, and at times his whole body would be paralyzed for a few moments. He was nearly always feverish. On some mornings he found himself powerless to rise from his bed, and by the time the attack passed, he realized in despair that he would be a whole hour late for work. Finally the day came when he was officially reprimanded for reporting late for work and he saw that this was the beginning of what he dreaded most in life—he was falling out of the ranks.

Twice Akim helped him by shifting him to other work, but the inevitable happened. A month after his return to work Pavel was confined to his bed again. It was then that he remembered Bazhanova's parting words. He wrote to her and she came the same day, and told him what he had wanted to know: that hospitalisation was not imperative.

"So things are going so well with me that I don't need any treatment, eh?" he said lightly, but the joke fell flat. As soon as he felt a little stronger he went back to the Central Committee. This time Akim was adamant. He insisted on Pavel's going to the hospital.

"I'm not going anywhere," Pavel said wearily. "It's useless. I have it on excellent authority. There is only one thing left for me – to get a pension and retire. But that I will not do! You can't make me give up my work. I am only twenty-four and I'm not going to live out my life as a labour invalid, roaming from hospital to hospital knowing that it won't do me any good. You must give me something to do, some work suitable to my condition. I can work at home, or I can live in the office. Only don't give me any pen pushing to do, putting numbers on outgoing papers. I've got to have work that will give me the satisfaction of knowing that I am still of some use."

Pavel's voice, vibrant with emotion, rose higher and higher. Akim felt keenly for Pavel. He knew what a tragedy it was for this passionate-hearted youth who had given the whole of his short life to the Party, to reconcile himself to the thought of being cut off from the struggle and forced to retire deep into the rear. He resolved to do all he could to help him.

"All right, Pavel, calm yourself. There will be a meeting of the Secretariat tomorrow and I'll put your case before the comrades. I give my word that I will do all I can." Pavel rose heavily and seized Akim's hand. "Do you really think, Akim, that life can drive me into a corner and crush me? So long as my heart beats here" – and he pressed Akim's hand to his chest so that he could feel the dull pounding of his heart – "so long as it beats, no one will be able to tear me away from the Party. Death alone can put me out of the ranks. Try to remember that, my friend."

Akim said nothing. He knew that this was not merely an empty phrase. It was the cry of a soldier grievously wounded in battle. He knew that people like Korchagin could not speak or feel otherwise.

Two days later Akim told Pavel that he was to be given an opportunity to work on the staff of a big newspaper, provided, of course, it was found that he could be used for literary work. Pavel was courteously received at the editorial office and was interviewed by the assistant editor, an old Party worker, and member of the Presidium of the Central Control Committee of the Ukraine.

"What education have you had. Comrade?" she asked him. "Three years of elementary school." "Have you been to any of the Party political schools?" "No." "Well, some people have been known to make good journalists without that. Comrade Akim has told us about you. We can give you work to do at home, and in general, we are prepared to provide you with suitable conditions for work. But work of this kind requires considerable knowledge. Particularly in the sphere of literature and language."

All this foreboded defeat to Pavel. The half-hour interview showed him that his knowledge was inadequate, and the trial article he wrote was returned to him with some three dozen stylistic and spelling mistakes marked in red pencil.

"You have considerable ability. Comrade Korchagin," said the editor, "and with some hard work you might learn to write quite well. But at the present time your grammar is faulty. Your article shows that you do not know the Russian language well enough. That is not surprising considering that you have had no time to learn it. Unfortunately we can't use you, although as I said before, you have ability. If your article were edited, without altering the contents, it would be excellent. But, you see, we need people who can edit other people's articles."

Korchagin rose, leaning heavily on his stick. His right eyebrow twitched. "Yes, I see your point. What sort of a journalist would I make? I was a good stoker once, and not a bad electrician. I rode a horse well, and I knew how to stir up the Komsomol youth, but I can see I would cut a sorry figure on your front." He shook hands and left.

At a turning in the corridor he stumbled and would have fallen had he not been caught by a woman who happened to be passing by. "What's the matter. Comrade? You look quite ill!" It took Pavel several seconds to come to himself. Then he gently pushed the woman aside and walked on, leaning heavily on his stick.

From that day Pavel felt that his life was on the decline. Work was now out of the question. More and more often he was confined to his bed. The Central Committee released him from work and arranged for his pension. In due time the pension came together with the certificate of a labour invalid. The Central Committee gave him money and issued him his papers giving him the right to go wherever he wished.

He received a letter from Marta inviting him to come to visit her in Moscow and have a rest. Pavel had intended going to Moscow in any case, for he cherished the dim hope that the All-Union Central Committee would help him to find work that would not require moving around. But in Moscow too he was advised to take medical treatment and offered accommodation in a good hospital. He refused.

The nineteen days spent in the flat Marta shared with her friend Nadya Peterson flew quickly by. Pavel was left a great deal to himself, for the two young women left the house in the morning for work and did not return till evening. Pavel spent his time reading books from Maria's well-stocked library. The evenings passed pleasantly in the company of the girls and their friends.

Letters came from the Kyutsams inviting him to come and visit them. Life there was becoming unendurable and his help was wanted.

And so one morning Korchagin left the quiet little flat on Gusyatnikov Street. The train bore him swiftly south to the sea, away from the damp rainy autumn to the warm shores of the southern Crimea. He sat at the window watching the telegraph poles fly past. His brows were knit and there was an obstinate gleam in his dark eyes.

CHAPTER EIGHT

D own below, the sea broke on the jagged chaos of rock. A stiff dry breeze blowing from distant Turkey fanned his face. The harbour, protected from the sea by a concrete mole, thrust itself in an irregular arc into the shoreline. And overlooking it all were the tiny white cottages of the town's outskirts perched on the slopes of the mountain range which broke off abruptly at the sea.

It was quiet here in the old park outside of the town. Yellow maple leaves floated slowly down onto its grass-grown paths. The old Persian cabby who had driven Pavel out here from town could not help asking as his strange fare alighted: "why come here of all places? No young ladies, no amusements. Nothing but the jackals... What will you do here? Better let me drive you back to town, Mister Tovarish!" Pavel paid him and the old man drove away.

The park was indeed a wilderness. Pavel found a bench on a cliff overlooking the sea, and sat down, lifting his face to the now mild autumn sun. He had come to this quiet spot to think over the course his life was taking and consider what was to be done. The time had come to review the situation and take some decision.

His second visit to the Kyutsams had brought the family strife to a head. The old man on learning of his arrival had flown into a rage and raised a terrific rumpus. It fell naturally to Korchagin to lead the resistance. The old man unexpectedly encountered a vigorous rebuff from his wife and daughters, and from the first day of Pavel's arrival the house split into two hostile camps. The door leading to the parents' half of the house was locked and one of the small side rooms was rented to Korchagin. Pavel paid the rent in advance and the old man was somewhat mollified by the arrangement; now that his daughters had cut themselves off from him be would no longer be expected to support them.

For diplomatic reasons Albina remained with her husband. As for the old man, he kept strictly to his side of the house and avoided meeting the man he so heartily detested. But outside in the yard he made as much noise as possible to show that he was still the master.

Before he went to work in the co-operative shop old Kyutsam had earned his living by shoemaking and carpentering and had built himself a small workshop in the backyard. Now to annoy his lodger, he shifted his work bench from the shed to a spot in the yard right under Pavel's window where he hammered furiously for hours on end, deriving a malicious satisfaction from the knowledge that he was interfering with Korchagin's reading. "Just you wait," he hissed to himself, "I'll get you out of here...."

Far away a steamer laid a small dark trail of smoke over the water at the very horizon. A flock of gulls hurled themselves seawards with piercing screams. Pavel, his chin resting in his hand, sat lost in thought. His whole life passed swiftly before his mind's eye, from his childhood to the present. How had these twenty-four years of his been lived? Worthily or unworthily ? He went over them again, year by year, subjecting them to sober, impartial judgment, and he found to his immense relief that he had not done so badly with his life. Mistakes there had been, the mistakes of youthful inexperience, and chiefly of ignorance. But in the stormy days of struggle for Soviet power he had been in the thick of the fighting and on the crimson banner of revolution there were a few drops of his own life's blood.

He had remained in the ranks until his strength had failed him. And now, struck down and unable to hold his place in the firing lines, there was nothing left for him but the field hospital. He remembered the time when they had stormed Warsaw and how, at the height of battle, one of the men had been hit. He fell to the ground under his horse's hooves. His comrades quickly bandaged his wounds, turned him over to the stretcher-bearers and sped onward in pursuit of the enemy. The squadron had not halted its advance for the sake of one fallen soldier. Thus it was in the fight for a great cause and thus it had to be. True, he had seen legless machine gunners riding into battle on gun carriages. These men had struck terror into the enemy's ranks, their guns had sown death and destruction, and their steel-like courage and unerring eye had made them the pride of their units. But such men were few.

What was he to do now that defeat had overtaken him and there was no longer any hope of returning to the ranks? Had he not extracted from Bazhanova the admission that the future held even worse torment in store for him? What was to be done? The unsettled question was like a yawning abyss spreading at his feet.

What was there to live for now that he had lost what he prized most – the ability to fight? How justify his existence today and in the cheerless tomorrow? How was he to fill his days? Exist merely to breathe, to eat and to drink? Remain a helpless bystander watching his comrades fight their way forward? Be a burden to the detachment? Were it not better to destroy the body that had betrayed him? A bullet in the heart – and be done with it! A timely end to a life well lived. Who would condemn the soldier for putting himself out of his agony?

He felt the flat body of his Browning in his pocket. His fingers closed over the grip, and slowly he drew out the weapon. "Who would have thought that you would come to this?" The muzzle stared back at him with cold contempt. Pavel laid the pistol on his knee and cursed bitterly. "Cheap heroics, my lad! Any fool can shoot himself. That is the easiest way out, the coward's way. You can always put a bullet through your head when life hits you too hard. But have you tried getting the better of life? Are you sure you have done everything you can to break out of the steel trap? Have you forgotten the fighting at Novograd-Volynsky when we went into the attack seventeen times a day until finally, in spite of everything, we won through? Put away that gun and never breathe a word of this to anyone. Learn how to go on living when life becomes unbearable. Make your life useful."

He got up and went down to the road. A passing mountaineer gave him a lift on his cart. When they reached town he got off and bought a newspaper and read the announcement of a meeting of the city Party group in the Demyan Bedny Club. It was very late when Pavel returned home that night. He had made a speech at the meeting, little suspecting that it was the last he was ever to make at a large public gathering.

• • • •

TAYA WAS STILL AWAKE when he got home. She had been worried at Pavel's prolonged absence. What had happened to him, she wondered anxiously, remembering the grim, cold look she had observed that morning in his eyes, always so live and warm. He never liked to talk about himself, but she felt that he was under some severe mental strain.

As the clock in her mother's room chimed two she heard the gate creak and, slipping on her jacket, she went to open the door. Lola, asleep in her own room, murmured restlessly as Taya passed her. "I was beginning to get worried," Taya whispered with glad relief when Pavel entered the hallway. "Nothing is going to happen to me as long as I live, Taya," he whispered. "Lola's asleep? I am not the least bit sleepy for some reason. I have something to tell you. Let's go to your room so as not to wake Lola."

Taya hesitated. It was very late. How could she let him come to her room at this late hour? What would mother think? But she could not refuse for fear of offending him. What could he have to say to her, she wondered, as she led the way to her room. "This is how it is, Taya," Pavel began in a low voice. He sat down opposite her in the dimly-lighted room, so close that she could feel his breath. "Life takes such strange turns that you begin to wonder sometimes. I have had a rotten time of it these past few days. I could not see how I could go on living. Never had life seemed so dark as lately. But today I held a meeting of my own private 'political bureau' and adopted a decision of tremendous importance. Don't be surprised at what I have to say."

He told her what he had gone through in the past few months and much of what had passed through his mind during his visit to the park. "That is the situation. Now for the most important thing. The storm in this family is only beginning. We must get out of here into the fresh air and as far away from this hole as possible. We must start life afresh. Once I have taken a hand in this fight I'm going to see it through. Our life, yours and mine, is none too happy at present. I have decided to breathe some warmth into it. Do you know what I mean? Will you be my life's companion, my wife?"

Taya, who had been listening to him with bated breath, started at these last words. "I am not asking you for an answer tonight," he went on. "You must think it over carefully. I suppose you cannot understand how such things can be put so bluntly without the usual courting and all that. But you and I have no need of all that nonsense. I give you my hand, young woman, here it is. If you will put your trust in me you will not be mistaken. We can both give each other a great deal. Now here is what I have decided: our compact will be in force until you grow up to be a real human being, a true Bolshevik. If I can't help you in that I am not worth a kopek. We must not break our compact until then. But when you grow up you will be freed of all obligations. Who knows what may happen? I may become a complete physical wreck, and in that case, remember – you must not consider yourself bound to me in any way."

He fell silent for a few moments, then he went on in a tender, caressing voice: "And for the present, I offer you my friendship and my love." He held her fingers in his, feeling at peace, as if she had already given her consent.

"Do you promise never to leave me?" "I can only give you my word, Taya. It is for you to believe that men like me do not betray their friends...I only hope they will not betray me," he added bitterly. "I can't give you an answer tonight. It is all very sudden," she replied. Pavel got up. "Go to bed, Taya. It will soon be morning." He went to his own room and lay down on the bed without undressing and was asleep as soon as his head touched the pillow.

The desk by the window in Pavel's room was piled high with books from the Party library, newspapers and several notebooks filled with notes. A bed, two chairs and a huge map of China dotted with tiny black and red flags pinned up over the door between his room and Taya's completed the furnishings. The people in the local Party Committee had agreed to supply Pavel with books and periodicals and had promised to instruct the manager of the biggest public library in town to send him whatever he needed. Before long large parcels of books began to arrive. Lola was amazed at the way he would sit over his books from early morning, reading and making notes all day long with only short breaks for breakfast and dinner. In the evenings, which he always spent with the two girls, he would relate to them what he had read.

Long past midnight old Kyutsam would see a chink of light between the shutters of the room occupied by his unwelcome lodger. He would creep over to the window on tiptoe and peer in through the crack at the head bending over the table.

"Decent folks are in their beds at this hour but he keeps the light burning all night long. He behaves as if he were the master here. The girls have got altogether out of hand since he came," the old man would grumble to himself as he retired to his own quarters.

For the first time in eight years Pavel found himself with plenty of time on his hands, and no duties of any kind to attend to. He made good use of his time, reading with the avid eagerness of the newly enlightened. He studied eighteen hours a day. How much longer his health could have withstood the strain is hard to say, but a, seemingly casual remark from Taya one day changed everything.

"I have moved the chest of drawers away from the door leading to your room. If ever you want to talk to me you can come straight in. You don't need to go through Lola's room."

The blood rushed to Pavel's cheeks. Taya smiled happily. Their compact was sealed.

• • • •

THE OLD MAN NO LONGER saw the chink of light through the shuttered window of the corner room, and Taya's mother began to notice a glow in her daughter's eyes that betrayed a happiness she could not conceal. The faint shadows under her eyes spoke of sleepless nights. Often now Taya's singing and the strumming of a guitar echoed through the little house.

Yet Taya's happiness was not unmarred; her awakened womanhood rebelled against the clandestine nature of their relationship. She trembled at every sound, fancying that she heard her mother's footsteps. What if they asked her why she had taken to closing her door on the latch at night? The thought tormented her. Pavel noticed her fears and he tried to comfort her.

"What are you afraid of?" he would say tenderly. "After all, you and I are the masters here. Sleep in peace. No one shall intrude on our lives."

Comforted, she would press her cheek against his breast, and fall asleep, her arms around her loved one. And he would lie awake, listening to her steady breathing, keeping quite still lest he disturb her slumber, his whole being flooded with a deep tenderness for this girl who had entrusted her life to him. Lola was the first to discover the reason for the shining light in Taya's eyes, and from that day the shadow of estrangement fell between the two sisters. Soon the mother too found out, or rather, guessed. And she was troubled. She had not expected it of Korchagin.

"Taya is not the wife for him," she remarked to Lola. "What will come of it, I wonder?" Alarming thoughts beset her but she could not muster the courage to speak to Korchagin.

Young people began visiting Pavel, and sometimes his little room could barely hold them all. The sound of their voices like the beehive's hum reached the old man's ears and often he could hear them singing in chorus:

Forbidding is this sea of ours
Night and day its angry voice is heard...

and Pavel's favourite:

The whole wide world is drenched with tears...

It was the study circle of young workers which the Party Committee had assigned to Pavel in response to his insistent request for propaganda work. Thus Pavel's days were spent.

Once more he had gripped the helm firmly with both hands, and the ship of life, having veered dangerously a few times, was now steering a new course. His dream of returning to the ranks through study and learning was on the way to being realised. But life continued to heap obstacles in his path, and bitterly he saw each obstacle as a further delay to the attainment of his goal.

One day the ill-starred student George turned up from Moscow bringing a wife with him. He put up at the house of his father-in-law, a barrister, and from there he asked his mother for money.

George's coming widened the rift in the Kyutsam family. George unhesitatingly sided with his father, and together with his wife's family, which was inclined to be anti-Soviet, he sought by underhand means to drive Korchagin out of the house and induce Taya to break with him.

Two weeks after George's arrival Lola got a job in another town and she left, taking her mother and her little son with her. Soon afterward, Pavel and Taya moved to a distant seaside town.

Artem did not often receive letters from his brother but on those rare occasions when he found an envelope with the familiar handwriting waiting for him on his desk in the City Soviet he scanned its pages with an emotion unusual in him. Today too as he opened the envelope he thought tenderly:

"Ah, Pavel! If only you lived nearer to me. I could do with your advice, lad." He read:

Artem

I am writing to tell you all that has happened to me lately. I do not write such things to anyone but you. But I know I can confide in you because you know me well and you will understand.

Life continues to press down on me on the health front dealing me blow upon blow. Barely have I struggled to my feet after one blow then another, more merciless than the last, lays me low. The most terrible thing is that I am powerless to resist. First I lost the power of my left arm. And now, as if that were not enough, my legs have failed me. I could barely move about (within the limits of the room, of course) as it was, but now I have difficulty in crawling from bed to table. And I daresay there is worse to come. What tomorrow will bring me no one knows.

I never leave the house now, and only a tiny fragment of the sea is visible from my window. Can there be anything more tragic than the combination in one human being of a treacherous body that refuses to obey him, and the heart of a Bolshevik, a Bolshevik who yearns for work, longs to be beside you in the ranks of the fighters advancing along the whole front in the midst of the stormy avalanche?

I still believe that I shall return to the ranks, that in time my bayonet will take its place in the attacking columns. I must believe that, I have no right not to. For ten years the Party and the Komsomol taught me to fight, and the leader's words, spoken to all of us, apply equally to me: 'There are no fortresses Bolsheviks cannot take.'

My life now is spent entirely in study. Books, books and more books. I have accomplished a great deal, Artem. I have read and studied all the classics, and have passed my examinations in the first year of the correspondence course at the Communist University. In the evenings I lead a study circle of Communist youth. These young comrades are my link with the practical life of the Party organization. Then there is Taya, whose political education and general enlightenment I am doing my best to promote. And then of course there is love, and the tender caresses of my wife. Taya and I are the best of friends. Our household is very simply run – with my pension of thirty-two roubles and Taya's earnings we get along quite well. Taya is following the path I myself took to the Party: for a time she worked as a domestic servant, and now has a job as a dishwasher in a public dining room (there is no industry in this town).

The other day she proudly showed me her first delegate's credentials issued by the women's department. This is not simply a strip of cardboard to her. In her I see the birth of the new, and I am doing my best to help in this birth. The next step is work in a big factory, where as part of a large working community she will gradually attain political maturity. But she is taking the only possible course open to her here.

Taya's mother has visited us twice. Unconsciously she is trying to drag Taya back to a life of trivialities, burdened down and hemmed in by the personal individualistic approach to reality. I tried to make Albina see that she ought not to allow the shadow of her own wretched past darken the path her daughter has chosen. But it was no use. I feel that one day the mother will try to stand in her daughter's way and then a clash will be unavoidable. I press your hand.

Your Pavel.

Sanatorium No. Five in Old Matsesta... A three-story brick building standing on a ledge hewed into the mountainside. Thick woods all around and a road winding dizzily down to the sea. The windows are open and the breeze carries the smell of the sulphur springs into the room. Pavel Korchagin is alone in the room. Tomorrow new patients will arrive and then he will have a roommate. He hears steps outside the window and the sound of a familiar voice. Several people are talking. But where has he heard that deep bass voice before? From the dim recesses of his memory, hidden away but not forgotten, comes the name: "Ledenev Innokenti Pavlovich. He and none other."

Pavel confidently called to his friend, and a moment later Ledenev was beside his bed shaking his hand warmly. "So Korchagin is still going strong? Well, and what have you got to say for yourself? Don't tell me you have decided to get sick in real earnest? That will never do! You should take an example from me. The doctors have tried to put me on the shelf too, but I keep going just to spite them." And Ledenev laughed merrily.

But Pavel felt the sympathy and distress hidden behind that laughter. They spent two hours together. Ledenev told Pavel all the latest news from Moscow. From him Pavel first heard of the important decisions taken by the Party on the collectivisation of agriculture and the reorganisation of life in the village and he eagerly drank in every word. "Here I was thinking you were busy stirring things up somewhere at home in the Ukraine," said Ledenev. "You disappoint me. But never mind, I was in an even worse way. I thought I'd be tied to my bed for good, and now you see I'm still on my feet. There's no taking life easy nowadays. It simply won't work! I must confess I find myself thinking sometimes how nice it would be to take a little rest, just to catch your breath. After all, I'm not as young as I was, and working ten and twelve hours a day is a bit hard on me at times. Well, I think about it for a while and even set about trying to ease the load a little, but it always ends the same way. Before you know it, you're up to your ears again never getting home before midnight. The more powerful the machine, the faster the wheels run, and with us the speed increases every day, so that we old folk simply have to stay young."

Ledenev passed a hand over his high forehead and said in a kindly manner: "and now tell me about yourself."

Pavel gave Ledenev an account of his life since they had last met, and as he talked he felt his friend's warm approving glance on him.

· · · ·

UNDER THE SHADE OF spreading trees in one corner of the terrace a group of sanatorium patients were seated around a small table. One of them was reading Pravda , his bushy eyebrows knitted. The black Russian shirt, the shabby old cap and the unshaven face with the deep-sunken blue eyes all bespoke the veteran miner. It was twelve years since Khrisanf Chernokozov left the mines to take up an important post in the government, yet he seemed to have just come up from the pit. Everything about him, his bearing, his gait, his manner of speaking, betrayed his profession.

Chernokozov was a member of the Territorial Party Bureau and a member of the government. A painful disease was sapping his strength: Chernokozov hated his gangrenous leg which had kept him tied to his bed for nearly half a year now. Opposite him, puffing thoughtfully on her cigarette, was Zhigareva—Alexandra Alexeyevna Zhigareva, a Party member for nineteen of her thirty-seven years. "Shurochka, the metalworker," as her comrades in the Petersburg Underground movement used to call her, was little more than a girl when she had been exiled to Siberia.

The third member of the group was Pankov. His handsome head with the sculptured profile was bent over a German magazine, and now and then he raised his hand to adjust his enormous horn-rimmed spectacles. It was painful to see this thirty-year-old man of athletic build dragging his paralyzed leg after him. An editor and writer, Pankov worked in the People's Commissariat of Education.

He was an authority on Europe and knew several foreign languages. He was a man of considerable erudition and even the reserved Chernokozov treated him with great respect.

"So that is your roommate?" Zhigareva whispered to Chernokozov, nodding toward the chair in which Pavel Korchagin was seated. Chernokozov looked up from his newspaper and his brow cleared at once "Yes! That's Korchagin. You ought to know him, Shura. It's too bad illness has put a spoke in his wheel, otherwise that lad would be a great help to us. He belongs to the first Komsomol generation. I am convinced that if we give him our support – and that's what I have decided to do – he will still be able to work."

Pankov too listened to what Chernokozov was saying. "What is he suffering from?" Shura Zhigareva asked softly. "The aftermath of the Civil War. Some trouble with his spine. I spoke to the doctor here and he told me that there is a danger of total paralysis. Poor lad!" "I shall go and bring him over here," said Shura.

That was the beginning of their friendship. Pavel did not know then that Zhigareva and Chernokozov were to become very dear to him and that in the years of illness ahead of him they were to be his mainstays.

· · · ·

LIFE FLOWED ON AS BEFORE. Taya worked and Pavel studied. Before he had time to resume his work with the study groups another disaster stole upon him unawares. Both his legs were completely paralyzed. Now only his right hand obeyed him. He bit his lips until the blood came when after repeated efforts he finally realised that he could not move. Taya bravely hid the despair and bitterness she felt at being powerless to help him. But he said to her with an apologetic smile: "you and I must separate, Taya. After all, this was not in our contract. I shall think it over properly today, my dear." She would not let him speak. The sobs burst forth and she hid her face against his chest in a paroxysm of weeping.

When Artem learned of his brother's latest misfortune he wrote to his mother. Maria Yakovlevna left everything and went at once to her son. Now the three lived together. Taya and the old lady took to each other from the first. Pavel carried on with his studies in spite of everything.

One winter's evening Taya came home to report, her first victory—she had been elected to the City Soviet. Thenceforth Pavel saw very little of her. After her day's work in the sanatorium kitchen, where she was employed as dishwasher, Taya would go straight to the Soviet, returning home late at night weary but full of impressions. Before long she would apply for candidate membership in the Party and she was preparing for the long-awaited day with eager anticipation. And then misfortune struck another blow. The steadily progressing disease was doing its work. A burning, excruciating pain suddenly seared Pavel's right eye, spreading rapidly to the left. A black curtain fell, blotting out all about him, and for the first time in his life Pavel knew the horror of total blindness.

A new obstacle had moved noiselessly onto his path barring his way. A terrifying, seemingly insurmountable obstacle. It plunged Taya and his mother into despair. But he, frigidly calm, resolved: "T must wait and see what happens. If there is really no possibility of advancing, if everything I have done to return to the ranks has been swept away by this blindness I must put an end to it all."

Pavel wrote to his friends and they wrote back urging him to take courage and carry on the fight. It was in these days of grim struggle for him that Taya came home radiant and announced: "I am a candidate to the Party, Pavlusha." Pavel listened to her excited account of the nucleus meeting at which her application was accepted and remembered his own initial steps in the Party. "Well, Comrade Korchagina, you and I are a Communist faction now," he said, squeezing her hand.

The next day he wrote a letter to the Secretary of the District Party Committee asking the latter to come and see him. The same evening a mud-spattered car drew up outside the house and a minute later Volmer, a middle-aged Lett, with a spreading beard that reached to his ears, was pumping Pavel's hand. "Well, how goes it? What do you mean by behaving like this, eh? Up with you and we'll send you off to work in the village at once," he said with a breezy laugh.

He stayed for two hours, forgetting all about the conference he was to have attended. He paced up and down the room, listening to Pavel's impassioned appeal for work.

"Stop talking about study groups," he said when Pavel had finished. "You've got to rest. And we must see about your eyes. It may still be possible to do something. What about going to Moscow and consulting a specialist? You ought to think it over..."

But Pavel interrupted him: "I want people, Comrade Volmer, live, flesh and blood people! I need them now more than ever before. I cannot go on living alone. Send the youth to me, those with the least experience. They're veering too much to the left out there in the villages, the collective farms don't give them enough scope, they want to organise communes. You know the Komsomols, if you don't hold them back they're liable to try and spurt out ahead of the column. I was like that myself."

Volmer stopped in his tracks. "How do you come to know about that? They only brought the news in today from the district."

Pavel smiled. "My wife told me. Perhaps you remember her. She was accepted in the Party yesterday." "You mean, Korchagina, the dishwasher? So that's your wife! I didn't know that!" He fell silent for a few moments, then he slapped his forehead as an idea occurred to him. "I know whom we'll send you. Lev Rersenev. You couldn't wish for a better comrade. He's a man after your own heart, the two of you ought to get along famously. Like two high-frequency transformers. I was an electrician once, you know, and those electrical terms have stuck. Lev will rig up a radio for you. he's an expert at that sort of thing. I often sit up till two in the morning at his place with those earphones. The wife actually got suspicious. Wanted to know what I meant by coming home at all hours of the night."

Korchagin smiled. "Who is Bersenev?" he asked. Volmer ceased his pacing and sat down. "He's our notary public, although he's no more notary public really than I am a ballet dancer. He held an important post until quite recently. Been in the movement since nineteen-twelve and a Party member since the Revolution. Served in the Civil War on the revolutionary tribunal of the Second Cavalry Army; that was the time they were combing out the White-Guard lice. He was in Tsaritsyn too, and on the Southern Front as well. Then for a time he was a member of the Supreme Military Court of the Far Eastern Republic. Had a very tough time of it there. Finally tuberculosis got him. He left the Far East and came down here to the Caucasus. At first he worked as chairman of a gubernia court, and vice-chairman of a territorial court. And then his lung trouble knocked him out completely. It was a matter of coming down here and taking it easy or giving up the ghost. So that's how we come to have such a remarkable notary. It's a nice quiet job too. just the thing for him. Well. gradually the people here got him to take a nucleus. After that he was elected to the District Committee. Then before he knew it he had charge of a political school, and now they've put him on the Control Commission. He's a permanent member on all important commissions appointed to unravel nasty tangles. Apart from all that he goes in for hunting, he's a passionate radio fan, and although he has only one lung, you wouldn't believe it to look at him. He is simply bursting with energy. When he dies it'll be somewhere on the way between the District Committee and the court."

Pavel cut him short. "Why do you load him down like that?" he asked sharply. "He is doing more work here than before!"

Volmer gave him a quizzical look: "and if I give you a study circle and something else Lev would be sure to say: 'Why must you load him down like that?' But he himself says he'd rather have one year of intensive work than five years on his back in hospital. It looks as if we'll have to build Socialism before we can take proper care of our people."

"That's true. I too prefer one year of life to five years of stagnation, but we are sometimes criminally wasteful of our energies. I know now that this is less a sign of heroism than of inefficiency and irresponsibility. Only now have I begun to see that I had no right to be so stupidly careless about my own health. I see now that there was nothing heroic about it at all. I might have held out a few more years if it hadn't been for that misguided Spartanism. In other words, the infantile disease of leftism is one of the chief dangers."

"That's what he says now." thought Volmer, "'but let him get back on his feet and he'll forget everything but work." But he said nothing.

The following evening Lev Bersenev came. It was midnight before he left Pavel. He went away feeling as if he had found a brother whom he had lost many years before.

In the morning men might have been seen on the roof of Korchagin's house rigging up a wireless antenna. While Lev busied himself inside the house with the receiving set, regaling Pavel the while with interesting stories from his past. Pavel could not see him but from what Taya had told him he knew that Lev was a tall fair-haired blue-eyed young man with impulsive gestures, which was exactly as Pavel had pictured him the moment they had first met

When evening came three valves began to glow in the twilight room. Lev triumphantly handed Pavel the earphones. A chaos of sounds filled the ether. The transmitters in the port chirped like so many birds, and somewhere not far out at sea a ship's wireless was sending out waves of dots and dashes. But in this vortex of noises and sounds jostling one another the tuning coil picked out and chine to a calm and confident voice: "this is Moscow calling..."

The tiny wireless set brought sixty broadcasting stations in different parts of the world within Pavel's reach. The life from which he had been debarred broke through to him from the earphone membranes, and once again he could feel its mighty pulsation. Noticing the glow of pleasure in Pavel's eyes, the weary Bersenev smiled with satisfaction. The big house was hushed. Taya murmured restlessly in her sleep. Pavel saw very little of his wife these days. She came home late, worn out and shivering from cold. Her work claimed more and more of her time and seldom did she have a free evening. Pavel remembered what Bersenev had told him on this score: "if a Bolshevik has a wife who is his Party comrade they rarely see one another. But this has two advantages: they never get tired of each other, and there's no time to quarrel!"

And indeed, how could he object? It was only to be expected. There was a time when Taya had devoted all her evenings to him. There had been more warmth and tenderness in their relationship then. But she had been only a wife, a mate to him; now she was his pupil and his Party comrade. He knew that the more Taya would mature politically, the less time she would be able to give him. and he bowed to the inevitable. He was given a study group to lead and once again a noisy hum of voices filled the house in the evenings. These hours spent with the youth infused Pavel with new energy and vigour.

The rest of the time went in listening to the radio, and his mother had difficulty in tearing him away from the earphones at mealtimes.

The radio gave him what his blindness had taken from him – the opportunity to acquire knowledge, and this consuming passion for learning helped him to forget the pain that racked his body, the fire that seared his eyes and all the misery an unkind fate had heaped upon him.

When the radio brought the news from Magnitostroi of the exploits of the Young Communists who had succeeded Pavel's generation he was filled with happiness.

He pictured the cruel blizzards, the bitter Urals frosts as vicious as a pack of hungry wolves. He heard the howling of the wind and saw amid the whirling of the snow a detachment of second-generation Komsomols working in the light of arc lamps on the roof of the giant factory buildings to save the first sections of the huge plant from the ravages of snow and ice. Compared to this, how tiny seemed the forest construction job on which the first generation of Kiev Komsomols had battled with the elements! The country had grown, and with it, the people.

And on the Dnieper, the water had burst through the steel barriers and swept away men and machines. And again the Komsomol youth had hurled themselves into the breach, and after a furious two-day battle had brought the unruly torrent back under control. A new Komsomol generation marched in the van of this great struggle. And among the heroes Pavel heard with pride the name of his old comrade Ionat Pankratov.

CHAPTER NINE

The first few days in Moscow they put up in the archive premises of an institution whose chief was arranging for Pavel to enter a special clinic.

Only now did Pavel realise how much easier it had been to be brave when he had his youth and a strong body. Now when life had him in its iron grip to hold out was a matter of honour.

* * * *

IT WAS A YEAR AND A half since Pavel Korchagin had come to Moscow. Eighteen months of indescribable anguish. In the eye clinic Professor Averbach had told Pavel quite frankly that there was no hope of recovering his sight. Sometime in the future when the inflammation would disappear it might be possible to operate on the pupils. In the meantime he advised an operation to halt the inflammatory process.

Pavel's permission was sought and he told the physicians to do everything they thought necessary. Three times he felt the touch of Death's black wings as he lay for hours at a time on the operating table with lancets probing his throat to remove the thyroid gland. But Pavel clung tenaciously to life, and, after hours of anguished suspense, Taya would find her loved one deathly pale but alive and as calm and gentle as always.

"Don't worry, my dear, it's not so easy to kill me. I'll go on living and kicking up a fuss if only to upset the calculations of the learned Aesculapiuses. They are right in everything they say about my health, but they are gravely mistaken when they try to write me off as totally unfit for work. We'll see about that."

Pavel was determined to resume his place in the ranks of the builders of the new life. He knew now what he had to do.

· · · ·

WINTER WAS OVER. SPRING had burst through the open windows, and Pavel, having survived another operation, resolved that weak as he was, he would remain in hospital no longer. To live so many months in the midst of so much human suffering, surrounded by the groans and lamentations of the doomed was far more difficult for him than to endure his own suffering.

And so when another operation was proposed, he answered coldly: "no. I've had enough. I have sacrificed part of my blood for science. I have other uses for what is left."

That day Pavel wrote a letter to the Central Committee, explaining that since it was now useless for him to continue his wanderings in search of medical treatment. He wished to remain in Moscow where his wife was now working. It was the first time he had turned to the Party for help. His request was granted and the Moscow Soviet gave him living quarters. Pavel left the hospital with the fervent hope that he might never return.

The modest room in a quiet side street off Kropotkinskaya seemed to him the height of luxury. And often, waking at night, Pavel would find it hard to believe that hospital was indeed a thing of the past for him now.

Taya was a fully-fledged Party member by this time. She was an excellent worker, and in spite of the tragedy of her personal life. She did not lag behind the best shock workers at the factory. Her fellow workers soon showed their respect for this quiet unassuming young woman by electing her a member of the factory trade union committee. Pride for his wife, who was gradually emerging as a true Bolshevik, made Pavel's sufferings easier to bear.

* * * *

BAZHANOVA CAME LO MOSCOW on business and paid him a visit. They had a long talk. Pavel grew animated as he told her of his plans to return in the near future to the fighting ranks.

Bazhanova noticed the wisp of silver on Pavel's temples and she said softly: "I see that you have gone through a great deal. Yet you have lost none of your enthusiasm. What more do you want? I am glad that you have decided to begin the work for which you have been preparing these past five years. But how do you intend to go about it?"

Pavel smiled confidently. "Tomorrow my friends are bringing me a sort of cardboard stencil, which will enable me to write without getting the lines mixed up. I couldn't write without it. I hit upon the idea after much thought. You see – the stiff edges of the cardboard will keep my pencil from straying off the straight line. Of course, it is very hard to write without seeing what you are writing, but it is not impossible. I have tried it and I know. It took me some time to get the knack of it, but now I have learned to write more slowly, taking pains with every letter and the result is quite satisfactory." And so Pavel began to work.

He had conceived the idea of writing a novel about the heroic Kotovsky Division. The title came of itself: Born of the Storm. His whole life was now geared to the writing of his book. Slowly, line by line, the pages emerged. He worked oblivious to his surrounding, wholly immersed in the world of images, and for the first time he suffered the throes of creation, knew the bitterness the artist feels when vivid, unforgettable scenes so tangibly perceptible turn pallid and lifeless on paper.

He had to remember everything he wrote, word by word. The slightest interruption caused him to lose the thread of his thoughts and retarded his work. His mother regarded her son's work with apprehension. Sometimes he had to recite aloud whole pages and even chapters from memory, and there were moments when his mother feared that he was losing his mind. She did not dare approach him while he worked, but as she picked up the sheets that had fallen on the floor she would say timidly: "I do wish you would do something else, Pavlusha. It can't be good for you to keep writing all the time like this..."

He would laugh heartily at her fears and assure the old lady that she need not worry, he hadn't "gone off his rocker yet."

Three chapters of the book were finished. Pavel sent them to Odessa to his old fighting comrades from the Kotovsky Division for their opinion, and before long he received a letter praising his work. But on its way back to him the manuscript was lost in the mails. Six months' work was gone. It was a terrible blow to him. Bitterly he regretted having sent off the only copy he possessed. Ledenev scolded him roundly when he heard what had happened.

"How could you have been so careless? But never mind. It's no use crying over spilt milk. You must begin over again."

"But Innokenti Pavlovich! I have been robbed of six months' work. Eight hours of strenuous labour every day. Curse the parasites!"

Ledenev did his best to console his friend. There was nothing for it but to start afresh. Ledenev supplied him with paper and helped him to get the manuscript typed. Six weeks later the first chapter was rewritten.

A family by the name of Alexeyev lived in the same apartment as the Korchagins. The eldest son. Alexander, was a Secretary of one of the District Committees of the Komsomol. His sister Galya, a lively girl of eighteen, studied at a factory training school. Pavel asked his mother to speak to Galya and find out whether she would agree to help him with his work in the capacity of "secretary." Galya agreed with alacrity. She came in one day. smiling pleasantly, and was delighted when she learned that Pavel was writing a novel.

"I shall be very glad to help you, Comrade Korchagin." she said. "It will be so much more fun than writing those dull circular letters for father about the maintenance of hygiene in communal apartments."

From that day Pavel's work progressed with doubled speed. Indeed so much was accomplished in one month that Pavel was amazed. Galya's lively participation and sympathy were a great help to him. Her pencil rustled swiftly over the paper, and whenever some passage particularly appealed to her she would read it over several times, taking sincere delight in Pavel's success. She was almost the only person in the house who believed in his work, the others felt that nothing would come of it and that Pavel was merely trying to fill in the hours of enforced idleness.

Ledenev, returning to Moscow after a business trip out of town, read the first few chapters and said: "carry on. my friend. I have no doubt that you will win. You have great happiness in store for you. Comrade Pavel. I firmly believe that your dream of returning to the ranks will soon materialize. Don't lose hope. my son."

The old man went away deeply satisfied to have found Pavel so full of energy. Galya came regularly, her pencil raced over the pages reviving scenes from the unforgettable past. In moments when Pavel lay lost in thought, overwhelmed by a flood of memory. Galya would watch his lashes quivering, and see his eyes reflecting the swift passage of thought. It seemed incredible that those eyes could not see, so alive were the clear, unblemished pupils.

When the day's work was over she would read what she had written and he would listen tensely, his brow wrinkled. "Why are you frowning, Comrade Korchagin? It is good, isn't it?" "No, Galya. It is bad."

The pages he did not like he rewrote himself. Hampered by the narrow strip of the stencil he would sometimes lose his patience and fling it from him. And then, furious with life for having robbed him of his eyesight, he would break his pencils and bite his lips until the blood came.

As the work drew to a close, forbidden emotions began more often to burst the bonds of his ever-vigilant will. These forbidden emotions were sadness and all those simple human feelings, warm and tender to which everyone but himself had the right. But he knew that

were he to succumb to a single one of them the consequences would
be tragic.

Taya would come home from the factory late in the evening to
find him still working, and after exchanging a few words with Maria
Yakovlevna in a low voice so as not to disturb Pavel, she would retire
for the night.

· · · ·

AT LAST THE FINAL CHAPTER was written. For the next few
days Galya read the book aloud to Pavel. Tomorrow the manuscript
would be sent to Leningrad, to the cultural department of the Regional Party Committee. If the book was approved there, it would lie
turned over to the publishers—and then...

His heart beat anxiously at the thought. If all was well the new
life would begin, a life won by years of weary, unremitting toil. The
fate of the book would decide Pavel's own fate. If the manuscript was
rejected that would be the end for him. If, on the other hand, it was
found to be bad only in part, if its defects could be remedied by further work, he would at once launch a new offensive.

His mother took the parcel with the manuscript to the post office. Days of anxious waiting began. Never in his life had Pavel waited
in such anguished suspense for a letter as he did now. He lived from
the morning to the evening post. But no news came from Leningrad.

The continued silence of the publishers began to look ominous.
From day to day the presentiment of disaster mounted, and Pavel admitted to himself that total rejection of his book would finish him.
That he could not endure. There would be no longer any reason to
live.

At such moments he remembered the park on the hill overlooking the sea, and he asked himself the same question over and over
again: "have you done everything you can to break out of the steel
trap and return to the ranks, to make your life useful?" And he had

to answer: "'Yes, I believe I have done everything!" At last when the agony of waiting had become well-night unbearable, his mother, who had been suffering from the suspense no less than her son came running into the room with the cry:

"News from Leningrad!"

It was a telegram from the Regional Committee. A terse message on a telegraph form:

Novel heartily approved turned over to publishers congratulations on your victory.

His heart beat fast. His cherished dream was realised! The steel trap had been rent asunder, and now, armed with a new weapon, he had returned to the fighting ranks and to life.

The End